Just Who . . . or What . . . Is Camden Archer?

ONLY REAL BOYS HAVE SOULS, and if Camden's not real . . . Jake Turner doesn't even want to think about that.

Camden Archer lives at the Center, along with seventeen other orphans.

Jake Turner is Cam's teacher at a Denver middle school. A storm throws them together, igniting Jake's suspicions that the boy isn't what he appears to be.

Cam grows an inch in one weekend, and his physical responses are too quick for Jake to follow—when the boy thinks Jake isn't watching.

The clincher for Jake? When Cam recovers miraculously from a deadly car accident that Jake was certain killed the boy.

Even Cam's subsequent attendance at Sacred Heart doesn't entirely convince Jake the boy is heaven-bound. Who is there to hear his confession, if he's not real?

The boy's abduction, and his ensuing pursuit by the Center's highly trained team of ex-military types, pull Jake into a life-or-death quest to save the boy he's come to care about as if he were his own.

In the deadly conflict that follows, Jake has to come to terms with his doubts about Cam. He also has to answer the bigger question: What does it mean to have a soul?

It matters very much to Cam, especially if the boy doesn't survive long enough for Jake to save him.

The
Center's Child

Farley Dunn

 THREE SKILLET

THE CENTER'S CHILD, Dunn, Farley L

First Edition

 THREE SKILLET

www.ThreeSkilletPublishing.com

ISBN 978-1-943189-02-1

For Steven . . . a very real boy.

Chapter 1

What's Real Is What's Real

"You're not a real boy. You know that."

I glanced at the kid sitting next to me, gauging his reaction. He might seem real to most people, because he's good, but I wasn't fooled. Let me tell you how I know, starting with a description. You'll need that to understand.

Cam has long hands and narrow feet, with strong legs, like a lot of fourteen-year-olds. Brilliant blue eyes, too, the sort girls fall into because they're so clear. He even looks and acts like a real boy. But he's not real. I've come to know him too well to believe that.

He looked at me and grinned. His expression was bright and open, the honest look of an ordinary boy. When I was a kid, I was a choirboy back in Casper. St. Anthony's. I had to put that innocent look on my face every Sunday, and that's how I know. That grin was part of his disguise.

I smiled back, casually suggesting, "Let's go have some lunch." The back gate approach. Catch him off guard. At the same time, I slapped him on the knee with the back of my hand, a friendly gesture, but stupid on my part. It was that tear in his jeans, the one I knew was there. Pain shot through my finger, reminding me of my torn fingernail, and I jerked my arm away. Then I laughed and stood, only to find myself biting at the fingernail.

Now, you probably think there's nothing odd about what happened, and you'd be right, if this was anything but a Center kid. The thing is, there *was* nothing odd about what happened, and that's what was odd. Any other kid, and he'd jerk his knee sideways, grab my arm, something. This one just laughed it off. Anyway, I was a little put out by the rip in his pants, but mostly because my nail stung, and I was giving the pants the blame.

By then, actual hunger pangs had kicked in. I glanced at him to see him still on the bench. I looked away, deciding on how long to wait on his response. I knew he hadn't eaten all morning; he'd been with me the entire time. Maybe today I'd learn the real truth. He didn't require food. He was made out of aerated titanium and woven glass instead of bone and tissue, with a fusion heart instead of beating muscle. Maybe his brain really did operate on a nano scale with chips and processors. It couldn't be only my imagination that his eyes glowed brighter than humanly possible when reaching a new level on his favorite video game, could it?

See what I mean about needing his description? You have to know what he looks like to understand what's got my suspicions up. He looks normal, okay, but that's only most of the time. Other times, well, that's what I'm trying to get across to you.

I was distracted when the park bench made a noise. That caught my attention, because it hadn't done that when I stood, and I'm a good forty pounds heavier than he should be. Maybe he really was all machine under that skin. If you think about it, that's the only explanation. All that machinery to run those high-speed processors has to weigh a ton.

"Pizza?"

His question broke my concentration. I turned, and there he was next to me, his wallet out, like he'd stood and then was there, instantly, without taking the time to move. Then there was the wallet, polished, woven stainless steel mesh, of course, as if leather was foreign to the touch, and he couldn't bear to think about it next to his skin. When he saw my disbelieving look—I knew he didn't have an allowance living at the Center—he pulled out two twenties.

"I've been mowing yards. I get repeat business. I'm fast, and I do the yards exactly the same every time. People like that." He gave one of those half grins, one side of his face pulling up. His eye even had this twinkle, a real-to-life sparkle like you see only in the movies. It looked normal, ordinary, even—the grin, at least—but it struck me as more. Studied, even, like it was meant to look ordinary.

See? You have to know what Cam *looks* like, or all this makes no sense at all. Now, you might call me paranoid, but this next thing is proof positive of my theory that Cam can't be a real boy. I reached for the bills, only to have him pull them away. I lunged, and he gave in. I watched him slow down and let me grab them. It was that small amount of hesitation that real humans aren't capable of just as I drew close that gave it away. What real person can do that, and especially a fourteen-year-old? If I hadn't been looking, I'd have missed it, but I was looking now. For all sorts of things I was looking, and I was finding it, proof that he was something besides a real kid.

Heck, I know how this sounds, even to me. Ridiculous, right? Artificial kids? Like, how would they do that? Cloning? Gene-splicing and perhaps a bit of surgery? Maybe a helium nuclear fuel cell that could power the kid's energy needs for at least a century? Let's pull out the cloned heart and stick this fuel cell in. He'll never need food again.

Was I a nut or what?

Now, I don't get to Mass as often as my mom wishes. I get the willies seeing confessionals, thinking of bleeding my sins, real and imagined, to a man I can't see, but I do go now and then, and there's something that bothers me. What does it mean if Cam was made in a laboratory? Would he even have a soul? Could he? I get the chills thinking about that.

Am I getting across why this is important to me? Everybody deserves a shot at heaven, and if the kid can't confess—and I'm pretty sure computers aren't welcome in the confessionals at Sacred Heart, even if they can walk and talk and have blue eyes—I don't want to think about what that means.

Holding that money, I felt foolish, because I really liked the kid. And he seemed to enjoy spending time with me. I guessed he did, anyway. He kept coming to our Saturday games, and that must mean something. I chuckled to cover a flush of embarrassment, and I said, "Sure, you can pay. You charge forty for one yard?"

I held the bills out to him.

"I don't charge them. If they like my work, they give me money. Why would I charge them? I don't need the money." He slipped the money and his wallet back into his jeans, and he knelt to tie his shoe.

I recognized what he was doing. He was refusing to look at me. Maybe he realized I'd finally seen through his thinly-veiled charade, and he couldn't face me any longer. He knew if he did, I'd see the machine-boy in his eyes. His cover'd be blown, and he'd have to be dismantled so all his individual parts could be recycled into other robot boys. That was funny and yet disturbing in a bizarrely scientific sort of way. After all, think about it. That's what they do with outdated computers and other sorts of machines.

"You don't need the money." I had to laugh at him, so intent on tying his shoes, but I wasn't laughing inside. It was the feeling that I was being handed yet another proof that Cam couldn't be a real boy. Real boys always need money. Then I shook my head. He wouldn't have suggested pizza if he had fusion power cells inside, now would he? Only real boys needed to eat.

"Well," and he looked up with a teasing grin, like he was back in real-boy mode; and he stood and punched me on the shoulder, dancing like Ali sparring in the ring. "Only if you let me pay for the pizza. I might need money for that."

I laughed. It was only later that I realized it was exactly what he intended. Maybe it was me getting light headed, because we took off to Snarky's Pizza, and I let it go. It didn't matter, anyway. I was hungry, and he was paying. That was enough for the time being. If I still felt like it, I could figure out the rest later.

Chapter 2

Home Sweet Home

The Center for Innovative Software Specialization and Intellectual Enhancement, or CISSIE, had been the butt of Denver's standup crowd for years. Of course, there was nowhere in the Center's charter or paperwork that the acronym CISSIE showed up, but the letters plastered across the side of the campus, the ones backlit in red LEDs, telling everyone on the distant highway that only the most esoteric and brilliant work went on here, were spaced in such a way that at a glance, only the uppercase letters C-I-S-S-I-E were easily visible at a quarter mile. Then, the human mind twisted the acronym, and it was history. SISSY.

No one knew just what went on inside the huge, ultra-modern facility. The walls were glass, clear in places, and frosted or mirrored in others. Massive beams jutted out at the most inexplicable angles, and it seemed the architects had left their plumb lines at home the day they designed the complex.

Inside, there were vast corridors with doors that were always closed, and visitors rarely met the employees. After all, to get any place in the complex, any place where any real work was done, required badges, thumbprint identification, and retinal scanners. Visitors were certainly welcome, and schools sent their students on

11

field trips to the Center all the time, but they had to be content with the stunning architecture, the cafeteria with its glass tables and high-tech food service lines, and the elaborate landscaping visible from every window. Most views even included original fountains and modern sculptures commissioned just for the Center's grounds.

Those areas behind the closed doors and the retinal scanners were just as bright and beautiful. The ceilings were tall with sky-lights that let in the sun. The floors were polished, and noise-canceling software kept the spaces hushed even as work was being done. Through a series of glass doors, lights flickered on banks of computer servers. There was no cloud processing done here. The research the Center did was totally proprietary, and nothing left the premises. Even the backup systems were all in-house, buried in basements that were sunk deep into the hillside.

One set of glass doors was labeled Dorms. No one was going in or out at the present. Down the long hallway, there were rows of doors on each side, each one made of glass with a name etched into its surface. Inside could be seen a white leather lounger, looking rather like a dentist's chair, and little else. There were closed cabinets lining the back wall of each compartment.

The fourteenth door had a familiar name on it. Camden Archer. It wasn't what most people expected as a home for orphaned children, but then Cam wasn't exactly orphaned, not in the way the good citizens of Denver believed.

Chapter 3

When Rain Falls, Everyone Gets Wet

The pizza place was closed, of course. The sign said Snarky was out of town, but the place was a dive. I suspected the health department had been by for a visit. More than once I'd gotten dirty napkins, but the pepperonis were spicy, and no one could beat Snarky's price.

"So," and I grabbed Cam by the neck. His skin was warm, and as I squeezed, I felt for high-tension cables instead of tendons, and for servo-motors moving his head from side to side. All I could find were muscles that felt very real around a neck that didn't seem mechanical at all. I let him go with a push. Then, just for a joke, I teased, "You want to skip food for today? We can find something else to do."

I watched him, fighting a smile. Would he say, sure, let's see a movie, instead? I can catch a meal next week or next month. What good's food to a fusion-powered body? He might laugh, but it might be the truth.

"There's your place. We can get a sandwich there. You had a couple cans of root beer last time I was over, that and we picked up some ice cream on the way. Remember? I'll pay, if you want." He ran his finger over the closed sign, tracing the words, as if he didn't want to look when I gave him my answer.

Didn't he trust me? Or was this a test of his own?

"And you ate everything. Do you remember that? The best I can do is maybe rustle up a sandwich or two."

I pressed my fist against his shoulder, pushing him, like I was giving him a punch in the ring. A prize fighter, maybe, like Ali, the best ever by anyone's measure. Then I let my fist slide off. I waited, daring Cam to call my bluff.

"We don't have to. I mean . . ." His voice trailed off. He looked at me, then away again.

"Sure," I said. "My house, my food, my money. I'll expect you to treat next time." Hesitation? From Cam? I felt bad for teasing him.

There was that smile again, breaking across his face, spontaneous, just like a real boy's, as if he wanted to spend time with me, even without the root beer and ice cream. Well, I guess if I were an orphan, I'd find an adult to latch onto, also. It'd make me feel better about my situation. If he were picking me, I guess anyone would do, too. Don't know what I had to offer, but he was welcome to it.

Then a siren sounded in the distance, high and lonely, insistent and forlorn at the same time. I glanced down the street but didn't see anything. Cam had a puzzled expression on his face, and then it cleared. As it did, the siren shut off, and it was quiet.

"Cam?"

He kicked at an empty can on the street, leaping at it, his arms out like a ninja warrior. That rip in his pants caught my eye. He was ignoring me.

"Cam, what do you know about that siren?"

"It's cool. Everybody's okay." He hit the bill of my cap, knocking it off my head and catching it in the same motion. I never saw his hand move until he held the cap out to me.

There it was again, more proof. First the money, and now my cap. I reached and took it from him, putting it back on my head. I don't know why it mattered to me so much. I wasn't raising the kid. Weekend a while back, shooting hoops at the park, I happened to see him and recognized him from one of my classes. We hung out on the courts and bumped fists when it was over. After that, he showed up again at the park a couple weeks later, then every weekend. I didn't mind. I liked his company, that and to kick his backside at video games a couple times when he stopped by my apartment afterwards. However, real parenting of a fourteen-year-old? That was for suckers dragged down by responsibility.

Single was better, and I was living proof of that, but that's beside the point. It was spending time with him that was giving me the opportunity to figure out that this kid at my side couldn't be real. Are you getting the big picture, yet? Do you see what I mean?

Then he punched me on the shoulder with his fist. "You need mustard. We'll pick up some on the way. We'd better hurry if we don't want to get wet."

How did he know I needed mustard? I didn't even know I needed mustard. Like I've said a million times, or at least twenty, there's no way he's a real boy.

Just then there was a crack of thunder, and the sky opened up. I began to run. Cam just laughed; his hair was plastered to his head. It seemed we had no choice but to get wet. We were already soaked.

Chapter 4

Take Two and Call Me in the Morning

Thank the lucky stars my apartment has two bathrooms. Oh, one isn't really mine, but it might as well be. My neighbor, that's Mrs. Osgood, locked herself in her apartment one Sunday, and since the building is an old mansion from two centuries ago, it's been chopped up so many times that each of the original rooms is now several rooms. Well, I have a door I never had a key for, and we found out it opened into Mrs. Osgood's bathroom. Odd, but handy. I picked the lock, and now she lets me use it when I have guests over.

The rain never let up. Instead, it got worse. I do have a car, but of course I'd left it at home, so we just had a good time getting wetter and wetter. We found puddles to jump in, and at one point Cam stood under a downspout letting the runoff hit him in the head until he nearly disappeared in the shower. I half hoped sparks would shoot out, because that would prove my theory, but he exploded out of the flood, laughing, and jumped on me, shaking his head from side to side to make sure all the water in his hair landed in my face. I just turned him upside down and carried him back to the downspout, letting the water hit him from the other end. Fourteens love stuff like that, the roughhousing thing. Of course, I got it, too, but as I was already soaked, it didn't really matter much. And we got a good laugh out of it.

I don't have a mop, so before going inside, Cam and I stripped most of our clothes off. We wrung them out as best we could in the rain, tossing them through the door into a pile in the hallway. If I had any neighbors watching, they'd probably think we'd been to the beach or something, except the nearest beach is nine hundred miles away, and that's only if you're a bird that can fly over the mountains. We didn't care what they thought. Cam and I were so hyped up on the rain, and with just being stupid, that if we saw Mrs. Osgood running around outside, we'd just laugh, and she's nearing eighty! Cam's met my neighbor, and he says she's a nifty old lady, but of course, being Cam, he was much politer about it.

I do have a washer, one of those two-in-one jobs, the kind where you wash one towel, then you put it in the little dryer on top and let it heat up the apartment while the towel tries to get dry. Well, when Cam and I got inside, you can imagine the two of us in soaked boxers, holding dripping clothes. I pointed him to my bathroom, and I headed to Mrs. Osgood's. Only thing, Mrs. Osgood didn't do her washing, so I had no towel. Still, I did have hot water, and I was warm when I got out. Last night's towel was still in the dryer, and when I went down the hall to get it, I could hear Cam in the shower. I knocked on the door, yelling out that I'd leave him a towel on the knob, so don't hurry. I only have the one, so I dried my hair, patted the rest of me, and slipped a pair of jeans on. Then I opened the bath door and hung the damp towel on the knob as I'd promised. The water was loud, and I think Cam was supposed to be singing, but it was more of a howl than a melody, so maybe the water was too hot, and he was in pain. I glanced at him. The curtain is patterned, but as far as I could tell, his legs were real legs, not mechanical pistons or articulated metal stalks like in *War of the Worlds*. The curtain is only about shoulder height, and he was rinsing his hair. I called to him, and he pushed his hair out of his face and waved.

"Towel's on the door, Cam. Damp, but I've only got the one. Sorry." I made a face that I thought would make him laugh. It did.

"I'm good. Thanks. We never did get mustard." He stuck his head back under the water. With shampoo running down his face, he called out, "I found your mothballs. They stink. I put them on the floor," and the singing started up again.

There they were, a science experiment I was working on called Foaming Mothballs. They were supposed to rise and fall on air bubbles in a jar of water if I mixed in baking soda and vinegar, but I think I got the wrong kind. All they did was smell like something died, and I'd forgotten about them.

I shook my head and picked them up, and I stepped outside and closed the door. I wondered if Mrs. Osgood used mustard. She might. She was gone to her brother's for the rest of the month, but she wouldn't mind if I looked. Not after I saved her life. I cut through her bathroom, which was the easy part, because I don't think Mrs. Osgood has thrown anything out since she moved in, and that must have been forty years ago, at least. On the way through, I flushed the mothballs down, glad to see them gone. That was an experiment I wished I'd never started. To get to the kitchen, I walked over forty years of clothes and newspapers, but I guess I was lucky. She hadn't thrown out her old mustard, either. There were maybe ten jars, and since mustard doesn't spoil, Cam and I would have plenty on our sandwiches.

He was at the kitchen table when I got back. His hair was sticking up on end, and water was running down his neck. He had the towel around his waist, and he was peeling a very brown banana I'd forgotten to throw out. It was something only a real boy would do, eat an old banana, when food was on the way.

"Cam, mustard!" I tossed it to him, and he caught it without looking. "You want sandwiches now, or do you want to take care of the towel thing?" I pointed. It was tucked at the waist, but barely. A sudden move, and it would be gone.

"Food." He worked in the top of the towel tighter. "Where'd the mustard come from?"

"Mrs. Osgood. There's more where that came from, too." I didn't expect we'd need it, since he was here just for the day, but it was nice to know there was plenty. He could eat all he wanted.

"Her brother's, again?" He was chewing the banana. Somehow he'd managed to eat around the really brown spots. "She's a good neighbor. She really likes you."

Really likes me? Where'd he get that from? All I did was save her life that one time, and now I use her bathroom when she's gone, and well, sometimes when I have company, like today.

We prepared our sandwiches. Cam ate two, like a normal boy would. I found him a pair of my clean boxers, and I tossed the towel in the washer. We sat around and played *Gods of War* and *Warcraft*, switching out one for the other when one of us got too far ahead, all the while listening for the rain to stop. It never did, just got harder and harder, with thunder rattling the windows. A real frog strangler. That and with Cam there, I decided I was skipping Saturday evening Mass. When I do go, that's the service I choose. I like to sleep in on Sundays.

Later, about ten, Cam asked if he could stay the night. We have to call the Center, I told him. He said they wouldn't care since it was the weekend, but I said I wanted to hear them say that. I got a pleasant woman on the phone, and she said, "Oh, so you're Camden's friend. We do like for our children to make friends outside of the Center. It helps them acclimate to the real world. We'll make a note that he's with you for the rest of the weekend."

She never did ask my name. That, and when I picked up Cam in the rain, he was really heavy for a skinny kid. However, I didn't think of that until the next morning. I had to rustle up an old blanket for Cam to use on the sofa, and I let him use one of my pillows, the one with the freshest cover. I hadn't changed the bed in several weeks, but I only slept on the pillows one at a time. I didn't think he would mind, since his visit was a surprise.

Once the TV was off, Cam and I sat in the dark and talked for a long time, mostly about me. It was like he needed to know all about me. I was telling him things I didn't even remember. Real things, just that I thought I'd forgotten them until he asked, then there they were all over again.

That was odd, too, but not at the time. Not until the next morning. It was just me and Cam, my little brother that I never had, sleeping over, as if he did it all the time. It was like he'd planned the whole thing. He couldn't have, though, could he? Nah! While Cam might not be a real boy, even he couldn't pull all that off, just to spend time with me.

And dang it, the entire visit he seemed just as real as a real boy could be. Still, I had to look at the bright side. Maybe he did have a shot at heaven after all.

Chapter 5

Sleep Tight till the Bedbugs Bite

There were eighteen doors altogether in the dorms at the Center, one for each of the orphans that called the Center home. It was night now, and the electrochromic glass in the doors was darkened, providing an element of privacy. They all glowed with a bluish light, except for number fourteen. Camden was away for the evening, and the door with his name etched into the glass was still clear.

The kids in their recliners were sleeping soundly, or at least anyone who happened into the dorms would think they were asleep. They were reclined, covered with identical blankets, but oddly enough, each child had a cap on, with wires running from the cap to the back of the chair. From the smallest child behind door number one to the tallest girl who slept behind door eighteen, all appeared to be at rest.

It was the bedbugs that were the problem. During the storm, lightning had struck the building holding the Center's servers. Of course, lightning rods protected each of the campus' buildings, and the servers were grounded. That would have protected the servers, except for the mower that had clipped one of the cables the week before. A work order had been turned in, but the welder scheduled to complete the repair was married, and his wife was due. She went into early labor, and the repair was delayed by a day.

Even then there would have been no problem, for there were backup servers, and backups for the backups. It's just that a power surge—bedbugs—hit the compromised system just as the children were undergoing their routine, nightly updates. The updates only took a fraction of a second, as the Center had the most powerful computer processors money could buy, but that was exactly when the backup servers kicked in, and that was all it took. Seventeen children suffered bedbug bites, and they didn't awaken the next morning, not as normal children, anyway.

The repairs would take a while, too. The children had to be normal, after all.

Chapter 6

One Plus One Equals One

I'm not much of a TV watcher. Really, I'm not, not since college, but missing last night's service, I tried to catch the Archdiocese's televised Mass at seven. It's nice in Denver they do that. Keeps the faithful faithful. And being only thirty minutes, it doesn't take up much of your day.

Might even keep me in the running for heaven, I chuckled, as I watched out of the corner of my eye.

Cam was on the sofa, his face buried in my pillow, and the blanket on the floor. I would've thought he was freezing, but when I felt his back, he was plenty warm. Still, I shook out the blanket and covered him. To give me something to look at besides Cam, I angled the set towards the table and turned the sound down low. I only get a couple stations, what with the free cable box, and after my program, all I had was the local news. Of course there was Snarky's, and I was right. Rat turds in the storeroom. Heck, I've probably got rat turds in my refrigerator, but I still eat the food. Oh, well. Then they showed the dead woman from the park, the one I knew about from three days ago. They had a lead on her identity, but they didn't say who. I started to tune out when the Center popped up on the screen. I glanced at Cam. He was on his back by then. He'd tossed the blanket off, and I stood to put it over him when the newscaster caught my attention.

"As you can see behind me, there's all sorts of activity going on at Denver's Center for Innovative Software Specialization and Intellectual Enhancement."

The camera zoomed in on the name, and at the angle, all I could really make out was CISSIE. I grinned, even as I felt sorry for Cam. He was too nice a kid to be saddled with that. I looked more closely, and there were emergency vehicles—helicopters and the like—crowding into the picture. Then the camera zoomed out again, and the newscaster was back in the scene.

"We have no idea just what is taking place in this super-secretive location, but we do know this is approximately where the dorms for the Center-sponsored orphans are located." A satellite shot of the campus appeared on the screen, and a red arrow pointed to one part of the image. "The storm that hit Denver last night damaged several area businesses, and it appears that the Center may have taken its share. There are reports of a lightning rod on the campus clipped by a mower several days ago. We don't know as of yet if the two incidents are connected, but there is some concern for the welfare of the Center's children, as the number of arriving emergency vehicles continues to grow. Wait." She reached to her ear as if listening. Then she took a piece of paper from someone nearby. She read it before turning back to the camera. "We have received confirmation from the Center that one of the dorm residents was away for the evening. His name is Camden Archer. Camden, if you are listening, we wish you the best, and we hope that each of your housemates is able to welcome you home when you return.

"This is Stella Whittinger with ABC 7News from Denver."

I looked at Cam and frowned, not really comprehending what she had said. Her mentioning Cam, though, bothered me. Like, that was where he lived, and if the storm had damaged the dorms—as suggested pretty plainly by the newscast—well, that was his home. What did that mean? Reaching to turn the TV off, I bumped a glass from the night before, and it fell over, spilling its contents. I grabbed a paper towel and began sopping it up. I set the glass up, hoping I hadn't disturbed my visitor, but I could see him yawning. I glanced at the TV, glad to see it had gone on to another report, a house fire, or something.

"The news is on?" It was Cam. "I thought you never watched TV." He yawned again and stretched. It was a real-boy thing, and I was sort of disappointed. I liked him as a robot or a cyborg better, with a mechanical pump for a heart and piston legs.

"Aren't you cold?" The storm had dropped the temperature, and it was probably sixty in the apartment. I hadn't really paid it much attention before, but I didn't want to talk about the Center just yet. The cold was a safer topic.

"I never get cold, not at night, anyway." Then he let out a screech and sat up. "Whew! That wakes me up! How about breakfast?" He grabbed the blanket and tossed it at me.

When I caught it, he grinned, like it was something we did all the time. A father and son thing, one of those simple and very ordinary actions that speak years of nuanced understandings, this time triggered by a toss of a blanket. Yeah, sure, that's part of the fun of having Cam around. We "get" each other. However, I like the whole relationship better as big brother, little brother. Then I can send him home when I've had enough.

His eyes twinkled. "I'll take mustard on mine."

I felt a sudden urge to tell him about the newscast, but he stood and was gone to the bathroom before I could get the words out of my mouth, leaping over the sofa in a burst of energy that I never feel so early in the morning.

He was still in my boxers, but I didn't look at what he was wearing. What caught my eye instead were his bare shoulders flexing and his long legs pumping, flinging him over the sofa like Superboy leaping a tall building in a single bound. There was nothing mechanical about that, just real muscle and real skin stretched over real bone. Normal boy body parts on a normal body.

It was just Cam, my pretend little brother over for the night.

Once he was out of the room, I began to shake. Weird, I know. I don't normally get the chills. Like Cam, I don't get cold at night unless it's close to freezing. Now, though, I wrapped the blanket around myself and wished I hadn't turned the TV on at all. Stella Whittinger had made me responsible to tell Cam the news. I didn't want to be responsible. I wanted to play basketball with him, beat him at *Warcraft*, maybe *Gods of War* a time or two, and send him home. I wasn't a *parent,* and I had no desire to do the parenting thing.

Thank you, Stella, I thought bitterly. You're going to make this

24

all my fault. Then I thought about Cam. What if all those other kids were injured? What if he couldn't go home to the Center? Was it that bad out there?

What if he needed a home, God forbid? Could I do it? *Would* I? A boy sleeping on my sofa every night?

Could I afford it, was more like it. I had no idea if two could really live as cheaply as one, but I knew one thing. I had no desire to find out.

Chapter 7

Two Crutches and a Crazy Man

"I was on my way to the show, and I had a man cut me off. That's why I'm on crutches. He took my other leg." The standup comedian grinned in a self-effacing manner, and the crowd hooted and clapped. He was actually on crutches, and he waved one in the air. "Tomorrow he can expect to see me coming and going, because I'm whacking him in the face with this crutch, and on the back of his head with the other one." He switched crutches, holding the second one up for a moment. The crowd roared as he hobbled back to the microphone stand, slipping the microphone inside.

"There, that's easier. Now I can walk with both hands. Oh, and did you hear about those scientists out there at CISSIE?" Of course, it sounded like *sissy*, but that was what made it funny. "They have a new intern reading program. Each new employee is required to read *Frankenstein*. Last night several of them got carried away. That was no ordinary lightning storm. You probably saw it on the news this morning. What they didn't show you was the roof of the building open, and the giant electrodes sticking through, channeling electricity into the dorms where they keep those orphaned kids." He did air quotes when he said the word kids, and the crowd laughed. "The latest news out of CISSIE?" Again, *sissy*. "They're alive!

They're alive!"

The crowd roared with laughter as the comedian waved one crutch and began to hobble off the stage. The lights went down for a moment, and when they came back up, the emcee held the microphone in her hand.

"And that was the phenomenal Barry Carter! Thank you, Barry, for keeping us rolling. Now, for our next guest, please put your hands together for Kinky Sutterland!"

Chapter 8

Goose Bumps Don't Lie

How can people be so mean? Maybe no one was hurt out there, but to make jokes like that after the news this morning?

I hadn't turned the TV off quickly enough, and I caught the end of *Comedy Sunrise*. That man on crutches soured my stomach, and the audience loved him. It just wasn't right, even if I would have laughed at it like everyone else yesterday. Still, today? It just wasn't right.

I dreaded Cam returning. Then I remembered his leap over the sofa. He had been in my boxers, still. His clothes, had they gone in the washer? I got up to check, and there they were, still balled up in the hall. Maybe no home, and now no clean clothes. The shower was running when I carried them to the washer. I was glad the water was included in the rent with the amount he was using. Oh, well. Fourteens. I guess I should expect it. I dropped his clothes in and hit start, only to hear him yell in protest. Upstairs probably heard it, it was so loud. His head came out of the door, his hair full of shampoo. The towel was bunched up around his waist, one leg visible and dripping water onto the floor.

"Hey! Where'd the hot water go?"

He wasn't grinning this time, and his eyes didn't sparkle. He was ticked. He didn't get angry very often, and the look on his face was priceless. It made me laugh, but I immediately felt bad about it, and I reached and stopped the washer.

"Thought you might like some clean clothes, but if you want to wear my underwear all day, feel free. Maybe a few people won't notice."

"Oh, sorry. I didn't think about that." He made an apologetic face, shrugging his wet shoulders, like a real boy would. "Do you mind waiting until I'm finished? Please?"

I missed my mechanical boy, though. Oh, well. At least he wasn't Frankenstein. He wasn't at the Center when the lightning hit, and he was alive all on his own. So, there, Barry Carter!

I had three eggs and some Oreos left from the night before. I scrambled the eggs with mustard, and Mrs. Osgood's milk still smelled pretty decent. I crumbled the Oreos for cereal and had it ready when Cam showed up, still in my boxers. I could hear the washer running, so I knew he'd turned it on, already. Probably ready to get out of here after sleeping on my sofa. It was pretty bad. I wouldn't want to sleep on it. I didn't even get it new. It was out by the dumpster when I moved in, and I told the movers to carry it up.

"Cereal, Cam." I set the Oreos in front of him and poured some milk over them. "You want eggs, too?" My stomach churned. I was putting off the inevitable.

"I'm all about the mustard." He grabbed the eggs and handed the Oreos back to me. "Here." He smiled, and it lit up his face. He's like that, able to tweak five facial muscles and change his entire expression. He sure works me with it.

I reached for the Oreos, and I spooned some into my mouth. They were pretty good, and I crunched a mouthful down. When I swallowed, I set the bowl on the table and took a deep breath.

"Cam, there was a report about the Center this morning." I so wanted to pick up the Oreos again, just to put something in my mouth and stop talking. He beat me to it.

"I know. Can I stay with you?" He had his clear blue eyes on me, and his face was so serious, so intent.

"I haven't even told you what happened." I kicked my chair out and sat across from him. He was wide-eyed and had such an innocent expression on his face that for a moment I thought I had misunderstood him. Then it dawned on me, this kid's playing me. He knew he was going to ask that before I even told him about the news report.

We sat in silence for a moment, long enough for Cam to eat the rest of the eggs. Then he said, "I won't be any trouble. You won't even know I'm here." He crossed his arms on the table, and he leaned forward in a way that said, Hey, you can trust me; would I lie to you? I believed him, too. Still, why would he say that?

"What do you mean you won't be any trouble? Were you listening to that report?" I watched him shrug, those bare shoulders doing a quick dance, and then he stood and tossed himself back on the sofa.

"I'm cold." He rubbed at his arms, and I was certain I saw goose bumps there. Like real boys have. He felt on the floor for the blanket and saw it over by me. "Throw me the blanket."

He smiled, his face lit up, and for a moment, I wanted him to stay. I didn't hesitate. I threw him the blanket like he asked.

Just like that.

He never did tell me if he'd heard the news report. Even if he had, they hadn't said anything specific. How could Cam know he needed to stay here? I thought he was still asleep when it was on.

I still do.

Chapter 9

Cam Gets a Boost

That weekend I got three phone calls. Unusual. I don't get three phone calls a month. In fact, I had to look under three boxes and an old pair of skis to find the phone when it rang.

But that wasn't right away. First I had to get milk. I knew I couldn't take Cam back to the Center, and it didn't look like he had any intention of leaving on his own. I had more Oreos, so that was our lunch, unless Snarky's was open for delivery by then. I didn't expect so.

When I returned, the door was askew, but I didn't think too much of it. Cam had his jeans on, and my boxers were off in the corner. No shirt, though, and I could see the muscles in his shoulders and chest shifting under his skin as he worked a gaming remote. Normal boy muscles under normal boy skin. Oreo crumbs were scattered across the table.

"Cam!" I brushed them into a pile at the back, just a little irritated. I don't like to clean *my* messes, much less a fourteen-year-old's. After ten? Maybe. I'd be awake then.

"Yeah?" He was back on *Gods of War*, and someone had just splattered all over the screen.

"Shirt?" I saw it half under one of the sofa cushions and pulled it out, tossing it in his lap.

"Sure." He held the remote with one hand and worked the shirt on, one arm and then the other, the game going the entire time.

"Are there any cookies left?" Watching him work his way into his shirt made me smile, but I suspected not. I picked up the empty package and shook it. It didn't rattle.

"I don't think so. Why?"

"You ate our lunch." His, anyway. I'd be higher than a kite if I ate cookie cereal more than once a day. That was when the phone rang. The first time.

"What's that? Mrs. Osgood's phone?" Cam glanced at me, but the game made a noise. "Hey, no fair. I can't die here," and he was immediately back on the TV.

The ringing was muffled, so his question was reasonable. I had to give him that. Her apartment is right next door, and the walls are thin. I'd already gone on, though, and I ignored him, digging through my stuff in search of my phone. When I leaned over him to search behind the sofa, I growled, "You could at least help."

"Help?" His fingers actually paused on the remote. How about that?

"Phone. Black box with numbers you push." I started looking under the sofa cushions, pushing him aside when I got to the center one. It was up to the eighth ring. I didn't have much more time.

"Here, I think." Cam walked over to my old skis and pointed, like he'd known where it was all along.

At first I didn't think so, but I shoved three boxes aside, and there it was. It's an old multiline business phone, the kind with the blinking buttons at the bottom. Only one line works, but the light blinks, anyway. It used to get voicemail on the second button, but I'm not the type of guy people leave voicemails for, because I never listen to them. I grabbed it and picked up the receiver. I punched the first button.

"Jake, here." I hoped it was worth the work, because I was out of breath. Riding the line on thirty does that to you. However, if a person gets only three calls a month, sometimes those three calls are the important ones.

"Jake Turner?"

Cam looked at me, and I remembered something I'd never liked about this phone. No privacy. When I had company, everyone in the room could hear everything the person on the other end said. Oh, well. I guessed the kid could listen. I had nothing to hide.

"I'm Jake. Sure. What can I do for you?"

"Jake Turner, science teacher, I believe."

Good lands! Was I that transparent? Sure, rat turds, maybe, in the fridge, and I guess the mold in my bathroom could count as a long-term experiment, but from the sound of my voice? How big of a nerd was I?

"That's him!" Cam called from the sofa. "At Bruce Randolph." His eyes were back on the game.

Well, there I was. My stalker knew how to find me now. Right off 70 and Colorado. I'd better warn my principal. I covered the mouthpiece. "Not smart, Cam. You don't know who this is."

He did, though. His expression told me. She introduced herself as Beth Ziegler from Admin. That's top echelon in the school world, just shy of the School Board and the State Board of Education. Notice the caps. Those guys are the gods of the academic world, because they hold all the power. They hire and they fire. Anyway, Beth was very bright and cheerful, and she told me she had heard from the Center. Just like that, with no explanation. I guess she knew about Cam, that he was in my class at Bruce. I always dealt with the Center. I should have known Admin would be in the loop.

"Is there a problem, Beth?" With hanging out with Cam, I meant. I looked at him, his wrinkled shirt and shoeless feet. He looked like a vagabond waiting for someone to give him a hand up. Well, I was trying.

However, spending time with students outside of the school day wasn't exactly looked on with exceeding favor by the gods in charge. I didn't see anything wrong with it, not in Cam's case, anyway, being from the Center and orphaned, but some people are sticklers for legalities, and I needed this job. I had rent due. I hoped Cam didn't mess that up. I might not want to parent him, but I liked the boy, and I'd hate for something like money to come between us.

"Maybe not." She didn't sound like there was. "We got a call from the Center this morning, and it seems you have one of their sponsored children with you."

I sat down. This was it. Everybody knew. Maybe one of the neighbors had called about us stripping our wet clothes off outside. How was I going to explain that to Beth? Forget Beth! There was the entire School Board!

"Mr. Turner?" Beth still didn't sound as if I should be worried, but then, what would she know?

"This is Sunday, right?" I just thought of that. Admin wasn't open on weekends.

"I'm at home, Mr. Turner, if that's what you're asking. Camden Archer. You called last night and got the Center's approval for Camden to stay with you overnight. Am I correct?"

"Yes." I couldn't deny it. She was still so pleasant I could hardly believe anything was wrong, but still. Admin was calling on the weekend about a boy from my class staying at my house. Me, a single teacher. It didn't look good.

"Excellent for you. You saved him, you know."

That caught me off guard. It made me think of missing Mass the night before, and then watching that morning on the TV. I pictured Jesus on the cross, what with Beth using the word *saved*, you know, because that's what the man came to do. Save us, everyone. Even robot boys, I hoped. In my mind flashed an image of Cam in the clouds, with St. Peter handing him a saved diploma. It was sort of funny, but scary at the same time. If St. Peter looked close enough and saw the robot thing, maybe he'd slam the gates in his face. I didn't want that to happen. I took a deep breath and felt my heart settle. I hadn't realized it was pounding in my ears. Cam was watching me with that look, the one that says I'm sweet and lovable, like a puppy. I won't even pee on the carpet, if you just let me stay. I forgot. The phone call. He can hear everything.

"Is this about that news report this morning?"

"I can't tell you everything, Mr. Turner, but the Center is in a bit of a quandary. Camden needs a temporary place to stay, and they mentioned how much he thinks of you. I hear you've made quite an impression on the boy."

"Cam, Mrs. Ziegler."

I remembered her, now. Cam must have recognized her voice earlier. She didn't like to be called Beth, although she hadn't corrected me. Whew! I'd dodged that bullet, but only by the skin of my teeth. It still hadn't completely registered what she'd said, though. Some people say I'm slow to catch on, but these things take time to sink in. When it finally did, I felt my armpits dampen. It was my nerves, I guess, because they do that when I don't like what I'm hearing.

"Cam?" Mrs. Zeigler sounded puzzled. "I don't understand."

"The boy from the Center. He goes by Cam. Everyone who knows him calls him that. Not Camden." I knew I was rambling, but I needed time to get my thoughts around this new development, and it was hard. My sofa as a boy's bedroom? I muttered, "A place to stay, huh?" She was putting me on the spot, and that was uncomfortable.

Then I realized what was bothering me. It wasn't just the sofa. It was food for two, and who knew what else teenage boys cost? An allowance, probably, and shoes. Underwear. Jeans. Shirts. Deodorant. And *toothpaste*. There went next month's spare money, if I took him on. It wasn't so much the money, not really, but my car had begun making a rattling noise, and I'd hoped to get it in.

Oh, crum!

"Just that, Mr. Turner, a place to sleep at night and shower each day." Mrs. Zeigler threw out her easy, pleasantly spoken words, along with the faint sound of a chuckle, as if this were business every day. You know, just give a teacher a kid from his class, like it's no big deal. "Since the Center has requested this temporary student placement, Denver ISD has pulled together behind the request, as long as you are willing, of course."

She made it so matter of fact, as if, of course, I'll take him, Mrs. Ziegler. Throw me a bone, and I'll just snatch it right out of the air. That irritated me. Besides, I was single Jake, having fun on my own. What right did they have to tie me down with this unasked for responsibility?

Yet, for some reason I hesitated before saying no, although it was there on my tongue. Then I realized what it was. He might be an orphan, and I might not like him wearing my shorts or eating all my Oreos, but I did like Cam. He was a mean basketball player, and sometimes I could beat him at *Gods of War*. He hadn't complained about the sofa, either, and that was really saying something. So, in spite of my misgivings, I changed everything I had thought about him staying.

"Is he allowed to go to Mass? I do attend." Sometimes, anyway, but some people might balk. If she said yes to this, then I was good.

"That would be perfect, Mr. Turner. Camden will be glad to attend with you. The exposure will be good for him."

"Then I'm on board. What do I need to do to set this up?" The words just flowed out, and when I heard them I realized I actually meant them. Me. Jake Turner. Dad. Well, guardian, temporary only.

35

Like a trial run for parenthood. Couldn't hurt. If it bombs I just send him back.

The other two phone calls? I'll get to those later.

Chapter 10

Jake Decides He Needs a Pair of Scissors

I do live in Denver. The Mile-High City. Mostly it's beautiful, except in summer when the smog settles over us and makes us choke. The rest of the time I wouldn't live anyplace else.

I had to run to the Center to sign paperwork concerning Cam. Temporary custody, things like that, stuff that had to be filed or sent over to Admin to keep all the legal addicts satisfied. Of course, the Center has its own legal wing, probably to take care of all those copyrights they're keeping to themselves. Now if they'll just share some of that with me. When I got there, Cam in tow, he looked at me before getting out of the car.

"I'm not staying, right?"

It was those puppy dog eyes, and I laughed. I stifled it when I saw them shimmering. He was serious. To lighten the moment, I teased him with, "What part of the phone call did you miss out on?"

I thought he would find that funny. After all, he'd made himself as much a part of the conversation as me. I shifted into park and killed the engine, reaching to my door.

"The part that said I never had to come back here."

I turned to him, surprised. He looked like he really would cry. Just for a moment I wondered where my eighth grader had gone.

You know, being fourteen, and how fourteens do, tough guy act and all. No waterfall, though, and I was glad for that.

"Hey!" I let go of the door and punched him on the shoulder. "At least you're mine for a little while."

When I pulled my hand away, I rubbed my knuckles. He's just a skinny kid, but my hand hurt. He always fools me, because he's built like a rock, in spite of his size. He could be a hustler when he grows up. Like a pool shark, except in a boxing ring. He'd knock 'em dead, and they'd never know what hit 'em.

Instead of ribbing me back, he put his hands in his lap, balling them into fists like he didn't know what to do with them. All he said was, "Do I?" And that was little more than a whisper.

"Anyway, I thought you liked living here." I pushed on his shoulder with my fist, easy this time. My knuckles still stung. I wondered at his hesitation to head inside. Cam's a polite boy. I always knew that. However, I'd not heard him say a negative thing about the Center or the people who ran it. I'd never seen the dorm wing, but I imagined it with leather couches, giant TVs, and good home cooking, very much the way everyone else does. That's the way the Center would do things, first class.

"You know I don't have parents."

"That you're an orphan, sure." It seemed he had more to say, and I waited on him. Sometimes that's what you do with eighth graders. You wait. They talk when they're ready. But he refused to say more, and that's all I got.

Then, I watched a light switch flip, and he changed. The muscles in his face shifted, and he was bright, happy, and beautiful. I know how it sounds to describe a fourteen-year-old boy as beautiful, but if you saw Cam, you'd know what I mean. He has that clear skin boys at that age have, and with those eyes, I bet all the girls will one day be in love with him. He'll eat it up, too.

Then he yanked open the door and leaped out, jumping onto the edge of the seat and slapping his hands on the roof of the car. "Let's go, Mr. Turner. We've got paperwork to sign." He drummed against the metal, and it echoed inside the car.

"*I've* got paperwork to sign, Mr. Archer." I looked at him. His feet were on the seat, and all I could see was the front of his jeans. One of the knees had that torn spot that had snagged my nail, and threads were hanging loose. "And I've got to get me a pair of scissors. You've got threads to trim."

What do they say? Paper covers rock, but scissors cut paper? Hope it cuts threads, too. Then Cam was off the car, the door slammed, and he started in a run towards the building. He motioned for me to come along, getting carried away with his hands. He nearly tripped on a step, and he laughed and stopped at the door, standing and waiting on me.

I opened my door. I actually thought I might like this. For a while, at least. On the way in I looked out across what I could see of the city. For some reason I felt a mile high. It was a beautiful feeling, if it lasted.

Chapter 11

I Get a Boost

There weren't as many papers as I thought I'd have to sign. With Cam fourteen, he got a say in where he lived, so that was part of it. And it was only temporary, so how many forms could the legal junkies need for their fix?

Mostly, it seemed like a formality.

They didn't even explain what had happened, and Cam didn't ask. I started to, and then I looked at him, and he was so happy about all the stuff going on. He signed his paper, grinning ear to ear. He gave it to me rather than the company lawyer, and that got to me. I didn't want to spoil his happy moment, so I never did ask my question.

Even so, it got answered anyway, sort of. A very pretty woman I hadn't seen before brought in this envelope once we were finished, and she laid it on the desk in front of me.

"Mr. Turner, may I call you Jake?" She smiled, and it was that clear-eyed look of Cam's.

"Sure." I glanced at him, trying to see more similarities, but I couldn't find any. It was probably my imagination.

"Jillian Compos." She held out her hand, and I took it.

"Glad to meet you, Ms. Compos." I nodded, still holding her

hand.

"Jillian, or Jill, if you prefer." She glanced at her hand, fighting a smile.

"Which do you prefer?"

That was Cam, and I gave him a hard look. I could swear he winked at me. The little toot winked at me just before he looked away. I did let go of Jill's hand, though. I'm not sure if that's what he intended or not.

Jill seemed amused by it all. I needed to get off that track, so I leaned forward and tapped the letter on the desk.

"This? For me?" Probably some detail they'd forgotten, like I was expected to reimburse the Center for expenses incurred, blah, blah, blah. That might negate the whole deal, that was if I hadn't already irrevocably signed my entire future over to the company store.

"We have quite an investment in little Cam here—"

"Little Cam?" It was Cam again, grinning as he interrupted, his voice distinctive in that just-going-through-puberty way. Not a little boy's voice any longer, but not as deep as it would be.

I cut him a sharp look. Was he turning into a monster, already? Kids do that sometimes. It's like marriage. Be sweet until the deed is done, then bye, bye, Mr. Nice Guy. But no, he had a grin on his face, and his expression was clear and innocent. Jill didn't seem bothered by it, either.

"Okay, big Cam. I can give him that, since he's now fourteen. I understand you wish Cam to attend Mass with you. Sacred Heart, correct?"

I looked at her. I hadn't said that to Mrs. Zeigler. I had said Mass, but I didn't name Sacred Heart. How much did these people know about me? Still, I never tried to hide where I went. Anyone who knew my car would recognize it there.

"Saturdays. I'm not a morning person, so I do Saturday. Evening." I put in that final word to make it clear. The Saturday evening service meant I could sleep in on Sunday. I didn't say it was only the occasional Saturday. If they knew my church, it was up to them to figure out the rest.

"He may have to miss from time to time. There is something you need to understand, Jake. Cam will need ongoing medical supervision." She reached and slid the envelope forward.

"You mean doctor visits." I was covered by Denver ISD, but it cost a bundle to add a dependent. Then there was the deductible. And *copay*. I could feel my heart begin to pound. That might get expensive. What if he had AIDS, or liver disease? Sickle cell anemia . . . no, he would have to have African roots for that. A bone marrow transplant? And what did this have to do with Saturdays? Who scheduled doctor visits on Saturdays?

Maybe there was nothing really wrong with the car. The noise wasn't *that* loud. Yet.

I guess my face was pretty transparent, because Jill laughed, and I enjoyed the sound. It was like hand bells from church during the Christmas season. I could like this woman. Still, I was here for Cam, not a date. I took a deep breath and tried not to look too silly.

"Jake, Cam is completely covered by the Center for all his health needs. All we require is that he returns here for all medical procedures. We'll even set up his appointments for you, so that doesn't have to worry you. We want this to be as easy as possible."

"Anything else?" I glanced at him, relieved. Insurance premiums are a big deal when you teach. Heck, anything that costs money is, and I didn't need Cam to be a big deal. Not one that hit my pocketbook, anyway.

He grinned and did a thing with his hand, pointing it at me like it was a gun, and he was firing something unspoken at me. Appreciation, maybe? Happiness? I'm not especially good at reading fourteen-year-old emotions. I could tell one thing, though. He was flying high with his chance to spend extra time with his teacher. Fancy that, because sometimes I don't enjoy spending time with me. But then, who knows what motivates fourteen-year-olds? *Gods of War* and mustard, from what I'd seen.

It was that arm, I suppose, pretending to fire a gun, but something made me look for the servo motors and cables I sometimes imagined underneath his skin. Instead, all I could see was regular Cam, his arm in motion, and I couldn't help but smile. Then I turned away, reality hitting me in the face. Being here, signing this paperwork, was all the proof anyone needed that he was very real. He had been brought into this world, and then he had been abandoned to live his life in an orphanage, a castoff. Unwanted. What parent could do that to a great kid like Cam? Thank goodness he had grown up to be normal. The Center had been instrumental in that, and I was grateful, let me tell you, especially if he was going to live with me for a few days.

"Yes. This." Jill tapped the envelope again, getting my attention, and sliding it forward another inch. It was almost to the edge of the table. If she slid it forward again, it would fall in my lap. I reached for it. Instantly, I knew. It was cash. It had that feel.

"This is for Cam?"

"Oh, no. Not for Cam. He doesn't need our money."

There was that laugh again, clear as a bell, and twice as entrancing. I thought for a moment and realized it wasn't hand bells. That was how Cam laughed. I looked at him again, expecting to see this woman in the boy, but no, just the eyes and the laugh, along with a big dose of my imagination. They had nothing in common, except that they both connected at the Center somehow.

"I'll take it, though."

Cam's hand was there, and I hadn't seen him move. He was just there, and Jill made a motion. He froze and moved away much more slowly. Like a real boy would.

That made me think of the cap the day before, Cam knocking it off my head, and I hadn't seen him move then, either, and of course, with that, I remembered being surprised at how heavy he had felt when I held him under the downspout. Piston legs and aerated titanium bones would explain that, but not the Center never asking my name, or Cam pulling up things about my life I thought I had forgotten, like he was memorizing me or something.

All that flooded over me at once, one thing leading to another, one of those gestalt moments, where it's all there at the same time. You know, like those cartoons where the guy gets hit real hard, and little stars circle his head. That was what I felt like. Bam! All those memories, a bunch of little stars that I hadn't noticed before. I looked at Cam, searching for my robot boy, only to see him grinning back at me, as real as real can be.

Then Jill distracted me. She reached and tapped the envelope again, and I noticed her finger, slender, immaculately manicured. I had to tear my eyes away when she started talking.

"For you, Jake. A teenage boy is an expensive undertaking. Since you are relieving us of some of our duties, you are also relieving us of some of our expenses. We wish to share that with you. Please open it and see if that will do."

The look on her face told me it would. The envelope was quite thick. I ripped the end off, and it was fat with money. I slipped several bills out to find they were not small, either. This was easily as much as I got paid in a month.

"This is for what, clothes and stuff? A new pair of jeans won't cost this much." And if they did, I wouldn't buy them. Not even for Cam.

"For anything you need." That was one of the lawyers, and he stepped beside Jill. "For you or the boy. A new suit for church, anything. We hope it comes in handy."

"Sure," I said, "for the next six years. How long until you get the damage here repaired?" Then I wished I hadn't said that. Me and my big mouth. I glanced over, and Cam was worrying the hole in his jeans. I hoped he hadn't heard.

"We're being forced to put our in-house residency program on hold for a time. Perhaps later, but the way it stands now—" Jill didn't complete her thought, and I think she expected me to read her meaning into it.

I read it in just fine. Her unfinished statement had responsibility and parenting and entrapment stamped all over it. I listened but didn't hear the send-him-back-when-it-was-over part, and I needed that to be there, also.

"That sounds like—" I stumbled, my stomach churning. I thought of that insurance policy. The Center might cover that, but there was everything else. Shoes. Socks. Underwear. And that suit he mentioned? Those were expensive. This money would evaporate really fast. I coughed, not really trying to hide it.

"Mr. Turner, Jake, let me explain."

It was Jill again, but I wasn't sure I wanted to listen. I wished Cam wasn't in the room. I'd give them a piece of my mind. It wasn't taking Cam that goaded me. I knew that, even through my irritation. I liked him. Remember, I'd already let him stay the night, and I hadn't minded that at all. It was that they'd tricked me. Yet, I was holding that envelope, and I sat still and bit my tongue.

She continued, "Our goal with our children has always been to get them into good homes. Not to go into too great a detail, but that opportunity was almost stolen away from us last night. Cam is our last chance. He's fourteen. He needs you. He likes you. He says he trusts you, and I can see why. Do this. For him."

Guilt trip. Yet, it was working. Cam likes me? I guess I had hoped he did, but for him to tell the people here? I pride myself on being tough. You have to be in Denver public schools. But this yanked my heart strings.

"So, this is more than just a few days?" That was already pretty clear, but the question was, more than anything, to give me some time to let it soak in. Immediately, I knew I should have put more excitement in my words, for Cam's sake, and I felt bad that he probably overheard me. I could barely make my voice work, though. Dang, I wished they had given me some warning.

"For as long as you're willing." The lawyer actually sounded like he had a heart. Surprise there.

"Cam?" I motioned him over, making my decision. It wasn't his fault, and I wasn't taking my irritation out on him. I patted the desk, and he sat on the edge right in front of me. His hands gripped the top on either side, and I noticed his knuckles were white. His face was composed, though, and his blue eyes were locked on mine. "You want to do this, Cam? On the sofa?" The lawyer and Jill looked at each other, but Cam knew what I meant. The sofa, one towel, and Mrs. Osgood's bathroom. Thank goodness for Mrs. Osgood's bathroom. I watched his knuckles relax.

"Do you, Mr. Turner?"

Well, I heard the desperation in his voice, and that choked me up. I couldn't say anything. We sat there and looked at each other for maybe two minutes, until tears began to leak down his face. To keep mine from doing the same, I nodded, and he fell onto me, his arms around my neck. That surprised me, him hugging me, but Jill and the lawyer were clapping, so I didn't say anything. Now, I can't be sure, but I think the kid whispered something in my ear. Of course, I only remembered when I thought about it afterward, but it sounded like it could have been thank you.

On the way out Jill stopped me, telling me there was one last thing to take care of. My bank account number. That envelope was just for starters. Another would come every month Cam lived with me. That was news I could use. That was news my bank account could use. And yes, she told me again, Cam could make his own way. This was money for me.

I think I can get along with Cam for a very long time, and eighteen is a very long way away. I might even have a new car by then.

Now, that's a thank you even my bottom dollar will appreciate.

Chapter 12

Jake Remembers a Boy's Name

I hate Monday mornings. Well, that said, I hate every morning. It's why I do Saturday Mass. But Mondays are the worst. I've had recovery time over the weekend, and I can't get back into the groove in one day.

Cam wouldn't get up, either. Wouldn't wake up, was more like it. He lay there on the sofa, and he was unresponsive. His color was good, and he was breathing, but no life. No open eyes, no smile, no screech. Nothing.

He was up late last night. At first I blamed that. Not just up late, he was doing everything. Video games. Reading. Talking. To me. Two showers. He would have probably showered a third time except his towel was too wet, and I don't have another. Then the food he ate! We used some of the money to stop by the store, and he put mustard on everything, even his frozen pizza. God help us, Snarky, please get your place cleaned up so we can go out once in a while.

I called the Center, but the advice they gave me was loony. There's a cell phone in Cam's bag, I discovered, and a crazy cap, the kind I wear, with a bill, but not like I wear, either. Turn on the phone, connect to the Internet, and plug the cap into the phone. Cam needs to sleep in it a couple nights a week. I had to get them to tell me how to do that, the Internet thing. I don't carry a cell phone, I said. I think they were laughing at me, but I know plenty of people who don't carry them. Poor people. Teachers. Me. Still, it was simple enough once they explained it.

I wish Jill had been there. She would have clarified what it was all about. Brain stimulation, I guess. Well, I'd be late for work if he didn't get stimulated pretty quickly, so I hooked him up.

"Cam," I called out. He had the cap on. Lot of good that's going to do, I thought. I grabbed his shoulder and shook him, and then I patted his face. I thought I saw his cheek twitch. I sat on the edge of the sofa. "Cam, twenty minutes and I'm out the door. You going with me?" I was relieved to see the beginnings of a grin.

"Do I have to?"

"You're kidding me, right?" I stood and dumped him to the floor. "You're awake and just lying there?"

The phone clattered to a stop, coming to rest beside him, and he reached for it. Then he found the cap on his head, and he pulled it off. He didn't look happy, either.

"What?" I slapped a plate on the table, all in a hurry, because it was about time to leave. I made sure it was loud to get his attention. I watched him for a moment, waiting for him to explain what was under his skin. When he didn't answer, I turned back to breakfast, spooning eggs onto the plate, and adding more than a dash of mustard. I looked across the room, and he was gone. The bathroom door slammed, and it was quiet, until the pipes kicked in, telling me the shower was running full blast. I noticed the towel on the back of Cam's chair. He'd be back for that.

Then I saw the phone and the hat. It was wadded up and stuffed into the cushions. That told me something. He didn't like this getup. I wondered why. I picked them up. It was the oddest contraption. Wires fed from the inside to a bundle at the back, terminating in a mini-USB connector, just the kind for a standard Android or Windows phone. I slipped it on and plugged it into the phone. I didn't feel anything, except for a distracting tingle. And that was probably my imagination. Cam had me distracted, and the tingle? I don't like being late for work.

When he came out of the bathroom, Cam was already dressed. Wet, but dressed. He saw the cap in my hand, and a look flickered across his face. I was watching him, and I knew it was there, and then he visibly got control, and the look was gone. He brightened, and he sat and began to devour his eggs. I looked at the hat, and then I looked at Cam. Okay, kiddo, what bad memories do you have associated with this? The timer on the microwave beeped, and I called out, "Time to go." We grabbed our things and hustled out the door.

That was our morning, and we still haven't made it home. Today is baseball practice, and I coach. Did I say coach? I sit and watch. John Franklin coaches. Two of us have to be here, though, so he lets me manage from the sidelines.

Maybe we'll stop off at Billy's for a hot dog on the way home. It's out of the way, but he makes the best hot dogs in town. Now, if he just offered apple pie with his ice cream. That said, you can't get everything, and I've got a kid to think about now.

While watching the boys hit the ball at each other, it occurred to me that Cam might want to go out for the team. When I lifted my hand to motion him over, he was across the field talking to a boy with a cast on his arm. The name came to me. Kenny Urbringer. Don't know how I remembered that. I'm not usually good with names. Kenny got hit by a pop fly several weeks ago, and he landed on his wrist. Snapped it clean.

Maybe Cam doesn't need to go out for baseball after all. Maybe I should suggest a safer extracurricular activity, like cage fighting, or war games. I remember how Kenny screamed. It still makes my skin crawl.

Chapter 13

The Other Two Phone Calls

Now, here's what's weird. You already know I'm not a friend to my phone. It stays buried as much as it sees the light of day, and I'm okay with that. If people want to talk to me, I've got a face. Come talk to me. Phones are for emergencies, not chatting just to fill the time of day.

I don't have a cell phone, either. Well, I have Cam's, now, but that's Cam's, for the Internet. He might not care if I carry it around, but it's his, not mine. I don't buy into the cell phone thing, not yet, anyway. Wait until they become really useful, like printing twenties, that's what I say.

I was using the toilet, the one that's not really mine. Well, Mrs. Osgood's phone began to ring. I thought it was mine at first, because it was faint like before. I called to Cam to get it, and when it kept on, I dried my hands and stepped into the living room. Mine was still out on the table, and Cam was gaming. I started to say something to him, like, there's the phone, Cam. All you have to do is pick it up and say hello. Then I realized it wasn't ringing.

I went back to the bathroom and closed the door. It was still ringing, probably up to five or six by then. I opened Mrs. Osgood's side of the bathroom, and it got louder. Hm, I thought, do I really want to talk to some old person wearing a hearing aid? Then I remembered that Mrs. Osgood was forgetful, and if she needed to contact me, she might call her own number by mistake. I pushed through the door and climbed over the piles of stuff. The phone was in the front hall, so it didn't take me too long. I caught it on ring nine, just before most people hang up.

"Jake, here." Once again I was out of breath. I'm not looking forward to thirty in a couple months.

"Ah, Mr. Turner."

"Okay." I didn't recognize the voice, and he didn't identify himself. That puzzled me, so I waited a moment. Lots of people know where I live, and if they've been around awhile, they know about Mrs. Osgood, too. She came over on the Niña. I was puzzled, but I wasn't concerned. Not yet. The next thing he said jerked my hair on end.

"With Camden Archer." Nothing else.

"May I ask who's calling?" I mean, like, it wasn't even my number. Who had Mrs. Osgood been talking to, anyway? Did she have a son she'd never mentioned? She was forgetful, after all. Maybe. Who knows what old people forget?

"Do you really want to do this, Mr. Turner?" His voice was heavily accented and reminded me of cast iron being scraped with a blade.

"Do what? Ask for your name?" I didn't like his voice, and I didn't appreciate being challenged over God knows what. What right did this stranger have to ask me a question like that?

Then I realized he knew about Cam, and I thought of Beth Ziegler's call. He was threatening me! I slammed down the phone, only to look at my hand and realize I was shaking. I'd sign every paper the Center wanted me to in order to protect that kid back in my apartment. If he needed a place until the Center got their program back on line, then he had one with me. I could manage for as long as he wanted to stay. Even Admin approved. Who did this joker think he was?

Cam was still on his game when I returned. I was glad he wasn't watching me, because I could feel sweat on my forehead, the kind that comes from stress and anger. I didn't want the kid to think I was angry at him.

The TV caught my eye. I knew this game, and I often beat Cam when we played. He was good, but he struggled at times. I was better, because I struggled less. Neither of us was outstanding. Still, he was playing fast. There were no pauses, and he didn't stop to think. I'd never seen him play so well before.

"Cam," I said carefully. I still had my eyes on the screen, and I swear, he slowed down just like that. Seamlessly. He hadn't known I was there, and when I said his name, he changed how he was playing.

"Hey, Mr. Turner. Like a game?" Without looking, he nudged the second remote. I watched his fingers, though. Were they slower than before? I couldn't be sure.

"Been practicing without me?" I sat beside him, touching the remote but not yet willing to pick it up, like it was hotwired, and it might burn me right through to the base of my brain.

"What do you mean?" He ran his first three words together, *whaddya*. He hit a button, and he hooted, holding the remote high over his head. I could see his arm clear down to his chest, and he was beginning a thatch of blond hair in his armpit. Robo kid wouldn't grow that.

"How'd you play so fast?" I pointed to the screen. "You weren't even slowing down. I've never seen such good play."

"Nah, man." He fell back onto the sofa, punching me in the shoulder. "Just practicing. Trying to get better than you."

"But—" I wanted to push the matter, but Cam sat up suddenly and grabbed the phone.

"For you." He held it out. It wasn't ringing. He smiled, those blue eyes inviting me to believe he was just what he presented himself to be, a warm, likeable kid who only wanted to please.

Then the black box jangled into life. Cam set it on the coffee table in front of me with a thump and jumped up with that sudden leap fourteen-year-olds do. He slapped the side of my leg hard and winked.

"Probably your latest girlfriend." He jumped over me, and I heard the bathroom door slam.

On the third ring I picked it up and pushed the blinking button. "Jake, here." There was nothing. After a moment the dial tone started. I put the receiver back and looked down the hall. That was convenient. Too convenient. And Cam never answered my question.

Somehow, I think that was the point all along.

51

Chapter 14

Snarky Says Hello

It had been two weeks, and things had about settled in. Cam on the sofa. A second towel. We made it to Sacred Heart once. We haven't had the opportunity to get him a suit, but I did make sure his jeans were clean. I even had the car repaired with some of the money from the Center. I felt guilty at first, but Cam rode me, reminding me what Jill had said. The money was mine. He could get his own.

He did, too, magically showing up with twenties in his stainless steel wallet. I made a point to check it every few days, mostly when he was in the shower, just to keep track. I intended to slip a few twenties inside without saying anything, but it was clear he didn't need my help. Not with cash. And it wasn't stolen. He was doing yards. Two days he skipped afterschool practice, and when I drove home, he was in a flowerbed down from the school pulling weeds. Somebody offer me free money, and I wouldn't be pulling weeds. But then I'm not Cam. Responsible Cam who's too good to be real. Responsible Cam who hangs up his towel and lets me win when we game together.

Yeah, I was watching. Cam was smooth, but he slowed down when we played each other. Not much, but just enough for me to win more often than not. Then he would jump on me and play-punch me in the stomach, teasing me about being mean to the little kid, like he'd really tried to win. Maybe he had. Maybe I'm really that good. I used to think so. I'm not so sure any longer.

He still peed in the toilet and poured mustard over his eggs. I've never seen a person eat so much mustard in my life. One night I was walking through the living room, and he was asleep. I hadn't seen the cap in a few days, and I dug around for it. It was under the sofa with the cell phone stuffed inside. I slipped it on his head and plugged it into the phone, then connected to the Internet. I remembered the tingle it had given me.

"Sweet dreams, Cam," I whispered to him, quietly so he wouldn't wake. Heck, I was grateful he was a sound sleeper and didn't come alive every time I walked through to get a glass of water. I didn't want to mess that up.

He shifted on the cushions, and I adjusted his blanket. Then I tucked it around his shoulders just in case. There was a dab of mustard on the side of his face, and I smiled. I realized I was getting attached, and somehow that didn't seem too bad. We'll see how that feels when all this falls apart, because he's not mine, no matter what they said when we signed those papers. He's an orphan that nobody wanted, and he belongs to the Center. I reminded myself I'd do well to remember that. Fourteens become fifteens, and they move on out of my life. It happens every year at my school, and about that time I knew I was feeling sorry for myself. Angry, also, because who had the right to give up on this kid, to just throw him away? The Center, too. They had at least given stability to him. Or they had before dumping him on me. A little glitch, and he was out the door. What kind of life was this for a kid, sleeping on the sofa and mustard three times a day? It's no kind of life for me, and I get to choose.

By that time I was a mess, and if I woke him, he'd want to know what was wrong. So, I climbed in bed and stared at the ceiling. I guess I dozed off, because the next thing I remember was a siren going on and off, and the sun was in my face. I threw the covers back and sat up, rubbing my hair with my hands. The door burst open, and Cam flew in, still in his boxers. He flung himself on the bed, grabbing my pillow and hitting me with it.

"What?" I wasn't awake, and I'm never a morning person, anyway.

"Snarky's is back open." I looked at him to see him grinning from ear to ear. "Listen."

"To what?" I could barely see. How could he expect me to listen, too?

He rolled to the window. My bed is pushed up against it because the room is so small. He released the catch and slid it up. The siren was louder. Each time it wailed to a stop, an electronic voice called out, "Snarky's Pizza, open for business. Discount coupons available at the door." Then the siren started up again.

Thanks, Snarky. I love you, too.

And I meant it.

Chapter 15

It's All in the Math, Sherlock

Things went along fine for another week. Cam and I, we headed off to Snarky's a couple times. Couldn't really tell any difference, except maybe the glass over the buffet line was cleaner. I like Billy's, but hot dogs go sour on me after a couple nights, and I was ready to get back to real food. Pizza. All the nutrients a body needs: meat, cheese, and bread, all done up in one pie. Cam inhales it. Makes me glad for buffet. I was talking to Snarky, and he said he has three boys. Grown, now, and working in the back, but that's why the buffet. Yeah, Snarky's a good man.

I didn't see Cam much at school. In class, of course, but I didn't monitor his lunch, and he was never in detention that I knew of. The Center kids never were. Before the accident, I said something to that effect in the workroom one day, and one of the other teachers laughed. "Out on their ear, if they do. They know they've got it good out there. Eighty-inch screens, pool tables, and each one has his own PlayStation." I just shook my head. Cam never said anything about that, so I took it for jealously. When you're a teacher, everyone's richer than you. Some of us can't deal with that.

Cam was with me when the awards were announced for next year's placement. Well, not with me, exactly, but in my class. The kids were working on experiments comparing densities of different liquids. He was with Kenny the one-armed boy. Funny how Kenny got transferred into my class just after he and Cam took up on the practice field. Good for Cam, though. Probably better for Kenny. He's been a different kid, even hobbled by his cast. Brighter. Friendlier. Cam does that to people.

The speaker crackled, like the wires were loose, and I quieted the kids down. Vivian, back in group seven, took second in science. The girls sitting with her squealed, nearly knocking over a beaker of blue fluid. I winked at her, and she blushed. I'm pretty sure she was pleased. First place wasn't in any of my classes, and I didn't recognize the name, but I'd find him and make sure he got a good word from the science department. It was math that surprised me. Of course they called out the third place first, then second, and saved first 'til the end, drawing out the suspense. The kids who cared were on pins and needles. Those who didn't—either they hadn't bothered with the test or had no hope of winning—found something else to do, which was okay as long as they were quiet. Cam was drawing on Kenny's cast, totally ignoring the awards, when first place for math was called.

"Camden Archer, first place in mathematics."

It was the final award, and all the winners were asked to head to the central office to pick up their certificate, for second and third, or their medal, for first.

Well, the class fell apart when Cam's name was called. Several of the bigger boys, jocks on the football team, began to laugh, pointing. I was in shock, myself. Cam, smart? I don't mean that the way it sounds. I know he's smart, but he hadn't told me he'd taken the math test. Not even hinted at it. Like, he never pays attention to the math part of science, just slips by on banana peels. I guess I was wrong about that. But then, I'd never seen his math grades, not on his report card. Those don't come out until next week, and I'll have to sign my first one ever.

Anyway, the class cheered, and the girl who got second in science ran up to him and kissed him on the cheek. Not exactly permissible behavior, but I was glowing by then. My Cam. First in math. She could kiss him anywhere she wanted, and I wasn't saying anything. He stood and waved before he exited, and he pointed to me.

"For you, Mr. Turner." He clapped his hands together and threw them out with his thumbs raised before making a royal exit.

I think several of the girls are now officially in love.

After practice a group of boys went with us to Snarky's, and I bought them all pizza as a way of bragging on Cam. As they filled up and filtered away a couple at a time, Cam and I were the only ones left at our table, with the remaining few at the video games. I wanted to talk to him, but not with anyone else around. And not at home. That was our space to just chill. Some things need to be broached outside of your own four walls.

Then, the last few came by for a high-five with Cam and a thanks, Coach, for me, even though I'm not a real coach. I waved and told 'em I'd see 'em at practice tomorrow.

"So, you took the math test." I had a napkin in my hand and wiped up a water ring off the table. It was my way of pretending I didn't really put too much into what I said.

"Yeah. Aced it."

I looked up, and he was grinning. I could tell he was pleased with himself. Very pleased. Well, I guess I would be, too, except I'd never seen that in my class, and science takes a lot of math. Cam was smart, but he never "aced" it.

"So," I began hesitantly, not really wanting to cast a shadow on things, "you just *aced* it, just like that?"

"I didn't cheat, if that's what you're saying. I don't need to *cheat* to get the right answers."

Well, I would have been ticked off already, someone doubting me, when I'd just won top math honors in the school. Not Cam. I looked at him, and I swear, deep in those blue eyes, he was finding this funny. He *wanted* the chance to prove he hadn't cheated.

"So, let's start over. Why'd you sign up to take the test?"

That was a simple question, and I began to run the dates down in my head. He was with me when the test was given. I knew that. I just didn't know he'd taken it. The signups ended—I had it counted out by then—the day after he moved in with me.

I don't have a good poker face. I've always known that. I guess Cam is good at reading expressions, because about the time I got that sorted out, he grinned and leaned back.

"Got it figured out, yet?"

"Um," I held out a hand, for what I didn't know, "not really. You signed up after you and I, um—"

"Started rooming together." His eyes twinkled.

"Yeah, that. You ended up on my sofa. And you just *aced* it? The math test? Just like that?" He was enjoying this entirely too much, and I decided there would be paybacks. Later, just not now.

"Yeah. I thought you would like that, me, you, top student and favorite teacher."

I caught his eyes, you know, when he said that, and they glanced away for a second. His cheeks flushed, too. I wondered if he said that on purpose, or if it slipped, the favorite teacher part.

"Then why not science? I teach science, you moron." I grabbed his shoulder and shook it, not hard though, because I was laughing at the time. He held his arms between us and pushed me away, ducking down into his seat.

"I couldn't do that."

"Not smart enough. Too hard, huh?" I leaned over the table and grabbed a handful of skin, twisting hard enough to get a response.

"Too obvious." He had both hands on mine, trying to force me off. By that time he was on his back, and the people left in the restaurant were watching us.

"Too obvious? What does that mean?" I let him go, and he was red-faced with laughter. I guessed I was the same, because I felt the temperature had gone up ten degrees.

"You're my science teacher. And I live with you now. People might think I *cheated.*" He balled his hand into a fist and punched me in the shoulder as he said the word cheated.

How smart can an eighth grader be? Smarter than an eighth grade teacher, that's for sure. But I tell you this, I sure am proud of him, even if I now have a bruise on my shoulder. Cam's got a wallop, and he knows how to use it.

Chapter 16

The Late Late Show

"President Obama, remember him? Tall, skinny guy who disappears in the dark and behind phone poles? Well, he has a new job, now." The comedian paused, the silence pregnant with expectation. He gave a wide smile. "Butterfly advocate. It seems that one of his granddaughters accidentally released all the butterflies at the new insect exhibit at the Honolulu Zoo. The president was going door to door handing out butterfly nets, encouraging people to return the butterflies to the zoo." He raised a long-handled butterfly net from behind his desk and began swatting at paper butterflies that fell from above the curtains. Laughter tittered from the audience.

"In other news, have you been keeping track of the latest edition of the Frankenstein novel? It seems Mary Shelley didn't have the last word. Not only do we have the monster himself, and the bride of Frankenstein, but now we have," and he held up a book for the camera to zoom in on, "the children of Frankenstein, or as we like to call it, *SISSY Frankenstein*." The title was written in bold letters, spelled like it sounded rather than the true acronym, but the image was telling, also. It showed the Center for Innovative Software Specialization and Intellectual Enhancement, with metal towers sticking out of the roof. A black cloud hovered overhead, with twin lightning bolts striking the towers. The crowd roared as the lights in the studio flashed off and on several times, mimicking lightning flashes.

"Have you ever noticed," and the comedian held out his hands, continuing to a new joke as he waited for the lights to remain on and the crowd to settle, "how people wait at signal lights, even when no one else is in the city? It can be midnight on Saturday, and everyone's asleep. Who is there to hit?"

The crowd roared, although not as loud as at SISSY Frankenstein. They loved that one.

Chapter 17

The Joke Falls Flat

So some people have a warped sense of humor. I know, because I have a boy crying on my sofa.

Now, fourteen's fourteen, and Cam's not really crying, but I know crying when I see it. He has his feet up on the cushion and his chin on his knees, and he's not talking to anyone. Anyone means me. That and his eyes are red. Real-boy red.

I think of my torn fingernail. It's better now. In the past three weeks, it's grown out enough to leave little more than a rough spot, but it still antagonizes me. It catches on things, just when I've forgotten it's there, and it tears all over again. I think Cam's like my fingernail. He's been damaged. He gets better, and he starts to forget he's damaged, and then he catches on something.

I pulled my basketball from the corner, and I bounced it a few times on the floor. If I do it too many times, Old Man Cheney from downstairs will start in with his broom, but I can usually get away with six or eight hits before he begins to beat on his ceiling.

"Go with me, Cam." I put the ball under my arm and kicked off my work shoes. I slipped on my athletic ones, trying to tie them with a hand and a half.

Cam looked at me a minute, then unraveled himself and

squatted beside me. "Let me do that."

He sniffled and wiped it on his sleeve, but at least he was moving. He had both shoes done before I could start to thank him. Then he hit the ball out of my arm, catching it as it went wild.

"At the court, man. You're toast." Before I could respond he was out the door.

What was that about? Tears, then a challenge? I teach 'em in my science class, but home time is out of my league. Then I glanced across the room to where the TV still flickered. It was the news, as usual. They were showing a clip from The Late Late Show. The sound was down, but I could see the picture well enough. The camera zoomed in on a book, and it was titled *SISSY Frankenstein*.

Zingo! Rip that fingernail right off the boy's hand. Off his heart, was more like it. Good going, Late Late Show. You get a good laugh, and I get tears. Well, I didn't intend to stand for it.

I hit the door after Cam. I intended to toast his buns. He might be good enough to win, but I'd make him work for every point. He'd be so tired when he finished, he wouldn't even *remember* that lousy joke. SISSY Frankenstein, my foot! I had the best SISSY Frankenstein in the whole world, and I had the paperwork to prove it.

I was going to make sure he knew it, too.

Chapter 18

The Center Giveth, and It Taketh Away

The Center called today. They want to see Cam. I told them he has classes every day, and after school I have to coach. You know what I mean, but to say I coach tells them I have to be there.

"Oh," they said, ever so politely, "how about this weekend?"

I didn't like that. My weekends are mine, mine and Cam's, now that he's with me. That's when we get to do what we want to do, like sleep in, just hang out, game till two in the morning. I suppose I've gotten used to having someone else in the apartment.

"How long do you need him?" I could work it in, I guessed, if it wasn't too long.

"If you could drop him off Friday evening, no matter how late, we can have him ready for you to pick up Sunday afternoon. How does that sound? We get his checkups done, and you get a weekend off. Two thumbs up, right Mr. Turner?"

Two thumbs up yours, I thought. You can't give him to me, *insist* that I take one of your Frankensteins—meant in only the nicest of ways, of course—and then take him away for an entire weekend. I bit my tongue, though, and I was polite.

"Cam's doing fine, Miss, er—"

"Mrs. Linkston." She was *so* well-mannered.

"There's nothing to bring him in for. His hat? Is that it? I make sure he sleeps in it at least three nights a week." I felt a sense of desperation. I didn't know why, but it was as if I wouldn't get back the same boy if I took him in. I guess it must have been Comedy Sunrise and The Late Late Show. Frankenstein, and all that nonsense. Still, the desperation was there, even though I knew it was silly.

"We knew you would be a good parent figure for Camden. He always speaks so highly of you. How about this Friday at eight?"

Eight. I could say he has a game. There is a baseball game on Friday, just that Cam's not playing. I could go, though, as a coach, and say Cam has to be with me. Scorekeeper. That's it. Cam's my scorekeeper. Then there's Mass on Saturday. That would be two weekends in a row, but I'd do that. At least I'd intend to.

"We'll see you then, Mr. Turner. Camden doesn't need to bring anything with him."

The line went dead, as if she knew what I was going to say, and she knew she had to cut me off first. I growled. I would take him, though. They knew I would. I picked up my bank statement off the table, and I pulled it out. Good to their word, there was a deposit from the Center, exactly the same as they'd given me that first day. That, what with my regular check from the school, and my balance was bigger than I'd ever seen it. I thought of what it would buy. Just not another Cam.

Cam burst into the room. His hair was plastered to his head, and one side of his clothes was streaked with mud. He was breathing hard.

"Cam—" I started.

"Kenny," he interrupted, laughing, "got his cast off today. We're playing tackle with some of the guys at the park." He dodged around me and grabbed several bottles of water off the counter, rolling them up in his shirt. The water bottles had come with the money from the Center. It beat the water from the faucet. I noticed he was wearing shorts. He'd started that since the weather'd warmed. One leg was scraped, but there was no blood. It looked pretty harsh, though.

But he was gone again, the door left open for me to close. I didn't have a chance to tell him about the weekend. I wondered if he'd mind. He'd lived there until he was fourteen. Longer than he'd lived with me. I wondered if they missed him when he was away.

I thought about the other orphans. Only one had gone to our school, seventh grade. She hadn't been back, and I'd assumed she'd been transferred to another facility. What other facility? I hadn't heard. Most Center children that came through were in advanced placement classes, which I didn't teach, so I had little direct contact with them. Then of course, if any fostered out when they were younger, the school staff at Bruce wouldn't know, even if they wound up at our school. Sealed records, and all that. Teachers. Don't tell them what the courts don't think they need to know. Let us stumble through in the dark.

I shook my head to clear that out and decided I had to make plans for the weekend, something to fill the time. I wondered if Jill out at the Center would be free. I even picked up the phone, but I didn't call. Conflict of interest. That's what we call it at the school. You don't date your students or the parents of your students. And it's frowned on to date a coworker. I didn't know the Center's policy, but asking Jill out on a date seemed rather like a parent of one of my students asking me on a date. I shuddered at that idea.

I wandered down to the park to watch the boys play. Football, I chuckled. Cam's branching out. When I first saw them, it looked one-sided to me. There were maybe ten guys, with eight clustered on one side, and two on the other. Eight shirts and two skins. As I got closer, Cam and Kenny were the skins. Kenny was without his cast, but he wasn't any good. That was clear from the moment I saw them. However, the shirts were desperately trying to gain a point, and it was hopeless. Cam was all lightning and bulldozer rolled into one. All Kenny did was stand back and cheer him on.

I watched for about ten minutes, and then something I did must have caught Cam's attention. He looked at me and waved, and then he did that thing, the one where he slows down, and he becomes the fourteen-year-old he thinks I need to see. Shirts took him down en masse, and he disappeared from view.

My heart stopped for a moment. I guess I didn't think he'd come back up. It must have been the call from the Center, like I'd thought he wouldn't come back from there, either, even though I knew it was silly. I held my breath, though, as Kenny jumped in, trying to pull the shirts off. Cam finally emerged, holding both hands high, victorious even in his defeat. The game went on for another quarter hour, but shirts dominated. Cam kept yelling to get my attention, as if he was glad I'd come. I wish I hadn't, though.

Without me, Cam was the superhuman robot boy I'd imagined him to be. With me, he was just Cam, real boy, normal as the rest of us. I hadn't decided yet which one I liked best.

I missed my robot boy, though. Tendons of steel, and pistons for legs. That would be too, too cool.

Chapter 19

Three's a Crowd, but Being Alone Is Worse

After school on Friday, we had a short practice. Game night and all. John likes to have short practices on game night, mostly to keep the juices flowing the right direction. Last minute hitting practice. Maintain the kids' focus on the game. That sort of thing. Coach things that I'm not really into.

Cam sat across the field and helped mentor Kenny. It didn't help Kenny's game, but I think it helped Kenny. He was eating up the attention. I don't know how Kenny qualified for the team, except we barely have enough for a full roster, and we need every warm body we can get.

Cam invited Kenny out with us afterward, since there was no point in Kenny going to the game. He never played, not with his cast at first, and John had never worked him into the lineup. I would've liked to have had Cam for myself, sort of a going away party, but Kenny's growing on me. Being in my class now, I'm getting to know him, and he's okay. Good grades, although not much personality. I probably wouldn't have paid him any notice but for Cam. Cam has that effect on people. What he likes, they like. He draws you in, and you're there, and even if you don't know how you got there, you find you enjoy it anyway. I try to drag people into what I want, and I wind up with enemies. How's that for good people skills? And I'm a teacher, and of eighth graders. It's a wonder I still have a job.

They went to the back and beat around on the video machines, and Snarky was cleaning tables. He got to mine, and since the late Friday crowd was still at the ball game, he folded his towel up and asked if he could sit for a chat. Sure, I said. What I didn't say was that I had an empty weekend coming up, my new roomie was leaving me, and I was afraid to ask my new squeeze for a date. Then, she couldn't be my new squeeze if I never worked up the nerve to ask her out. All that stayed bottled up inside.

"I like your boy, the blond one," he said. "Reminds me of my youngest, back in the day."

"How's that?" I was pleased with his remark. It sounded like a compliment, and the part about him being my boy wasn't too bad.

"From the Center, I gather." He sat and refolded his towel, not looking at me. "How'd he make it through?"

"Through what?"

"Come now, Mr. Turner. Your first name's Jake, right? Can I call you that?"

I nodded as his eyes cut my direction.

"Well, Jake, you teach over at the school, right?"

I nodded again. Everyone knows that.

"That boy living with you's about the age you teach, I guess. Might even be in one of your classes."

"What are you getting at?" I thought of the night of the storm, and Cam and me pulling our wet clothes off outside. His question smacked of that, and I felt uncomfortable. I slipped out my wallet, thinking maybe I could pay right then. I'd been by the ATM and had some of the Center's money.

I pulled several bills out, and I realized the money felt wrong, like they were buying me off. I knew what it was. I didn't want Cam to go tonight. Then, before I could decide to hand Snarky the money, he asked me another question.

"He's smart?" He nodded his head Cam's direction.

"Top math award for eighth grade." In spite of my unease, I couldn't help saying that. I was still proud.

"Thought so. Center kids are like that. Had his first appointment, yet?" His eyes were on Cam, watching him hoot and cheer with each successful conquest. When I didn't answer, he turned to

68

me. "They always do that, Jake, tests and the like. You'll see. Your boy'll start to grow, and you won't know why. It's the Center that does it."

"Tonight's his first." *Appointment.* I didn't say that, but he nodded, and I knew he understood. I didn't know why I told him that, but I guess I had begun to relax. I sensed this man wasn't out to accuse me of improper behavior with one of my students. And telling someone helped bleed the frustration, I suppose. Anyway, it felt good that someone else knew. I slipped my wallet away with the Center's money still inside, the urge to escape gone with the shift in the conversation. "What do you know about the Center's kids? I haven't heard where the rest of them went after the incident out there."

"Didn't go nowhere. How's your boy still out, though?" Snarky turned back to me, waiting, as if this were important.

"He got trapped at my place during the storm." I thought that's what he was asking. His earlier question had begun to make sense to me, now. "When I called in, the Center told me to keep him overnight. The next morning he had no home to go to." I chuckled to myself. It sounded ordinary, even ho, hum when I said it like that, and it was the truth, too. So much for stressing over nothing. I knew what it was. It's that teacher thing, you know, about maintaining proper student-teacher relationships. Stripping in the rain, even innocently like Cam and me . . . well, in education, sometimes innocence is tainted by the eye of the beholder.

"So I hear." A frown creased the place just between Snarky's eyes.

"Yeah," and I tapped the tabletop. "Lucky for him that storm stranded him that day, I guess."

"And at your place." Snarky looked bothered, the frown deeper, like there was something else he wanted to ask.

"We didn't start off at my place." I laughed. "Not at first. We were headed here for lunch." I remembered why we didn't stop, and I hated to mention it. Snarky didn't, though.

"And I was closed by the health department." He nodded matter-of-factly.

"Since you mention it, yeah. We headed to my place for sandwiches, and that was when the storm hit."

He smiled, glancing at me then to the boys. He looked like he wanted to say something, but he didn't. That puzzled me.

"What?"

"Health department never did shut me down. I was out of town, visiting my nephew at the Air Force Academy, Colorado Springs way. Would've been open, but my eldest, he got sick, and my second can't cook to save his life. The youngest was driving me."

Why had he told me all that? I looked at Snarky, and he seemed years younger, as if he had needed to get it off his chest, like it explained something he hadn't been able to figure out before. It didn't make any sense to me, though. It was just what had happened, and now Cam was mine. Then it really hit me what he'd said. Cam's still out. And the others aren't? What did that mean? I meant to ask him, but the boys came running over. Cam had beaten the game, and Kenny was falling over his words to tell me. Snarky moved to the next table and began to wipe it down.

We were in the car when I remembered the rest of what Snarky had said. Cam'll start to grow. Don't all boys grow? How's the Center got anything to do with that? Anyway, we dropped Kenny off at his grandmother's, and I headed out to the Center. The drive was quiet, the only sound that of the wind pouring in through the open windows, and I didn't know what to say. I'd never had a son, and while I couldn't claim Cam, he was as close as I was going to get for a very long time. Maybe forever. How did I tell a fourteen-year-old that I didn't want him to get out of the car, and that my weekend would be hollow and empty without him? I didn't take that course in college, and I was always glad to be rid of my students for the weekend. Cam was more, though, now that he lived with me. What was my sofa for if I had no Cam to sleep on it?

"Want me to come in?" I parked right in front of the door. All the lights were on, and the building glowed in the gathering dusk. It was really pretty, but I didn't feel it just then. The moment was awkward, and I didn't want to go in, but I felt I had to ask.

"No."

His voice was small, and I knew he felt the same as me. I was tempted to drive away with him still inside the car, but I knew better.

"You're okay, then, on your own." I touched the seat between us. I almost hugged him, but I didn't. "Get out, then, you little turkey. The weekend's mine."

I tried to sound light, like I meant it, but I could feel the lie burning in my eyes, and I looked away. He didn't move. He just sat there, his hands in his lap, looking forward. I turned back to him, catching his darkened profile against the lighted backdrop of the Center. He was so still he didn't look real, and something caught in my throat.

"Cam?"

"I'm okay."

He took a deep breath, and I knew he wasn't okay. I teach eighth graders. I might not know how to tell them I'll miss them, but I know when they're not okay. Well, sometimes I can tell, and this was one of them. I shut off the car.

"What is it?" I saw someone inside, but they walked on by and didn't come out. That's when I had an epiphany, one of those things where you suddenly put the facts together. I remembered the cap, and Cam stuffing it in the sofa. "You know what they're going to do, don't you?" He nodded. "But you'll still be Cam when I pick you up on Sunday, right? No scars, no memory wipes, no sixth finger." I tried to be funny.

"No sixth finger." He held up one hand and looked at it. I saw him visibly pull himself together, and his expression changed, as if he had accepted something he didn't want to but had no choice. "Definitely no sixth finger, and I hope no memory wipes. I'm worth too much money. They wouldn't dare." He grinned, and his face was bright and happy again, his blue eyes sparkling in the fading light. He opened the door and climbed out. When I started the car, he shut the door and began to walk off. Before I could pull away, he ran back and leaned in through the window.

"Forget something?" Lame, but what else could I say? I love you? I didn't quite think so.

"You are coming back on Sunday? You'll be right here when I come out?"

"Right in this very spot. Count on it." I watched him take a deep breath. Was that desperation I saw in his eyes?

"Good." Then he walked away and didn't turn back.

We've got to work on that fingernail.

Chapter 20

The Real World Can Hurt

The weekend was tough without Cam.

I did call my mom in Casper, though. I don't do that often enough, if I believe what she says. After Dad died, I just sort of lost connection with my hometown. Mom reminds me of something I wish I could have held onto a little longer. I've tried to get her to move here, but she won't think of it. So, she has her life there, and I have mine here. I started to tell her about Cam, but I couldn't. I was afraid I'd bleed all over the phone, and I didn't want to get messy. Then I'd have to call back and explain all about the Center and why he lives here. Mom wouldn't get it. She'd just ask me why I wasn't married so I could give her real grandchildren.

Saturday night I actually played *Gods of War*. It wasn't much fun by myself, though, and I began to wish I'd made it to Mass. Something to break the routine. Get out of the house. About two I knew I had to get some sleep, and I considered the sofa. I even got my pillow, but once I was settled, I remembered why I never slept there. The center cushion is like a cavern, and it makes my back hurt. While I was trying to get comfortable, I found the cap and the cell phone. I held the phone up and unlocked the screen. It glowed in the dark, and I scrolled through, looking for anything to remind me of Cam. Then I plugged the cap in and slipped it on, pulling the bill down low, and connecting the phone to the Internet. I got that same tingle as before. Maybe that's why Cam didn't like it. But then, maybe that's why he aced that math test. Couldn't hurt me to get smart. I decided to keep it on a while.

I guess it was an hour later that I woke nauseous. My head was spinning, too. I brushed the hat off and stumbled to the bathroom, drinking some Pepto right out of the bottle. I made my way to bed and fell in. I had crazy dreams after that, full of strange colors and warehouses of body parts. The sun was in my face when I jerked awake. I felt better, except for the dreams. If I'm going to dream, I want a beautiful woman in there with me, not what I got that night. I found the cap and phone and stuffed them back into the sofa. I felt sorry for Cam.

I ate some Oreo cereal about eleven and moped around until the afternoon. I hadn't thought to ask what time I was supposed to be there, so I figured two might be good enough. I didn't want Cam to think I wasn't coming. I pulled on a pair of jeans and a tee. I wasn't dressing up for those jokers, not after they ruined my weekend. Loafers and no socks. That'd show them how they rated in my book.

Cam was waiting when I got there, outside, sitting on the steps. He waved when he saw me drive up, but it wasn't like I'm used to. When he moved to the car and climbed in, he didn't dance, either. He walked. For Cam, that was unusual.

"Hey, bud. Hard weekend?" I didn't tell him about mine. I'm the adult. I'm supposed to be able to handle it.

"Hey, Mr. Turner." He grinned, and I could see the old Cam. He leaned back and stretched his legs. Then he held out his arm and spread his fingers. "Have I grown?"

That was an odd question. It'd only been two days. But I looked him over appraisingly like I was seriously evaluating him, and by jiggery, he was right. His neck, not much, but I knew Cam and how his clothes fit. And his sleeves hit at just the wrong spot on his arms. Not much off, just off. His feet were under the dash, but his jeans seemed a bit snug in the crotch.

"Those are the same clothes, aren't they?" Of course, they were. I recognized the tear in his jeans.

"The same. I'll need new stuff this week. I should have said that before. We could have shopped last week, and my new clothes would have fit."

Shopped last week for clothes that fit this week? What I didn't know about kids would fill a parenting manual.

"We can stop on the way home." I started the car, pulling out towards the highway.

"Can't. I hurt too much."

"Hurt?" I stopped the car and glanced back at the Center. "What did they do to you? Tell me, Cam, or I'm turning around." I was angry, now. Last night, and now they'd hurt him. I'd hire a lawyer and see if I could get full custody. Even if they quit giving me money, I thought we could both live on my salary. Maybe.

"It's my joints. They always hurt after the treatments."

He was rubbing his wrist. I gently took his arm and felt of it. He grimaced, and I released it. I couldn't be sure, but underneath the skin, it felt, you know, like when you add a weld to make a pipe longer. Just that little bit of a bump where it should be smooth. And the skin, it was too tight over his arm.

"Cam, why do your joints hurt after your treatments?" I thought about Snarky. They always grow after visiting the Center. What did that mean? I think I was finding out.

"It takes a while for my body to adjust. It always hurts at first, then it goes away. My skin, too. It's always tight for a day or two. I just need to be immobile for a few hours."

Immobile? The kid knows immobile? It sounded like he'd been through this a time or two. I felt sorry for him, even as I wondered how severe his medical problems really were.

Poor Cam.

Then his hand grabbed mine in a tight grip just for a second, and as quickly he relaxed it. I glanced over. He looked asleep. He wasn't, though. He whispered, "Thanks."

"For what?" I squeezed his hand back and put it on his leg atop his jeans that were mysteriously too tight.

"For coming back for me."

Like I would have done anything else. I turned to tell him that, but he'd started to snore. I laughed to myself. I knew one thing for sure. Robots don't snore, and I was pretty sure Superboy didn't, either. I was convinced by then that I had a real boy in the car with me. I wouldn't tell him that, though. Real boys aren't grateful, and they never, never say thank you. I was just glad it was Cam with me, and whether he was real or he wasn't, I liked him just the way he was.

Snore and all.

Chapter 21

It's Just Me, Mr. Turner

We got it all. Shoes, socks, fresh underwear. Not on Sunday, of course, because Cam could barely move after I picked him up. I remember some of that, though. I'm tall, and when I shot up about Cam's age, my joints hurt all the time. I'd lie in bed and cry when it was really bad. I don't think anyone knew, well, my mom, maybe. She might ride me about grandchildren now, but she's pretty perceptive. A pretty good mom at fourteen, too. Anyway, I let him have my bed. I'd changed the sheets the week before, and after being on the sofa, I didn't think he'd really mind. The sofa doesn't smell too good, either.

He just crashed. He hobbled in, trying to smile at me, but I saw the tears in his eyes. I tried to imagine my mom, me being her and Cam being me, and I picked him up in my arms and carried him to my room. I rolled him onto the bed, whispering that I was sorry, and I pulled his shoes off and tossed my comforter over him. He half smiled and wrapped his arm around my pillow, working his head into a comfortable position. Then he was dead to the world for the rest of the day. So, I had Cam back, but I still had the day to kill. And I couldn't go anywhere. What if he needed me? I hadn't thought about that. It must be a parent thing. It also made me wonder if most parents would do it over again if they had a choice. You know, have children. Would they make the trade, giving up all their freedoms, if they knew beforehand? It gave me cause to think how I'd wanted Cam back for the weekend, wanted him back really bad, and now he had my hands tied. Being a parent is tough, even if I'm not really one.

He got up in the middle of the night and found me on the sofa. I had eventually dozed off after working my towel under my back. The room was completely black, and I knew he was there when I felt the cushion at my feet move. Then he picked up my legs and slid under them, resting his arms on top of the blanket. I heard him take a deep breath and let it back out again.

"Still hurting?" I could empathize. The sofa. My back. Cam's pain was different. He wasn't choosing to hurt. It was the Center's fault, and that didn't seem fair to me.

"Not bad."

"That's good." I could feel the blanket move, and I knew he was kneading it in his hands. His jeans rubbed the back of my legs, and I wished he would sit still or get up. I'm less awake in the middle of the night than I am in the morning, and little things like that get on my nerves. Even so, I tried to imagine my mom and what she would do. She would let me talk, even if it didn't fit her schedule. I thought maybe Cam needed to talk. I felt sympathy for my mom. I talked to her a lot growing up.

"Every four months." Cam's voice was barely more than a whisper.

"What?" There was something going on in that head. I usually saw just the surface, I realized. This was deeper. I didn't know if I wanted it to come out. When someone's an orphan, there's no telling the baggage they're saddled with.

"I was a baby when this started. People say kids don't remember, but I remember every time. Crystal clear like it was yesterday. When I was little they gave me tranks. They'd stick an IV in me and feed me the stuff like it was candy."

He laughed, and I could feel it through my legs. His hands were fists, though. They pressed against my shins. That told me more than his words.

"Then it'd get better, and I'd be proud that I'd grown. An inch taller, I'd crow. Like it made a difference. Everyone was an inch taller. And sometimes one of us would make our way out of the

76

Center, and a new one would come in, a baby to keep us awake at night."

That sounded incredibly simplistic to me, like a child's version of things, one painted from a perspective that didn't see the full picture. Still, it was Cam's picture, and who knew, maybe it was on the money. One thing, though. They showed up as babies? Always? People don't get orphaned when they are six or ten? However, the conversation had reached its end, like Cam had said what he needed to say, and he was cleansed. Emptied. Better, I hoped. Eventually, he leaned over on me, crowding me on the sofa. I put up with it for a bit, thinking he needed my attention, but when I heard the snoring, I knew he was just asleep. He had only come in to get his sofa back. That was fine with me, because I wanted my bed back. I slipped out from under the blanket, rolling it up over Cam, and I made my way in the darkness to the bathroom. Mine, not Mrs. Osgood's. It felt good to use my own bathroom.

The next morning, I told John I couldn't make after-school practice. He asked around and brokered a trade with Stefanie Hickson, art, for lunch duty. So, I got to do lunch duty. I got to watch Cam, too. After yesterday, I was keeping my eye on him as much as possible. There was something I couldn't put my finger on. Yeah, his jeans were too tight, and when he bent over, the waistband of his shorts showed, but no surprise there. We were shopping after school to fix that. It was something else. His arms, maybe. Was there more muscle there? I wasn't sure. He still looked like a kid, like fourteen, the way boys that age are little kids at one angle, and adults at another. I kept coming back to his face. It was still Cam's face, his brilliant blue eyes, his quick smile. That was all Cam. It was someone else, too, like I'd been away from him for an entire summer, and this was the boy who'd come to take his place. When I first started teaching, I took pictures of my students in September and posted them on my bulletin board. Then in May I did the same thing, only I still had the September pictures up. The kids were the same, but they weren't, either. They were eight months different. Cam was eight months different, except in his case, it was more like four months.

Every four months, he'd said. Every four months he grows an inch. Fourteen times three plus twenty-one at birth. That made sixty-three inches. Five foot three. How tall was Cam? Five-three? I bet he was now. Exactly. I'm six-two, and Cam was a foot shorter than me a month ago. We marked the door frame at the house. I bet he's eleven inches shorter now. Chills ran up and down my spine. I walked Cam's direction, just doing my job. Monitoring, keeping the monkeys under control. I tapped on one table where food was being traded, and I shook my head no. Cam was telling a joke as I got closer. There seemed to be a lot to it, because he'd stop and start. At one point his hand knocked over an open milk carton, and as it toppled, he grabbed it. He moved so fast I barely saw it. He checked to see if his shirt had any spots, but of course it didn't, because none of the milk had spilled. The girls at the table with him shrieked and then pulled at his shirt, certain there must be spillage. Cam caught me watching, and he grinned. Then I understood. He'd planned that. He knew that carton was there, and he'd knocked it over on purpose. He'd rescued it the same way, too.

It was his face, though. My word, I thought, it wasn't my imagination. His jaw, the cheekbones. Everywhere, the planes of his face had sharpened up. His eyes were the same, though, that clear blue that pulls you in, and you can't get out.

Then he winked at me, the barest flicker of one eyelid, and I knew he recognized what I'd seen. Superboy and his X-ray vision had been inside my head and read my thoughts. I walked up behind him and put my hand on his shoulder, and I squeezed his neck. I was feeling for cables and pulleys, the steel tendons that would tell me the truth, that Cam was something besides a real person. He was a construct of the Center, and they'd rebuilt him over the weekend, sending back a boy that was just a little bigger and just a little different from the one I'd given them.

I leaned in to whisper in his ear, "Hey, tight-pants. Don't get too fresh with the girls. Wait until after we go shopping this afternoon." I smelled his hair, and it was coconut, just like I keep in the bathroom. His neck was smooth and soft, with only bone and muscle underneath, nothing that said Superboy or Metalman. When I stood, he turned around to look up at me, and he smiled.

"It's just me, Mr. Turner. Trust me. I'm not any different."

Then one of the girls tried to push a french fry in his mouth, and he laughed, grabbing it with his hand and trying to keep from eating it. I let him go. We'd get his big boy pants that afternoon. Right then, I needed to let him have a good time. After yesterday, he deserved it.

Chapter 22

Welcome Home

Mrs. Osgood got home today. I heard the water running on her side of the wall, and I knew Cam was out with Kenny. It had to be Mrs. Osgood. I walked to the bathroom door and could hear her washing her hands.

I knocked, calling out, "Welcome home, Mrs. Osgood," and the door opened.

"What's that, Mr. Turner?" She smiled at me, for all her age, still with a set of perfect teeth. Her hands were wet, and she was drying them with a towel. My towel. Oh, well.

"I said, welcome home." I remembered what Cam had said. She liked me. I leaned over and gave her a kiss on the forehead. When I backed away, I think she beamed brighter than I'd ever seen before. Just that, and she was happy. Who'd have thought such a little thing could make so much difference?

"This yours?" She held up the towel. "I have more of my own. You've got company, I know. You've been using my bathroom." She nodded as if that said it all. There was nothing slow about Mrs. Osgood. She might dial a wrong phone number now and then, but she didn't miss much. She let me use her bathroom, too.

"A student from the Center. He's staying with me for a while."

"I know who, too." She shook the towel at me, waiting for me to take it. "That Cam boy. I've met him, you know."

Good heavens, I thought. Does everyone in Denver know Cam's living with me? Maybe everyone in Colorado. Next thing I know, Mom'll be calling, telling me that if I make enough money to house and feed an orphan, I make enough to give her a real grandson.

"He's grown since you've seen him last." I thought about picking him up from the Center and his tight pants that day.

"Boys do that, Mr. Turner. You've got to expect it." She turned back into the bathroom.

"Come for dinner tonight," I called after her. I usually didn't invite my neighbors over to my apartment. For one thing, it wasn't big enough. For another, we're enough in each other's business as it is. A little separation can be a good thing. When I didn't get a response, I added, "Cam will want to see you."

That got her attention.

"Good. I'll bake a pie." She smiled, and she pushed the door to.

Lets me know how I rate. Just below a fourteen-year-old boy. Great.

Chapter 23

Three's Not a Crowd

Have you ever had one of those dinner parties where everything goes so smoothly that you can't believe it's not a television show? Neither have I.

Yet, when Mrs. Osgood came through her bathroom door with her pie in hand, I could swear she and Cam were pressed from the same mold. Not in their looks, of course. What eighty-year-old is even similar to one fourteen? Yet, that pie drew me in, and I had to have a slice.

Call it what you want, but I was glad I'd invited Mrs. Osgood over. For the pie, for Cam, for Mrs. Osgood, I didn't know. The pie helped, though.

Cam was the one that surprised me. He was the host of the party. Understand my situation. I can fix Oreo cereal, and maybe eggs and mustard. After that I'm down to toast. Hot dogs challenge me, unless they come from Billy's. Even then, to get them home and reheat them, well, did I say I can fix Oreo cereal?

I'd invited Mrs. Osgood over, but the idea of planning food hadn't entered my mind. I just assumed that if I invited her, the food would somehow appear, like showing up at Mom's for Christmas Eve. Cam called out for pizza. Now I was eating my third slice of pie, and Cam had Mrs. Osgood playing *Gods of War*.

I was amazed. The kid had the patience of Job. He'd reach over and show her which button to push, and when she did something correctly, he'd smile at her, and she'd just light up. I don't think she'd ever touched a gaming remote in her life, and here she was playing one of the most complicated games out there. And loving it.

I didn't feel left out, either. You know, like when three people meet to go out, and two of them wind up talking all the time. Cam and Mrs. Osgood were doing all the talking, and it was okay. I was eating my pie, they were involved with each other, and I was happy with it. Like, how else would it be? And I was Cam's *Gods of War* buddy. You think I'd be jealous. No. Not tonight. The world was about perfect, and I couldn't see it any other way.

Chapter 24

Humpty Dumpty Falls Down and Breaks His Crown

I hate stupid drivers. I mean really hate them. I don't mean those that cut you off then honk at you like you're doing something wrong. I mean the really stupid ones that scare you 'til you've got to go home and change your underpants.

Cam and I had borrowed one of the bats from the school. Kenny's been struggling on the team, and I thought if Cam were better, he could bring Kenny up to speed on the weekends. As you know, Kenny needs all the help he can get.

Well, we were at the park, and I was hitting some pop flies to Cam. I'm not much of a ball player, liking b-ball much better, but there I was, helping out in the only way I knew. Pop flies. Except I was popping them all over the place. Cam was good with it, though, running after them wherever I hit them. I think he thought I knew what I was doing, and it was all part of the practice. I didn't tell him otherwise, either.

A couple times I hit the balls pretty close to the street. Now, that's not usually a problem, not if there's no cars, and there usually aren't. Cam dashes into the street, retrieves the ball, and we're back in business. But there are cars, sometimes, and being near the park where kids play, of course they have to be the ones with the stupid drivers.

Anyway, we heard the car before we saw it, or at least I did. Cam I would have thought heard it too, but he's fourteen, and we all know boys at that age. Hearing is selective. About the time I threw the ball up and swung, tires squealed somewhere around the corner. I have that moment frozen in my mind, the ball hanging in the air in front of me; the sunshine on the grass; and Cam looking my way, his glove in hand, his eyes glued on the ball. I was twisted around at the waist, my muscles tensed, and my lungs full of air. It was perfect, one of those moments in time when everything comes together, and you couldn't ask for anything more. Then I saw the car. Red. Low. Black tires spinning. I'd give anything if I could call back that moment and undo the least little bit of it. By then it was too late. My brain had already sent the impulses, and my muscles were firing. The bat swung around, and crack! The ball was gone, slammed through the air at fifty miles an hour.

Of course, Cam wasn't watching the car. He couldn't see it skip and skitter across the pavement. He was taking care of business. His eyes were on the ball, and his hands were in the air, held high over his head. I watched the ball arc toward the street, and I could feel my chest tighten. No, I thought. It was all in slow motion, or at least I remember it in slow motion. I called, "Cam!"

He called back, "I've got it," as he leaped sideways across the sidewalk and right into the path of that very red, very stupid car.

I just knew he was dead. Tunnel vision grabbed hold of me, and all I could see was the front bumper impacting Cam's legs, and Cam's body contorting sideways. Then he was flipped head over heels, landing hard on his back. The red car disappeared down the street, its engine revving, and its tires squealing.

"Idiot, idiot, idiot," I cried, running as hard as I could. I wasn't sure if I meant me, the driver, or Cam. All three of us had been stupid. The driver for hot rodding near a park. Me for hitting the ball into the street. Cam for going after it. If he was still alive, I was going to ream him out, tell him to pay attention next time, or there wouldn't be a next time. Got that, kid?

When I reached him, one leg was bent at an oddly contorted angle. I hoped that was the worst of it. I looked for blood, grateful that the street was clear. Internally, I didn't know, though. People could bleed to death inside, and they were just as dead as if they

84

bled on the outside. I dropped to my knees, wondering if I should pick him up or not. I wanted to. I wanted to pick him up and hug him to me, to protect him, to take back what the red car had done, and make it five minutes ago all over again. Then I'd hit the ball the other direction, or, better yet, we'd pack up and go home. Kenny could find another mentor. I didn't, though. I remembered broken backs, and if you moved someone, you risked paralysis for life. I wouldn't risk that for Cam. However bad this was, I wouldn't make it worse. I did put my hand under his neck, though, and I pressed my palm to his face. I stroked it, whispering for him to wake up, to please wake up.

The whole time I was thinking of St. Peter and the gates of heaven, and my delusional thoughts about whether Cam had a soul. Of course he did. The real question was whether Cam even believed. He hadn't professed his faith to me, and he hadn't been to a confessional at the church. I knew, because I'd been with him every time. It wasn't fair to take a kid out, and not give him at least a shot in the dark at making it. Who did that to a boy, a good kid like Cam, who only wanted to make other people happy?

Later I knew I must have heard the sirens, but I didn't know anyone was there until a paramedic took my shoulders and had me move aside. My vision was blurred as I watched them shift Cam to a stretcher and slide him into the waiting van. Someone came up to me and asked me questions, writing down my responses, as the flashing light tore away through the streets. They said I needed to go to the hospital as someone next of kin, and did I have a ride? I just nodded and shook my head and nodded again, whatever made them stop and write on their paper. Cam couldn't be dead. He couldn't. And I had caused it. The worst thing? If he missed heaven, it was my fault. I was accountable, and that was scary.

He wasn't dead, but I didn't know that then. I really thought it was the end for him. It was one of those crazy moments when the weirdest thoughts come to you, ones you wouldn't tell anyone in a million years. Mine was, Mrs. Osgood won't bring over any more pie. I guess I grabbed onto that, because the thought of Cam dead was just too much for me to get my head around.

They didn't even take him to the hospital. Or if they did, he wasn't there when I got there. The nurse told me the Center had sent a van, and he was in transit there. Would I like her to call a taxi?

I wouldn't, but what choice did I have? My car was at home,

and I was here. I needed to go there. Walking was not an option. So, I paid the fare, and I walked into the Center, demanding to see Cam. They weren't going to hurt him this time. I was going to make sure of that.

My complaints hit a blank wall, though.

"Mr. Turner, Camden has received some pretty serious injuries. I think you need to let us handle this."

"Is Jillian Compos here?" Hers was the only name I remembered, and I wanted to go over someone's head.

"No, sir, not today. I can leave her a message, and she can get back with you when she's available."

She'd been here the weekend I got Cam, I thought, but I knew to start trouble might be to do something I'd regret later. I turned away until I could get control.

"Can we call you a taxi?" Said so *very* politely to my back.

"Can I wait?" I wanted to take him with me. I wanted him back like he was. I wanted my Cam whole and in one piece.

"No, sir. He won't be ready to go home today. We'll call you when you can pick him up."

Just like that, and there was a taxi outside. I hadn't even said I wanted one. Everyone evaporated, and I was left alone in the vast, glass-filled space. That made me angry all over again. They didn't even escort me out. They *knew* I'd do just what they wanted, and they didn't even bother to check to see if I did. Although, when I was rational later, I knew they had video monitoring, and if I hadn't left, they'd have sent their goons in to make sure I did. At the time I could feel steam coming out of my collar.

At home I paced the floor. Two steps over, two back. Not much pacing room, but I couldn't sit. I wanted to go outside and walk, but I'd have to leave the phone behind. I didn't think about Cam's, but in any case, how could they reach me by Internet? Tingle me in order to contact me?

Finally, the phone did ring, and I was on it like a leopard on fresh meat. "Jake Turner."

"Mr. Turner. This is Jill, Jill Compos from the Center. How are you today?"

"Not well. How's Cam?" I wanted to be polite. Jill hadn't done anything wrong. But the Center had, and she was the Center at the moment. I really tried, though.

"Please be patient, Mr. Turner. I know our methods seem

unusual to you, but Camden will be fine. We just need a little time to work on him. I don't think he can be ready for you this evening, but we can certainly drop him off at school in the morning. Will that do?"

She had just yanked my soapbox out from under me. I wanted to scream and yell, tell them it wasn't right I hadn't been allowed to see him, and here she was offering to deliver him to school in the morning.

I was surprised he was even alive.

"Thank you, Jill. I would appreciate that. Who'll be bringing him? He'll need clothes, clean ones." How domestic that sounded! I couldn't help it, though. They wouldn't think of it, so I had to be the responsible one.

"Then by your house. Will that be acceptable? Seven? I'm sure Camden will be up and about by that time. Then you can dress him in fresh clothing for the day. Oh, and Mr. Turner, Jake, I'll be the one to deliver Camden to your door."

Jill was coming by the house. Well. That changed everything.

Chapter 25

Doubts About the Real Cam Creep In

I felt good for about twenty minutes. Jill's laugh. Her eyes. I remembered those, because they had been so much like Cam's. It was like a jolt of electricity to my adrenal glands. All energy and tingles, and yeah, a bit of hormonal attraction, I suspect. It didn't last, though. When I came off it, I was in worse shape than before. I had seen the accident, remember. It was still painted in my slow-motion memory, and I had no way to wipe it clean. No rewind button. No *erase* feature that automatically blanked the hard drive and left it fresh for new information. And I had touched Cam's face. He hadn't responded. People who didn't respond were usually dead.

And about his soul? Real people had those, and I'd been frightened that Cam wouldn't make it past the pearly gates. I had wondered earlier if he really had one. Crazy me, faithful believer, wondering something as ridiculous as that. Of course he had a soul, didn't he?

That got my head spinning. His wrists, and the way he'd changed after his visit to the Center. His words to me that Monday in the cafeteria: It's just me, Mr. Turner. I'm not any different. Yet, he had been different, in a hundred ways, none of which I could precisely put my finger on. I just kept searching for the one thing that was the same, and I found it every time. Those eyes. I searched for them, fell into them, and I didn't want to believe he was anything other than my Cam, the boy who liked to game with me, pound the basketball courts, and eat my eggs covered with mustard. I had seen what I wanted to see. Well, today I saw what was real. He was bent crooked, and there was no life in him. I hadn't even felt him breathe. I held my hand to his face, and it never moved. Not once. That's the real Cam, the one I knelt beside out there on the street, with his soul leaking away into whatever afterlife he had earned.

I pictured the day of the football game. Cam's leg. His skin was blistered with a scrape that was appalling. No blood, though. I remembered that clearly, because I thought he needed it treated, but there was no blood, so I let it go. No blood. Like today there was no blood on the street. Had I ever seen Cam bleed? Once? Boys always bleed. *Real* boys always bleed. They bump things, cut their nails crookedly, fall down, they *bleed.* What did that mean? He had to have a soul, didn't he? I mean, people can't just *not* have a soul. Otherwise, they aren't people.

I was on the sofa by then. I pressed on the cushion where Cam slept each night, the one where his back went. That first morning I thought he must be freezing, but he wasn't. His skin was warm. Warm, like anyone's. I was being stupid and paranoid. What had Cam said or done since returning from the Center last time that made me think he was any different? Nothing. He was just Cam, going to school, being a friend to Kenny, and catching my wild pop flies. That's a real boy. How could I think any differently? I fished around and found his cap and slipped it on. I didn't plug it in, not with the weird dreams from last time, but I pulled out the phone. I opened the main screen, and I began to poke around. I was about to turn it back off when it vibrated. I nearly dropped it. Then a number appeared over one of the icons at the bottom. I touched it, and a message opened up.

Hey, Mr. Turner. Are you okay?

I jumped, and the phone went flying. I grabbed at it, catching it just before it hit the floor.

"Yes," I said into it, before I had a chance to think. Then I held it to my mouth, "Cam?"

Nothing.

I can be slow, but I usually catch on eventually. This was a text, not a phone call. I had to text back. Touching the screen, I finally got a new box and a keyboard to come up. I typed in, *Cam?* It was his phone, after all. If anyone could contact me on this, it would be Cam.

I could tell you were messing with my phone. Hey, I'm sorry about the car. I should have been watching.

You're okay, though? Why didn't I know we could do this? I had his phone all weekend when he was gone. I wanted to kick myself, and I wanted to kick Cam, too. He was fourteen. He should know about these things. More importantly, he should tell me. I'm the adult, here. I'm not supposed to know about these things, or, rather, I *am* supposed to know, but I can't unless he tells me first.

I will be by morning. My legs will hurt tomorrow, so you might write me an excuse for PE. Thanks ahead of time. They don't know I can do this, so I better go. I don't want them to find out. See you in the morning, Mr. Turner.

I tapped and tapped, but nothing more happened. Cam was there, and he was gone. He was there, and he was gone, just like that, and they didn't know. Good for you, Cam. Good for you. Beat the system. Find a way to break out, show them who's boss.

I dropped the phone onto the sofa. What was I thinking? I was blaming the Center, and they weren't really to blame. I just didn't like the way they were doing things. Besides, I was a teacher. I was part of the system. I didn't want him to show *me* who's boss. I just wanted him back on my sofa. Back gaming on my system, playing ball with me, part of my life.

I shook my head to clear my thoughts. Enough of that. Keep that up, and someone will think I'm attached to the kid, that I love him or something. I just like the company, that's all. The bank deposits don't hurt. One day he'll be gone, and the money will be gone, and I can't afford to get attached to something I can't keep.

But that text kept coming back to me. *Hey, Mr. Turner. Are you okay?* Cam wanted to know if *I* was okay. That was the first thing he asked. What real boy does that? Not one that's fourteen, that's for sure. And if he's not real . . .

I let that thought die, and I headed for bed. I hoped a Broncos cheerleader would be there, and if not, maybe Jill. In fact, maybe both. I smiled. That would be too much to ask for, but I did sing in the shower, and I can carry a tune.

Unlike Cam.

90

Chapter 26

One Little, Two Little, Three Little Frankensteins . . .

There was something unusual about the Center for Innovative Software Specialization and Intellectual Enhancement. They didn't produce product, or not product that anyone from the Denver area would recognize. They also didn't hire from the Denver area. All their employees came from far-fetched places with impossible names to pronounce, except for a few high-placed personages, and of course, those who did some of the more basic chores, like squeegeeing all that glass or mowing the lawns. Those jobs didn't require direct access to the more sensitive areas of the Center's operations, so they didn't matter much.

Except for those mowers. That had made a big difference. Now the only product the Center had up and functioning was Cam, and they had to keep him functioning normally. They hoped to get the rest back on line soon, but soon was relative. When your timeline is decades long, and your pockets are very deep, you take your time, because to rush is to fail. Success was the essence of everything the Center did, and so far, Cam had been an unmitigated success.

Now, though, a trauma team worked on him. He had been damaged very badly. Tubes were hooked to his body, and his life fluids pumped steadily along, sparkling through the transparent polycarbonate material. He was opened up from his chest to his ankles, a dozen sets of hands working in his body cavities.

Cam was awake, even so. His blue eyes looked at the ceiling, anywhere except at the people who worked over him. He had been wheeled in past the old dorms. The residency program had indeed been put on hold, just like Jake had been told. However, it wasn't exactly what Jake had been led to believe. Seventeen doors still glowed blue, and one was clear. Camden Archer's door. The other seventeen had their occupants neatly inside, covered with blankets, wearing their caps, which were wired and plugged into their chairs. The updates weren't taking. The glitch had gone deeper than the Center had hoped, and they were just now beginning to dig down to find out what was wrong.

Then Cam's right foot twitched.

"Got this one," a technician with magnifying lenses on his glasses called out gleefully. "Let me fix this pin, and we can close this leg up."

Next to him, a female whispered, "Almost there," just as she snapped a metal bracket over a tube leading to a freshly installed liver. "Try the bile ducts." A smile grew on her face as she turned to a computer monitor and watched the results. "We're almost there, people."

In spite of the woman's assurances, they had hours to go, more bones to replace, and skin to repair afterwards. If Cam had been Superboy, he might have survived the accident without any serious injuries. But the red car had been going very fast, and Cam had hit the pavement very hard. A real boy can't survive such g-forces without severe and very detrimental consequences. And Cam was very real, in spite of what Jake Turner seemed to suspect. It was just a matter of how you defined real.

To put it another way, what's real is what's real, and Cam was very real and very much in pain, even if the team working on him had no idea just how much.

They only watched their machines, and they rarely bothered to look into his eyes.

Chapter 27

The Rusty Nickel Late Night Chat Line

"Welcome, Michelle from Mississippi. You are live on the Rusty Nickel Late Night Chat Line. This is Rusty. What do you want to talk about tonight?"

"Oh, oh! I got through. This is so exciting, Rusty!"

"Michelle, you might want to turn your radio down. It creates feedback through your phone. Thank you. Now, what's your question?"

"Well, I was wondering if Frankenstein really existed."

"That's a good question, Michelle. There is a Castle Frankenstein in Darmstadt, Germany, but the living, walking monster from Shelley's book? No, I'm sorry, Michelle. There is no evidence Frankenstein ever really existed outside Mary Shelley's head."

"Well, I have a friend from Denver, and he tells me there are real Frankensteins living in a modern castle in the mountains there."

"Come, now, Michelle. Don't you think if that were true, it would have made national news by now?"

"It could be a government conspiracy. Everyone knows there were aliens in that ship in Roswell, and the government covered it up. Maybe they're covering this up, too."

"Thank you, Michelle. That is very interesting. Perhaps you can call again, sometime, and we can discuss that. Welcome, Bill, from Colorado Springs. You are live on the Rusty Nickel Late Night Chat Line. This is Rusty. What do you want to talk about tonight?"

"Can I talk about something someone else has talked about?"

"Of course, Bill. Your time on the air is all yours. What is your question?"

"It's not a question, Rusty. I lived in Denver, and I met some of those Frankensteins."

"You did, Bill? And just what did they look like?"

"Like normal kids, except not normal, not when they thought you weren't looking."

"I see, Bill. And did they have stitches on their necks, maybe around their wrists? That's what I think of when I picture Frankenstein."

"Be serious, Rusty. They fix that with plastic surgery. You can see 'em if you go up there."

"Exactly where, Bill?"

"It's called the Center for Innovative Software Specialization and Intellectual Enhancement. The local comedians call it SISSY." He might have said CISSIE, but who could tell? It sounded the same.

"SISSY Frankensteins. That's funny. Thank you, Bill. I appreciate you calling. Welcome, Sheila, from Goldsboro, North Carolina. You are live on the Rusty Nickel Late Night Chat Line. This is Rusty. What do you want to talk about tonight?"

"Rusty, you think California might really fall into the ocean? Cause my sister lives out there, and I want the $250 she owes me, if it does."

"Well, Sheila, the experts are divided on that . . ."

Chapter 28

Superboy Gets a Day Off

I paced the floor. Two steps, then two back, just like before. It was early, too. I was ready for Cam to return. I hadn't slept well, even in my own bed. It wasn't a Broncos cheerleader, either, although that would have been a nice diversion. It was that conversation with Cam. Why didn't he want them to find out? Why would they try to keep him from texting me? It's like I knew there was something bigger than I knew, but I had no way to find out, and Cam wasn't talking, not really. He was like a clamshell, zipped up tight about what went on behind the Center's glass walls. Like he was brainwashed. Yeah, that's what it was. Brainwashed.

I sat, exhausted. I couldn't take much more. I still had to go in to work, and this consumed my brain. Must be a tiny brain, I joked with myself. I looked at the clock. Nearly seven. At seven-thirty I'd set the timer on the microwave, otherwise I'd wind up and be late for work, but I was focused on seven, now. That's when Jill said she was bringing Cam. I looked forward to seeing Jill, but it was Cam who really had me anxious.

I heard a car on the gravel lot where I park. I stepped into the public hallway, and I looked through the door. It was just getting light, but there they were, Jill and Cam. Cam was barely moving, though, and Jill was keeping pace at his side. I opened the door and stepped out.

"Cam?" I went to him, walking faster when he looked up at me. I expected him to smile, but all I got was nothing. I wanted to put my arms around him, but Jill was there, and besides, I remembered his wrist. I knelt in front of him and gently grabbed his shoulders. "Does it hurt? For me to do this?" I got my first glimpse of a smile.

"Hey, Mr. Turner. I'm glad to be back."

"That's not what I asked. Does it hurt for me to touch you like this?" Why can't fourteen-year-olds answer a plain question with a straight answer? It's not rocket science. Just yes or no will do. I looked at Jill, and she was smiling.

"It doesn't hurt, Mr. Turner. In fact, it feels good. I don't have to work so hard to stand up."

"But you hurt in other places." I looked at his legs. He was standing on them, but I'd seen the car. I knew what they'd looked like the day before.

"Yeah. Can I go in and sit down, please?" His face was drawn, and I knew he'd reached his limit.

"Sure. You want me to help? I can carry you—" I glanced at Jill, picturing Cam and me outside the night of the storm, pulling our wet things off. I didn't want her to mistake what I meant. She was watching Cam, though.

"Not yet, Mr. Turner. I got to sleep a couple hours at the Center. Let me try on my own."

He did make it inside. I invited Jill in, but she declined, saying she had obligations at the Center. I think she saw my apartment and knew it fit two, and barely, at that. She was polite, and I was polite back. It wasn't like I thought it would be, with more romance. However, it was seven in the morning, and I really wake at ten. I decided I would have her bring him back at ten next time. If there was a next time.

When I closed the door, I pulled up a chair from the table and had Cam sit. I wanted to see his legs, to see if they were his real legs.

"Off, Cam." I pointed to his jeans.

"Mr. Turner, please?" He sounded as if it was too much effort to move, and he really didn't want to expend any more energy than he had to. "Can we do this later?"

"I want to see what they did." I knelt and began undoing his shoes.

"You won't find anything. Just my legs."

He was resigned, though, and he began undoing his jeans at the waist. Together we worked them off, and I tossed them aside. He was right. They were just Cam's legs, smooth with barely a hint of hair down his shins. Normal, undamaged legs. That's what bothered me. That car had walloped him. If nothing else, he should be black and blue. Broken blood vessels do that, bleeding all under the skin, leaving bruises that last for weeks. I know. I've taken some hard hits before, with the bruising to show for it.

"We're staying home today." I stood and picked up the phone, punching in Admin's absentee request number.

"No school?" The relief in Cam's voice was as thick as refrigerated honey. "You're staying, too?"

"I did say we." I got a look of gratitude with that. I felt warm inside, like I'd done something real good for him. If they docked my pay, it would be worth it. "You and I need some hang time, even if you sleep all day. I'm not leaving you alone after yesterday."

The phone answered.

"Hey, Jake Turner here, Bruce, science, eighth. I need a sub today." I paused, listening, then continued, "Just one day for now, and yes, my lesson plans are out on my desk, just like always. I'll call back if I need to extend it. Thanks." I turned to Cam. "Bed or sofa?"

"Bed, please?"

"You bet. It's yours all day long, and tonight if you want it." I shouldn't have been surprised, my robot boy asking politely.

I don't know why it felt so good giving up my bed to a fourteen-year-old. I did notice as we went through the doorway that the mark we'd made was one inch shorter than him. He was still eleven inches less than me. Seeing that was a relief. They hadn't made him grow an extra inch. He was this height for another three months.

I got him settled and the living room blanket over the window, and I turned out the light. It was mostly dark, and when I went to shut the door, he called to me.

"I don't want to be too much trouble."

"Don't say that, Cam."

"I promised, though." He shifted on the bed, putting one arm

97

across his face.

"Don't do this, Cam." I knew what that arm meant, and I stepped back inside to sit on the edge of the bed. I reached and gently took his arm down. I was right. His eyes were red, and there were tears there. He put his arm back.

"I don't want you to see." *Me cry*, but he didn't say that. He didn't have to.

"It just tells me I was right to call in sick. You hurt too bad for anything as silly as school."

"That's not it." He moved his arm, and he looked at me. I could see tears glistening down his cheeks.

"What, then?" I had no idea what else it could be. He was home. He had my bed. What else did I have to offer? Eggs, maybe, and mustard.

"I said I wouldn't be any trouble. You wouldn't even know I'm here. All I've been is trouble." He kept those big blue eyes on me, his face expressionless, the light glistening on his tears.

Man, he was getting to me.

It was those eyes. The tears, really, like he wanted me to be something I wasn't, like in love with him. He's just a kid. I liked him, sure, and I'd missed him when he was gone, but that was all. Even so, I felt a lump in my throat, and I tried to shake it off.

"I like trouble." I laughed, forcing my voice to be bright, and I gave him a fake jab to the jaw. "Trouble comes my way, and I just say, come on in and make yourself at home."

"Thanks," he said, covering his eyes again. I could see more tears flooding out. Then he rolled over and buried his face in my pillow.

Oh, well, I thought. It'll dry, and it's about time to change it, anyway.

One thing, though, caused me to stand at the door and watch him for a minute before I stepped into the hall. He had quoted himself exactly, word for word, and from a month ago. What fourteen-year-old does that? Most boys his age can't remember what they said yesterday. It wasn't that strange in itself, but with his legs, and the text messages from last night, I had one unusual boy sleeping in my bed.

And, more importantly, I had the day off. Yes!

Chapter 29

Cam Surprises Even Me

My excitement wore off after a couple hours. I mean, sure, the idea of not having to go in at the crack of dawn was appealing. I never enjoy facing people when my brain is so fogged I can barely walk, but in my job I have to do it every day. This morning was a reprieve of the most welcome kind. Yet, I don't have the most stimulating environment here in my apartment. If I had a media room, or a pool table, it might be different. But if I had those, I'd have enough money not to work, and it'd all be a moot point. What I'm trying to say is, when the fog finally cleared from my brain, I had nothing to do. I'm not a reader, despite being a teacher. Science, remember? I do things, mix chemicals, blow things up (not always intentionally), and stay busy. I don't read if I can get out of it. Besides, I didn't have any best sellers just lying around. I'd left them all at the bookstore for someone else to buy.

I checked on Cam once or twice. He was balled up under my comforter, his face barely showing, and I figured he needed the rest. He hadn't moved since morning, he was that tired. So, I tried to be quiet. Sitting there, I thought about Mrs. Osgood and her pie. Not so much about the pie, but one goes with the other, so I thought of them both, and I decided she might like a visit. If I was bored, think how she felt. She sat around and did this every day. She must be crawling out of her skin.

I went to her bathroom and checked, making sure she wasn't inside. Then I stepped through to the door into her apartment, knocking.

"Mrs. Osgood? It's Jake, from next door."

I knocked again then tried the knob. It turned, but then it would. The lock was on the other door, and I'd picked it. It stayed unlocked, just in case.

Now, Mrs. Osgood's bathroom is pretty clean. Clear. Unclut-tered, whatever you call it. How much stuff can you keep in a bathroom? Maybe too many bottles of shampoo, but those get used up eventually, and you throw them away. At least I did, and since I used Mrs. Osgood's bathroom, I threw her empties away.

The rest of her apartment was hers. I never touched it. If she wanted to collect every newspaper that had been printed, let her collect every newspaper. I didn't have to live with it. So, when I opened the door, I was caught off guard. She had a floor.

That sounds stupid, and I know it. It's just that I'd never seen her floor before, and there it was. Wood. Real, hundred-year-old wood. It wasn't polished or anything, and you could tell it was stained, and the moldings were all chipped up, but the floor was there, staring me in the face, like a message from somewhere. The housing authority, perhaps, telling me that Mrs. Osgood wasn't going to be my neighbor much longer. That had deep ramifications. No more pies.

"Mrs. Osgood?" I called out, not sure if she even still lived here. I saw some pictures I recognized on the walls, so that was a relief, unless she'd died, and no one had wanted the rest of her stuff. "Mrs. Osgood, are you home?"

I heard something in the kitchen, glass clanking against glass, and I knew someone was in there. Packing, probably. The housing authority has to send someone to clear out forty years of stuff from vacant apartments.

"Mr. Turner? That you?"

It was Mrs. Osgood's ancient soprano, and I breathed a sigh of relief. At least she wasn't dead. I moved down the hall, walking on the real floor, and I found her setting a place for one at the table. A crock pot bubbled on the counter. I realized how good it smelled. With the morning, I hadn't even had breakfast.

"Moving anytime soon?" I asked the question as casually as possible, like it was no big deal. I didn't see any packed boxes, but I didn't see a lot of stuff that usually filled the apartment, and that was just as odd. I walked to the counter and leaned over her pot. It looked better than anything I'd cooked in my apartment in a very long time. Maybe ever.

"Now, come sit down, Mr. Turner. Have you had any lunch?" She smiled at me and patted the table. I guess my look was pretty transparent.

"Well, no, but I couldn't impose—"

"It's only an imposition if I haven't asked." She already had a second plate out, placing it on the table. I pulled the chair out and sat, my stomach starting to growl. "Now, this is my best china. I don't have guests often, and I want you to enjoy lunch."

"Thank you, Mrs. Osgood. That really smells good." I glanced, and my plate was different from hers. Mine looked new. Hers had chips out of the edges.

"Now, why are you not at work today? I didn't know we had a holiday coming up."

Like I said, Mrs. Osgood is sharp. She doesn't miss much. At the same time she dished out a generous serving of stew on my plate, with vegetables and ample chunks of meat. The meat looked like it would melt in my mouth. She pulled a biscuit out of a tin and put it on the back of my plate to complete the ensemble.

"Now, in my house, I always say a word of thanks before I eat. Bow your head, Mr. Turner."

I did, and she did, and I dug in. For about ten minutes, neither one of us said anything. I couldn't have, because my mouth was so full. About halfway through, a glass of water appeared, and I attacked that, too. I found out Mrs. Osgood likes spices in her food. It was when I was mopping up that she returned to her original question.

"Clearly, you're not sick. You being home, does this have anything to do with that sweet boy living with you?"

She took my plate, and magically, on the table, right before me, appeared a piece of pie. Oh, man, I was going to miss this when she moved.

"Cam's asleep over in the apartment."

"Oh? He's not at school, either?" That made her pause. "Then I guess he can have the rest of this when he wakes up. I'll send it over with you."

"Thank you. You can save all the pie for me." I dug in, cutting off a bigger bite than I should have, but my anticipation clouded my judgment. When I bit into it, it was just as good as ever, if not better.

"And why is that boy home, if I may ask?"

She sat down holding a damp rag in her hands, wiping up where her plate had been. I noticed she didn't have any pie, but I didn't see anything in it. Between bites, I answered her.

"He got hurt yesterday. He had to spend the night in the hospital—" The Center, but I didn't want to have to explain that. "—so I thought he deserved a day off."

"You, too, a day off, I see." Her eyes twinkled.

"Me, too. I noticed your stuff. Are you moving?" Watching her, I wondered if she'd been pretty when she was younger. I'd have to pay more attention to her pictures. She might be in one of them.

"What do you mean?"

"Your stuff. It's all gone." I nodded with my head at all the empty space. I caught her expression, and I could see it in her eyes. She knew exactly what I was asking.

"I have plenty of stuff, as you call it, left. I just don't have all the stuff I didn't need." As if that summed it up.

"So, you did all this?" Her brother, maybe, had been on her. But from what I knew, people who collected stuff didn't just up and toss it into the dumpster.

"That boy of yours, Mr. Turner. He's been helping me. He also tells me he's been going to services with you on Saturdays. You keep him in, and he might feel the call one day. That boy's got a good soul, and you're good for him, don't you think you're not." She stood, and she took my plate, replacing it with a bundle wrapped in foil. "Now, this is hot, still, so you be careful. And this," she placed a second foil package on top, "is for your boy. You don't eat his pie, and I'll know, because I'll ask." She also scooted me on out the door before I could argue.

I felt a little guilty as I stepped through the bathroom. I'd lived next door to Mrs. Osgood for years, and I'd never helped her throw anything away. I just assumed she wanted to keep it all. I guess maybe she couldn't carry stuff to the dumpster, and it was easier to live with it than ask for help. It didn't make me feel any better that her apartment now looked cleaner than her bathroom. I could have at least scrubbed in there. After all, I used it, too.

By the time I got to the kitchen, I'd decided Cam would enjoy half a slice of pie as much as a whole slice, and I unrolled the top of the foil. The aroma hit me in the face, and I leaned close. I was full, but it wasn't about full. It was about taste buds and endorphins in the brain. I could overlook full for this.

"For me?" An arm draped itself over my shoulder. Cam's face was right next to mine, and his eyes were closed as he drew in the aroma of my pie.

Dang! How did he know?

"From Mrs. Osgood. She sent you stew, too." I shrugged his arm off as I set the pie aside, and I pulled a plate from the cabinet, unrolling the foil and dumping the contents out. He was snatching chunks of meat and eating it with his fingers before I could get it on the table. Even I hadn't been that hungry.

After I got him seated with a spoon in his hand, I stood back and watched him eat. Normal, hungry Cam, just like any fourteen would be. No mechanical moving parts, no steam escaping with every movement, no nuclear warning symbols pasted on his forehead. His hair was sticking up in back, and he had drool stains on the front of his shirt. How ordinary was that?

"Thank you, Cam."

"What'd I do?" He looked up, pausing between bites to ask his question.

"Helping Mrs. Osgood."

He moved another spoonful to his mouth, his eyes on me. I thought of Jill and her blue eyes, but Cam wasn't Jill, and I let her go. I saw him start to smile, then he put the spoon in his mouth, and he was chewing.

"I want you to know how much I appreciate what you did. She does, too. That's why she sent you pie." That was stretching a bit, the pie part, not the grateful part, but I was sure she'd say that, too, if she were here.

"Okay. It was nothing. You can have the pie if you want." He reached to the counter and set it on my side of the table.

I can have the pie if I want. Just like that. Cam is dead, he comes back to life, all in one weekend, and I can have his pie if I want. I remembered what Mrs. Osgood said. I was good for Cam. I didn't know about that, but I did know he was good for me. I dug in the cabinets a long time, looking for just the right utensils, because I didn't want him to see. And I couldn't wipe my eyes, because then he would know. He might think I loved him, and I wasn't ready for that.

I did enjoy that pie, but I had to make Cam promise to tell Mrs. Osgood he ate every last bite. He said he couldn't lie to her. We can work around that, I explained. He could eat the last bite, and then he wouldn't have to lie to her.

His eyes twinkled as he placed it in his mouth. He chewed slowly, and when he swallowed, he took a deep breath and stretched, his arms high over his head.

"That was the best pie ever, to the last bite." Then he doubled over, laughing.

I grabbed him, hauling him out of his chair and to the sofa, forcing him to laugh until I thought he'd pee his shorts. Finally, sweating and breathing hard, we sat back, letting waves of inexplicable laughter ebb and flow. It was one of those moments where you're glad to be alive, to be able to enjoy the people around you, because they're the best thing that ever happened to you.

I wish I'd known then what I know now, because I'd have pulled Cam to me and hugged him. I didn't, though. I was on one end of the sofa, and he was sprawled on the other, his feet up on the cushions between us. I grabbed one of his feet and pulled it on my lap, looking at his toes.

"You need a trim."

I thought that meant for him to trim his own nails. Instead, he reached over his head to the small table at the end of the sofa where everything collects, and he fished around, coming up with a pair of clippers. He held them out to me. So, I trimmed his toenails. After the first foot, he switched feet, and I trimmed those, too. Normal, everyday boy stuff, taking care of business, just trimming toenails. That's what I did instead of hugging him.

Boy, was I ever stupid. Really, really, god-awful stupid.

Chapter 30

Someone Plays Hide and Seek

They never did find the driver of the red car, but after Tuesday, it didn't seem to matter much anymore. Monday night Cam wore his cap wired into his phone, and he got up Tuesday just fine. His pep was back in his step, and I got to work on time, fancy that. Early, even, and that's nice, because I always have extra work when I get back from an absence. Papers to go over, discipline reports to send in, that sort of thing. I sent Cam off to find Kenny. I knew the boy'd be lost without Cam, even for a day, and they needed to reconnect. Kenny was like that, a lost boy, at least socially. The opposite of Cam.

Stefanie had done Monday after school, so I did her lunch again. I didn't see Cam until halfway through, but he and Kenny came in with a big sign, jumping around and hooting to get everyone's attention. Apparently, the student council had a car wash planned, and they'd roped in the boys to deliver the message. It was bedlam for about ten minutes, and then I took the sign from them and taped it to the wall. It was good to see Kenny getting positive feedback from the lunch crowd. He was better with Cam, just like I was. When Cam grabbed him around the neck, and Kenny laughed, I knew just how he felt. Pretty good.

After school was when things went awry. I wish I could pinpoint just what went wrong, but it's no good blaming myself. I'd have to go back to that phone call, and even at that, I wasn't sure the two were really connected, although now they seem to fit together too nicely not to be one and the same. Anyway, Cam had yard work to do, and I had baseball. At fourteen, you feel you can trust kids to be out on their own. I mean, people snatch eight-year-olds, but fourteen? Cam's big enough, and heavy for his size. It'd take some tough dudes to catch him off guard. Or an idiot in a red car, but that's past tense. How many people get slammed with red sports cars in a whole lifetime? I think the odds are pretty much on the side of, don't worry about it, because it ain't going to happen.

Except to Cam.

Enough of that. After school, I headed out to the practice field, and Cam came running up to me. He punched me on the shoulder—harder than I would've liked—and danced around doing the Ali thing before saying, "I'm off to the butterflies," and he laughed and took off running, piston legs pumping. I knew what he meant. It was that quote from Muhammad Ali. Float like a butterfly; sting like a bee. It's still with me, because that's what I want to do. Not the float part, but the sting part. And maybe more than sting. Hit, crush, mutilate. Someone needs to hurt for what they've done.

The first thing I noticed amiss was the yard Cam was scheduled to work in. I wasn't sure he'd still be there, because although John let practice go at ten till, I waited on Benny's parents for another twenty-five minutes. Allow ten minutes for me to get to the car and on the road, and it was almost six-thirty by the time I drove by. The flower beds were disheveled, and there were tire tracks in the grass. Cam wasn't going to get paid if he kept this up, was all I thought. The tire tracks? Well, Cam didn't own a car, so it looked like the plant nursery's problem to me.

When I got to the house, I didn't think anything, just went in the front door and to the apartment. I grabbed the door, expecting it to be unlocked. Cam never locks it; sometimes he forgets to shut it, too, but we've been working on that. He's been better lately. When I nearly broke my nose because it was still locked, and I ran into it, I swore, but not loud. I didn't want Cam to hear. I'm still his teacher and all, and teachers aren't supposed to use vulgar language, supposedly anywhere. However, if you think about it, that's unrealistic. We are people, after all.

The apartment was silent and dark. There weren't many places for Cam to hide, either. The bathroom. My bedroom. He was either there, or he wasn't. Well, he wasn't, and I was irritated. I guessed the honeymoon was over, and I'd start seeing the darker side of fourteen. Great! Just when I was starting to really enjoy the kid.

After about ten minutes and a change of clothes, I decided it was too quiet. Not just in my apartment, but in the building. Mrs. Osgood usually prepares dinner between six and seven, mostly closer to seven. I can hear her banging around. And her TV comes through sometimes. She keeps it a little loud, because she has more windows than I do. The street noise comes in, and she can't hear the people speak.

"Mrs. Osgood?" I stepped through and knocked on her side of the bathroom.

Good neighbors are polite neighbors, I've been told more than once. I wanted to keep Mrs. Osgood as a good neighbor, so I never barged in. However, I was getting jittery. I could see it in my hand. It was shaking. When there was no answer, I opened the door just a crack.

"Mrs. Osgood? Have you seen Cam?"

Please, God, yes. I felt hope swell in me. There was a closet she hadn't cleared out yet, and Cam was buried inside, digging through the boxes. Please, God, was all I could think.

That was when the first picture on her wall caught my eye. It was crooked. All my pictures are crooked, but when I was here yesterday, every one of Mrs. Osgood's was lined up perfectly straight. That was Cam, I bet, because when he's interested, he's interested in doing it right. The third picture was on the floor, and the glass was shattered. And blood. It went up the wall. I hoped Cam wasn't in here, and if he was, I hoped the Center was on his speed dial.

I heard a noise in the bedroom, and I leaped over the glass. When I stepped through the door, I saw Mrs. Osgood. She was behind the bed on the floor, and her hair was a mess. When she saw me, she cried, "No! No! Stay away!" She held up her arms in front of her face, and one was covered in blood.

"It's me, Mrs. Osgood. It's Jake, from next door. I'm not going to hurt you." I stepped slowly to her, taking her arms in my hands. Good heavens, I thought, who had done this to her?

As I helped her up, I noticed the rest of her apartment. Everything had been ripped apart. Even the closet had been emptied. Once I got her on the bed and got a towel on her arm, I found her phone and called 9-1-1, describing the situation. Then I sat beside Mrs. Osgood and held her good hand. She was shaking, and her eyes were wide. I worried about shock, and I hoped the ambulance hurried.

"Do you want to talk about it, Mrs. Osgood?" I tried to be gentle. She turned to me and reached to my face, touching it as if she wasn't sure who I was.

"Mr. Turner? Is it really you?" Tears flooded her eyes. "They wanted your boy, Mr. Turner. I said he didn't live here, and they didn't believe me. I tried to make them leave, but I caught my arm on the picture, and I hurt myself. I'm so sorry, Mr. Turner. I'm so, so very sorry."

She began to sob violently, and I put my arms around her and held her tight until the paramedics arrived. I remembered the phone call that day and the way the caller had threatened me. He'd called Mrs. Osgood's number by mistake. He thought I lived here, instead of next door. The flower bed and the tire tracks. I knew now. He had found Cam, not at home, but at work, doing fourteen-year-old work in a very public yard where everyone could see. Why had I let him do that, go out in public? I was so stupid. Then I got angry. What right did anyone have to take Cam? What right? He was mine. I'd signed papers for him, taken care of him when he was sick, and I'd watched him die and been grateful that he'd come back to life. Did I say I was angry? I was furious. And I intended to do something about it.

As soon as I had a plan.

Chapter 31

Two Heads Become One

The police showed up about the same time as the paramedics, crowding into Mrs. Osgood's tiny apartment. One pair of men was bandaging her arm, and a man and a woman in uniform were attempting to discern just what had taken place. Was anything missing, stolen, perhaps? Was anyone else injured? Did she know the person who had attacked her?

I tried to stay close just in case they needed me, but each time they asked a question, it made me want to grab them and shake them, screaming, yes, you fools, something was taken. A fourteen-year-old boy. Cam Archer. He's gone, and I don't know where to start looking.

Twenty-four hours, they say. People are not really missing for twenty-four hours. You can file a report, but give them a day to come home. You might be surprised to know how many teenagers are just at a friend's house, and they forget to call home. Not Cam. No. He's missing, even if my proof is intangible. My apartment is in perfect order. The flowerbed down the street? Oh, officers, my neighbor's flowerbed is disturbed, so I know my child has been abducted. That would go over like a lead weight. The phone call from a month ago? The man didn't even call my number. I had nothing, and I wasn't waiting on these jokers.

I knew who to call, and it wasn't the police. After quizzing Mrs. Osgood, they might get involved, but that's not who I was contacting first. As soon as I could get away, I slipped through the bathroom, and I pulled out my old office phone. Rummaging through Cam's paperwork, I found the number and punched it in.

"You have reached the Center for Innovative Software Specialization and Intellectual Enhancement. Our main offices are closed at the current time—"

"Closed, my foot." I growled, punching the zero. I wanted a live person. Those people were out there twenty-four-seven, and one of them could good and well talk to me.

"If you know the number of the person you wish to reach, you may dial their extension at any time. If you wish to leave a message—"

Grr! How could I get through to someone? I had no practice at this. Zero was all I knew. "I just need to talk to Jillian Compos," I muttered at the phone.

"Thank you. Connecting to Jillian Compos now. Jillian is not at her desk. If you wish to leave a message, you may begin to speak at the tone—"

I raised my finger to hit the zero again, hoping that if I started over, I could find a different way to navigate to a living person. As my finger was going down, the instructions changed.

"If this is an emergency, say emergency now."

"Emergency!" The phone fumbled in my hand. When I picked it up off the floor, the voice in the receiver was pleasantly chatting away, informing me it was transferring me to Jill's cell phone.

"Yes? Jill here."

She sounded so very pleasant. And I hadn't been pleasant at all when I'd spoken to her over the weekend. Why would she want to help me now? Maybe if I appealed for Cam's sake.

"May I help you?" Jill interrupted my internal monologue, and so very politely. I started to answer when another voice broke me off.

"Who's that, Jill?" It was a male, irritated, and in the back-ground.

"I don't know. Go out to the car, Jared. I'll be there in a minute." A door opened and closed in the background. "Is anyone there?" Jill, again, to me.

"Jill, this is Jake Turner." I took a deep breath. She's married. Why hadn't I thought of that? That explained why she didn't come in yesterday morning. Duh!

"Ah. With Camden Archer. This is a surprise." She paused, and I thought, just wait until you hear the rest of it.

I began haltingly, "Um, I don't know where to begin, and it sounds like you've got plans." Crud! How stupid! I've got a missing boy, and I'm apologizing for interrupting her plans?

"Oh, I think I can take a few moments, Jake. How is Camden doing?"

"I don't know." I slumped against the wall, my eyes burning. Jeepers! Why couldn't I talk? Cam's probably being taken farther and farther away, and I couldn't even talk.

"Okay, Jake. Give me a minute." The phone muffled, and I could hear her opening a door. She called out, "Jared, can we do this another night? Center business."

I could barely hear his reply, but it sounded something like, "Give me a break, Jill! Not again!"

"Don't be a baby. Head on, and I'll see if I can make it up to you." Her voice grew louder. "Now I can take all the time you need. Jake, why don't you start from the beginning?"

It was a long time before I hung up, but I thought we wound up on the same page. At least she and I agreed on one thing. Calling her was the best thing I could have done, and I was to meet her at the Center as quickly as I could get there.

I hoped Jared was just a one-night fling. This was a desperate search for Cam, but if I had someone from the Center on my side, I wanted it to be Jill. And only Jill. In all the bad things dumped on me today, she was my one bright spot, and I ignored all the speed limit signs to get there as quickly as I could.

Chapter 32

We Reach an Understanding, and I'm Still Confused

As I turned off the highway, the Center was brilliantly lighted, even at this hour. It wasn't yet dark outside, and still, the campus glowed like a nuclear waste dump at midnight. It struck me just how deep the pockets were behind this place. At home I unplugged my toaster to keep my electric bill down. These people flaunted their disregard for efficiency.

I tried to keep one thing in mind: they'd done a dang-good job of taking care of Cam before he came to me. That was one mark in their favor. Against them, well, if I started that list, they'd be struck out, and the game'd be over. The point was, I was between a rock and a hard place. I didn't trust the Center, and I didn't have anyone else to trust. I was grasping at Jill, because she had been nice to me, and she had Cam's eyes. Someone couldn't be completely bad with Cam's eyes, and his laugh, of course.

I blinked away tears, not wanting them to come. It was that laugh. Not Jill's, although it was the same, but Cam's, at something stupid. The pie, the way he had laughed about that last bite and how good it was, how good his performance was, really. And I grabbed him, and we both laughed together. And then I trimmed his toenails instead of doing something important, like hugging the kid and telling him he was important to me. The Center had stuck their one remaining orphan with the crudest, most callus, stupidest person in Denver. And I couldn't even hold onto him. That made my slide into self-pity even worse. I tried not to picture Cam gagged, his hands tied behind his back, all stuffed into a dark trunk, watching the backsides of the brake lights flash on and off through the cracks in the lining, not knowing where he was going. He wouldn't know I was doing everything I could to get him back, even if that was just putting my car in park and turning off the engine.

I got out and shut my door, looking over the vast facade, the jutting rooflines, and the soaring walls of glass. The place looked so transparent, like nothing bad could be going on at SISSY. Yeah, I called it that, too. Not in front of Cam. Especially not in front of Cam. Not really anyplace else, either, just in my mind. Now I wanted to yell it out, scream it at the building, even get a can of spray paint and write it across those pristine glass walls. It would backfire on me, though. I intended it as an insult, but adding graffiti to the building would only make the place seem cool to my eighth graders. Cutting edge. The latest and greatest. The best around. Dear God, I hoped this place was the best, and as loaded as they seemed, because I wanted some pretty deep pockets to go out and help find me a lost boy.

Then I saw Jill inside, coming down a corridor, walking pretty fast. That surprised me. Not the fast part. I hadn't seen her car. Or any cars. I expected her to meet me here, but I pictured her driving up, and here I was, all pumped and ready to smash some child-abducting face. And she was already inside. I had ignored every speed limit sign I saw. How fast had she driven to get here? What really irritated me was that her being here first knocked the head off my steam. She was headed out on a date, I interrupted her, and she got here first, as if she cared about finding Cam more than I did. No, it wasn't going down that way. She might be pretty, and I'd overlook a lot for that, but where Cam was concerned, I wasn't taking second place to the Center for any reason. They might be big, and they might be powerful, but they were also cold and unfeeling, willing to snatch my boy away whenever it suited their whims, without any regard for what was best for him. I'd seen the tears. Did they even bother to look into his eyes? That was the real boy, living inside those eyes. Get in there with him, and they'd know. He needed more than a fancy building with eighty-inch TVs and leather sofas. He needed someone to remind him to close the door and who'd clip his toenails at night.

By that time, I was at the door, and I could feel myself about to boil over. Jill swiped an ID card across a scanner, and she placed her hand on a panel. The glass door whispered aside, and she waved me in.

"Thank you, Jake. I know you're concerned about Camden. Let's see if we can fix this problem."

That got my goat right there, and I snapped. I mean really snapped, and right at her, lashing out with all the pent-up anger I felt inside.

"Cam. That's the problem with you people. You don't even know his name. You just see Camden this and Camden that on all his paperwork, and you think his name is Camden. Well, it's not, lady. It's Cam, and only Cam. Got that? And he's not a problem. He doesn't need fixed. I take my car to the repair shop, and it gets fixed. It's a *machine*. People fix *machines*. They don't fix boys. Got that?"

I meant every word, but as soon as they came out, I wished I could take them back. I have to hand it to Jill. She took it on the chin, never blinking, and without an ugly word back. She had the right, too. I had my one ally standing in front of me, and I was shooting off laser blasts that could drill holes in steel. All she did was smile at me.

"Thank you, Jake, and you are right. About all of it. Cam it is, and I agree with you one hundred percent. We don't fix boys, only machines, and I'm glad you see Cam that way. But, we are going to fix this situation, if I may continue to use that word. Cam is a very valuable asset, both to the Center, and clearly, to you." By then we were walking briskly down the glass corridor, Jill swiping and palming every door we came to, and never missing a beat.

"Asset?" I growled the word. It sounded too much like *thing*, and I didn't like the connotation.

"Asset, Jake. An asset is anything you hold very dear." She paused and looked directly at me. "When Cam chose you as his outside mentor, he certainly made a wise decision. You have bonded with him very nicely."

"Wait a minute." A door slid open, and two green lights blinked directly above it, indicating permission to step through. We were entering a part of the facility deeper into foreign territory, one that was clearly an inner sanctum of the huge complex. I wasn't moving, though. "What do you mean Cam chose me?"

Jill just looked at me, then motioned, requesting, "This way, please?" She asked, and very nicely, but I was beyond asking, and I jumped all over her.

"No. There was a storm, and I, me, Jake Turner, called and asked if Cam could stay the night. Cam didn't call. He didn't want me to call. And all that business about the storm—" I was waving my arm around at that point, getting all worked up. "—wasn't Cam's doing. He doesn't control the weather. And I saw the news reports about this place. The lightning. You telling me that wasn't real? You people just faked that? I might as well believe that the aliens living in Roswell have taken over the U.S. government."

"This way, please, Jake. I'll answer all your questions as best I can, but not standing here in this doorway." When I refused to move, she sighed and gave in. Not much, but she gave in. "The storm was very real. You are the one who contacted the Center. Yes, all that's true. We did receive damage that night, and we still haven't resolved all the issues. And no, Jake, the aliens in Roswell have not yet taken over the U.S. government." She smiled at that, and I could see it in her eyes. She thought it was funny.

"Thank you, Jill. Thank you for answering my questions." I tried to regain my poise, and I stood straighter and adjusted my shirt. I walked through the door and listened to it whisper closed behind me. I glanced back to see two red lights blinking above the door, and I wondered if it opened on its own from this direction.

It wasn't until later that I realized Jill hadn't answered the important question. What did she mean, Cam chose me?

Chapter 33

Sometimes All You Can Do Is the Next Thing

When we finally reached the dead center of CISSIE—or *SISSY*, I wanted to snigger—I wasn't sure if we had reached the most high-tech place in the world, or the most neglected one. The door coming up was totally frosted. Lights were burning on the other side, but I couldn't make out anything except the words on the glass. They were clear enough. Secure Location. No Admittance. I got the impression that it meant everyone. Me. Jill. Probably every person who worked here. The other doors we'd come to had displayed two red lights blinking above them. When Jill swiped her card, one would turn green. Her palm would turn the second one. You start to notice things like that when you don't know where you're going, and there's not much to look at, just blank walls, dark windows, and the occasional lighted fountain burbling away outside. I didn't see any people, but I was pretty sure if I tried to go through a door without Jill's ID and her hand, they'd show up pretty quickly, and I'd be tossed out on my keister. With no apologies, too.

There were four red lights above this door. Four. My armpits were damp. I wasn't supposed to be here. I knew that, and I had stuck pretty close to Jill the whole time. I didn't mind that, not at all. It's just that another circumstance, like not here, would be preferable. I tried to think what could get us past four lights. If we didn't make it, I pictured the four lights turning into high-intensity, tight-beam lasers, slicing our legs off so we couldn't run away. Sort of like Indiana Jones trying to steal an ancient artifact, one protected by charms and juju beads. And deadly poisoned darts, ready to shoot us right between the eyes. I watched that first movie as a kid, and more than once. I changed my underwear a few times, too.

Then we were standing in front of the door. Jill swiped. Blink. One light was green. Her hand, and a second turned. Then she stepped forward, facing the door, and a grocery scanner flickered across her face. You know, the light that's inside the cash register, and it reads the bar codes. It read Jill's bar code. A retinal scanner, I figured, except it read a lot more than her retina.

That was only three lights, though. One more was still red. I waited for the lasers. I hoped they missed my vital organs. I could live without my legs. I wasn't so sure about my other parts.

"Jillian Compos, 17623Thumper, Security Code 3BF."

The final light snapped to green, like the little soldier it was, and the door whispered aside.

"Gosh, Jill." I felt eight years old inside. "This is better than Tom Cruise in *Mission Impossible*."

"Wait until you see what's inside." She pushed her hair behind one ear, and she motioned me in. "Just don't touch anything."

"No lasers gonna slice me up." I held my hands shoulder high, and then I dramatically slipped them into my pants pockets. I grimaced, like I thought it might really happen. Well, it might. This was that type of place. No Admittance. Secure Location, and all. That generally meant lasers. I knew. I watched a few of those movies growing up.

"Okay, Jake. Are we here to find Cam Archer, or do you want to play spy games?" She looked exasperated, and I think I'd finally gotten on her nerves.

"Sorry. What do I do?"

"Nothing, except watch. I need you here to give me information."

She walked over to an island in the middle of the room. It was the only thing inside, except for a couple of tall white leather and chrome stools, the kind you'd find at an ultra-modern bar. They were off to the side, and she didn't pull one up. I kept at her side, my eyes scanning the ceiling for possible lasers.

When we reached the island was when it got weird. She touched a spot on the countertop, right in the middle, and a stalk rose out of it. She took a device out of her pocket—I'd swear it was a smart phone, but not like Cam's. Hers was all clear glass and nothing else—and she clipped it to the stalk. It lighted up, then she began to type rapidly with one hand, occasionally speaking to it. That was when the walls came alive. Lights began to blink, ones that I hadn't even seen, and I'd been looking. Then images started popping up all over the walls, like TV images, but projected, I supposed. They kept moving around. Some overlapped, then the images would shift, fixing the overlap. It didn't take me long to look up and see that a device had dropped out of the ceiling, and it was covered with lenses. Projectors, probably, and that's where the images originated. Jill touched the phone, and one enlarged until it was bigger than the rest.

"There, Jake. Your house."

It was grainy, but sure enough, it was my hundred-plus-year-old mansion. I could see a whited-out spot, and I figured that was the security light in the trees by the front door. There was the sidewalk, and the edge of the lot where I parked my car.

"How are you . . ." I stopped and pulled one hand from my pocket, and then I stuffed it back inside. "These are security cameras, like, police cameras, aren't they?" Now I was really wet under the arms. They had access to this? Me, walking to my car in the middle of the night? That was frightening. Then I thought of something, and I pointed to the image. "But this, that's the apartment's security system. It's private. You can get access to this?"

"Yes. And you saw the door and what it took for me to get inside. That security code? I can only use it once. A new one is generated when I leave the room. I have to request special access each time."

"To, um, keep you people from watching all of us out there who don't know you can do this. People like me." I could hear my voice shaking. That was my sidewalk up there.

"That's why this is the most secure room in the building." Her eyes were on me, intent and serious.

I sorta doubted that. After all, I was in here, but I kept my mouth shut. I just listened as she went on. I caught a police car pulling up at the edge of the picture, and the car's lights went out. I figured they were there to keep a lookout on the crime scene for the night. If so, they were too late to do any good. That wasn't even where the real crime had happened. Look down the street, I wanted to yell at the picture, thinking maybe I should have gone to them first. Except all this. Wow! Did the police even have access to stuff this good? There were images flooding the room.

"This is live?" I interrupted Jill's very informative monologue, walking toward the image of my house. I got in the way of the projection, and I tried to brush myself aside in the image before I realized what the problem was, and I moved to the side. "I mean, this is a real-time image feed?" Hey, I am a science teacher, after all. I keep up with a few things.

"Yes. All of it. I thought if you tell me places you think Cam might be—"

"Forget that. What about where he was? Can you run these things backwards?" I was getting excited now.

"Not indefinitely. It's a massive amount of data. There's a four hour loop before unsolicited images start to sink beneath new input—"

By then she was over my head, and I cut her off again. "Run it back. This one. My neighbor, I told you someone called her apartment when Cam first came to live with me, threatening me. It's been," and I glanced at my wrist, only to find I wasn't wearing a watch. "Dadgummit, what time is it?" Had it been four hours yet? Then, "Sorry."

"For what?"

"My language. I usually don't talk like that." Not out loud, anyway, and never in front of a lady. It was the confessional thing. I'd have to visit one again, and you know how I feel about that.

Jill turned all efficient, as if she hadn't been a model of organization so far, and began to work at the phone. However, she had a smile on her face.

"What?" I glared at her, irritated that she found this funny.

"I've heard worse than that." She glanced at me, then turned back to her phone.

"Not from me you won't." I think she smiled wider.

"There, Jake. See if you can tell anything."

The police car backed away, then the scene was quiet for a while. The picture brightened slowly, and my car appeared. I got out and walked backwards to the door and backed inside, all in a hurry, jerky in reverse motion. Then the EMTs and the police were there. It was going too slowly. I turned, exasperated.

"How much time has it been?" I motioned with my hand, as if I thought that would hurry the video along. I do that, talk with my hands when I get worked up. "Come on, Jill. We're going to miss them." In the picture, I sauntered backwards to my car, now in my work clothes, and backed away.

"I'm sorry, Jake. Three hours forty minutes. At any moment the image will start to degrade. If we don't see it soon, we don't have it. Besides, there's no assurance they were on this side of the house."

"That's the door they have to enter to get to Mrs. Osgood's apartment, the same one I use to get to mine. If I'd only gotten home on time." I hit myself in the temple with the palm of one hand, thinking of Benny's parents. They were always late. Didn't they know other people had places to be? Like saving their own kids from rampaging maniac kidnappers?

"There's no guarantee you could have prevented—"

"There! There!" I hooted and jabbed at the screen with my right hand. A red car had appeared in the picture, one I recognized. "There they are!"

"Are you sure? Let's see—"

"Of course, I'm sure." I leaped forward at the image. It was breaking up, and I had to see who got out of the car. Someone was inside, but the windows were tinted, and the image was blurred. One was clearly a man, though, his face bulky and indistinct. "That's them, right there. Can you make the picture any clearer?"

"The degradation is irreversible. I can try to save what we have."

The image froze, and I could hear Jill working on the little phone. I studied the red car, the one that had tried to kill Cam. I knew that now. It hadn't been a stupid accident. It had been malicious, premeditated murder. *Attempted* murder, but only because Cam hadn't died. I hadn't been angry before. I was angry now, and it wasn't the same at all. I didn't want to crush and maim, I wanted to peel away exposed veins very slowly, watching the person scream in agony. I wanted to do that to the person who possessed the gall to take away the best thing that had happened to me since I had my dad alive.

Crum, I was hurting inside, and I wanted to strike out at someone.

120

"I have it, Jake."

I turned. Jill tapped the smart phone with a smile. I could see she was pleased with herself, and in reality, I was pleased with her, also. We almost lost this, and it was important information. However, I couldn't jump and cheer just yet.

"Can we make this thing search all these feeds?" I looked around at the images flickering around the room. Was that possible? I hoped so. If it couldn't, I'd stay here and search each and every one until I found that red car or Cam, no matter how long it took.

"Yes. It won't be precise. Face recognition isn't perfect, but it can pull up possibilities for us to go back and review later."

"Can your people do that? Faster than we can?" I continued to move from image to image, hoping to catch sight of Cam, that blond hair, those blue eyes, anything that told me where he might be. "Can they?" I turned, and she was typing furiously on her device. After a minute, she looked up at me.

"Already done. The search is running. Too bad we can't get a tag off that car." She was disengaging the phone from the stalk.

"Cam's picture. Did you tell it to look for Cam?" In my mind I could see him in every image, and yet I couldn't find him in any of them. I hadn't heard her say his name into the phone, and I didn't want to miss something so very obvious.

Rather than answer, she reseated the phone and tapped it once. "Camden Archer, Subject 1136M. All pictorial files." The room lit up with images. Cam about six. There as a baby. Another with a front tooth missing. Us on the park bench that day of the storm. In class, with me leaning over him, asking a question. It looked like that one was taken through my classroom window. They had everything, except in my apartment. They didn't have him crying because he thought he had disappointed me. Him tasting Mrs. Osgood's pie, laughing because he'd eaten the final bite. Me cutting his nails, the very last thing we did together, just the two of us.

I found the one of us on the way to practice, when Cam had come up to me like Muhammad Ali. I smiled at the image of us, just standing there in the sun, Cam's arm punching me on the shoulder, and me with a look of dismay on my face. The bright afternoon light made the image especially sharp and clear. In science we call it clarity, where you can see things that are invisible under any other circumstance.

"Is that one special, Jake?"

"Sting like a bee. I'm gonna get those suckers. Rip 'em limb from limb, no matter what price I have to pay." I shook with emotion, and I sniffled, trying to stop the tears.

"I think I can help you with that, Jake."

"What is all this?" I turned to her, no longer caring if she saw the tears. I looked around the room, sweeping my arm past all the images of a boy's lifetime. "What is Cam to you that you do all this? Why, Jill? Why?"

"Why are you here, Jake? You're not his father."

She was very matter of fact, and I looked at her, surprised at her reply. She had turned my question back on me, and that pulled me up short. She was right, though. He wasn't mine and had only lived with me a little over a month. Why was I here, indeed? The answer swelled in me, and I felt my chest fill up. I knew I would explode if I didn't get it out.

I leaned against the wall next to our picture and stood for a minute, looking at it, seeing what Jill couldn't see, the emotions that had filled the moment. Cam and I, we had shared something we hadn't needed to say, all because we were connected in some way. In the short time he had lived with me, we had, I don't know, become like dendrites that branch from cell to cell, and we had connected to one another in a way that made a new level of communication possible, one that no one else could see, because it was ours, and ours alone.

When I couldn't feel Cam in the image, I sank to the floor, letting my legs give way beneath me. I knew why I was here. It was because I had no choice.

"Mr. Turner?"

Jill's voice, firm, as if this was important. She waited, too, for a long time. Finally, I pulled myself together and looked at her through water-soaked eyes. I tried to speak, but the words choked in my mouth.

"You can walk away, and no one will blame you. The Center will take full responsibility for Cam. You do know that?"

"Do you love him?" My pent up emotions burst from me, like a flood across a broken dam, and I raised my voice at her, my arm in motion, emphasizing my point for me. "Do you sit at his side when he cries and carry him to bed when he hurts too much to walk, all because you people *fix* him when he doesn't need fixed? How can you take full responsibility for a kid you don't even know?"

"We do know Cam, Jake."

Her words were softer, as if I'd perhaps said something she wanted to hear. She didn't know him, though, not like I did. I had my arms in front of my face by then, with my fingers tangled in my hair, and I could barely draw in air. My chest jerked with the effort.

I managed to choke out, "Have you ever looked into his eyes? You don't know Cam if you haven't looked into his eyes."

She didn't say anything to that. I guessed she never had. That was why I was here. I had fallen into those eyes, and I hadn't been able to find my way back out.

Chapter 34

I Have Company in the Middle of the Night

The police were there for me.

When I got home that night, I was empty. Physically—I hadn't eaten—and emotionally. When I parked my car, I put my head on the steering wheel for a minute, unable to force myself to open the door and go inside, not wanting to face an empty sofa and an apartment with no one else inside. I guess I didn't really want to face the fact that Cam was gone. Not even Mrs. Osgood was here. Her brother had come and gotten her, refusing to let her live in such a dangerous area, even if she had survived in her apartment just fine for forty years. I had no one and no reason to be here. Still, I had nowhere else to go.

When I opened my door, so did the officers sitting in the police car. One of the men was a big guy my age, and the other, older with gray hair. They escorted me inside. I was too tired to argue with them and too drained to even wonder why they were here. I hadn't been attacked.

They introduced themselves as Officers Simpson and Prouty and explained with no shortage of efficiency, although I would have called it brusqueness. News of Cam's disappearance had gotten to them, as I suspected it would. What did I know? Anything? I didn't know what to say, because none of it would make any sense. I inherited Superboy, the robot kid from the stars, and he's been stolen back to his home world by his greedy forbears. I didn't guess they would want to hear that. Piston legs and woven glass skin don't impress most cops.

Instead, I told them of the flowerbed, which they'd figured out, and the phone call, which they hadn't. I didn't tell them about the red car in the video, because I didn't think they needed to know the Center had the Secure room. I had to trust Jill and her people with that one. Then the big one, Officer Simpson, asked about me, a single teacher, having a student from my class living with me, and I showed them the legal documents from the Center, all signed and in good order. Even after seeing the paperwork, Officer Simpson made a snide remark about me taking Cam to Mass, as if there could be anything inappropriate in that.

"So, what do we do?" I was on the sofa with my head back. My eyes were closed. I just wanted them to leave, if they had no ideas, and especially if the Simpson officer couldn't be polite.

"Go to work; wait."

Said very matter-of-factly, as if all parents with kidnapped kids go on with life as usual. That was from Officer Prouty, the old man with all the experience. He should know, I thought. It's not his kid gone.

"You want me to go to work tomorrow." I sat up, kneading my pants with my hands, wadding the material up, then flattening it again. I shook my head in disbelief.

"Yes, Mr. Turner. Clearly, this man wants something, and he will try to contact you. He knows your schedule, and you must stay on it."

I thought of the thirty kids I see in each of my classes and trying to maintain an interest in each of their individual problems, and I couldn't do it. I couldn't care about those kids, not when Cam was out there, stuffed into the trunk of a car, to California by now, probably.

"Camden's kidnapper needs to be able to contact you. Make sure you carry your phone with you at all times." The young guy. Cops must make more than teachers, if he expected me to have a phone.

"Cam. His name is Cam, and I don't carry one." I was leaning back again, my hand over my eyes. The light overhead was entirely too bright, and my eyes were scratchy by that time. I wanted them closed, for the night, and not with these tools here.

"Come now, Mr. Turner. Everyone has a phone."

The young gun. Sure. Everyone. Then I thought of Cam's, and without looking, I dug in the sofa. Yes, there was Cam's cap, and the phone was inside.

"I have this, but it's not mine." I held it out to them, opening my eyes with difficulty. "I can carry it, but it won't do any good. It's for Internet access only."

The older man took it, then handed it to the big man. "Look at this, Jerry. Can it receive calls?"

Officer Simpson took it and tapped it a few times. "It's got texts on it. It can receive calls." He handed it back to me. "Carry it, Mr. Turner. Somebody knows how to get through on this line."

"It belongs to Cam, the boy who's been kidnapped. He texted me once on it."

"And the kidnappers have him. If they want to find you, that phone's how they'll do it. Don't let it out of your sight." Both of them stood. "We'll be outside for the rest of the night. You'll see us when you head off to work in the morning. Mr. Turner, make sure you go to work. Remember, these kidnappers are thorough. They know your schedule like the back of their hands."

Just not well enough to know which apartment I lived in. When they left I locked the door to Mrs. Osgood's bathroom. I also threw both the deadbolts on my door, and I hung the blanket over the bedroom window. Then I wadded up my extra pillow under the center cushion and slept on the sofa. I don't know why I did that. I hate sleeping on the sofa. I guess I thought if Cam happened to show up, I wanted to know he was here, and this was the first place he'd come. His bed. The sofa.

Like he could have gotten in with all the doors locked. Exhaustion does strange things to a man's mind.

I didn't have a good night. Not at all. And it had nothing to do with the hole in my sofa. It had to do with the hole in my life, one that needed to be filled with a fourteen-year-old boy. I hadn't even known I needed a kid in my life, but I knew for certain now I needed him back. Maybe this was how my mother felt when I moved to Denver. Maybe it was why she wanted me to move back home. Maybe I'd go see her soon, after Cam came back.

Lots of thoughts go through your head when you can't sleep. And I tossed and turned all night long. I thought morning would never come.

Chapter 35

Cam Writes an Essay

Arriving at school wasn't any better. The night before, at the Center with Jill, I was full of anger and derring-do, like their deep pockets could actually get Cam back. I was going to head off on a campaign of vengeance, smash some heads together, with the Center behind me all the way. I pictured myself as King Arthur, vanquishing evil and saving Guinevere from the big, bad bullies. Then big guy Jerry made me feel like a low-life, and old guy sent me off to work. Who can teach tired and preoccupied, with fog in his brain? Not me, and not much teaching got done.

I held onto that phone, though. It was in my pocket all day, banging against my leg, reminding me of why I carried it. I took it out to check it at least once every class period, just in case I missed something. It was at lunch that I figured out how to set it to do something other than vibrate, not sure I'd feel it if it did. How would it be to get to the end of the day, only to find I'd received a message that morning, and I hadn't known all day? An hour that Cam was in the kidnapper's custody was an hour too long, and I didn't want to postpone his release by even a minute, if I could help it.

It was my fifth period that caught the text. I was leaning against my desk, letting the kids work in small groups, and about half asleep. No sleep at night makes for a very sleepy Jake, and I was awake only because I was standing. What got my attention was giggling in the back of the room. I shook my head, pretending to be deep in thought. When I leaned over to my desk to pick up a pencil, one of the girls called out, "Answer your phone, Mr. Turner." Her table burst into another round of giggles. Now, you have to know, students aren't allowed to have phones in my class. I don't mean they can't bring them, but they have to be turned off. And I never have one. When one goes off in class, I take it up and return it at the end of the period, just to make my point. No phones in class.

I was so groggy I didn't get what she meant at first.

Then I heard the chiming. Not vibrating, chiming. It was from my pocket. That got my attention. I reached in my pocket and pulled it out, turning my pocket inside out in the process. From the back of the room, I heard, "Mr. Turner's got a hottie calling him." It was a boy's voice, but the girl's table burst into giggles again.

"Hold on," I said, fumbling the phone, still half asleep and hardly able to focus. I couldn't remember how to pull up the text. My concentration was shattered, and I felt sweaty all over. You know how when nervousness makes you stink, even to yourself? I was there, and I needed space to think. I walked into the hall. I didn't even tell the kids to be quiet or anything. I just stepped outside. Closing the door behind me, I realized I had the phone upside down, and I found the power button, pressing it once. The screen lighted, and I remembered it would have a number at the bottom if there was a new text. One. It said one, and I reached to tap it, my heart pounding in my chest. I didn't want to hear from the kidnappers, and I didn't want to postpone Cam's confinement, either. The thought that kept hovering at the edges of my mind was that Cam might be dead already, and I wouldn't know. The kidnappers wouldn't tell me, would they?

I touched the icon, and a text box appeared.

Mr. Turner, are you there?

My heart dropped into my stomach. I held the phone to my face, my hand shaking, about to answer yes, when I remembered I had to open a reply box and type in it. I tapped on the screen unsuccessfully, ready to explode, when one of my girls stuck her head out the door and asked to go to the restroom. I couldn't answer her, except to motion for her to go on. Then I called, "Beth, make this reply to a text, please."

"Let me see, Mr. Turner." She took the phone, tapped it once, and handed it back to me. "There. Hit send when you're finished. Bye!" She smiled and waved, heading off to the restroom.

I'm here, Cam. Where are you? I hit send, and I watched the image shift. Now, both our messages were there. Cam's *Are you there?* and my *Where are you?* All I could do was wait. It didn't take long.

The words appeared, *I don't know.*

I typed back in, *We're trying to find you.* I waited for a few minutes, realizing my class was getting very loud. Beth came back down the hall, and she asked, "Did you get it figured out, Mr. Turner?" I nodded. When she went inside, I stuck my head in and called out, "Pop quiz in five minutes. Have your papers ready." I didn't have a quiz, but I could make something up, I hoped. Then the phone chimed. I looked down at it.

It's really dark in here. I'm scared.

I was scared, too. For Cam. I typed in, *Have they hurt you?* The reply took forever, it seemed, although it couldn't have been over thirty seconds. At times like that, even a second seems like an eternity.

Finally, the words popped up, *Sorry, Mr. Turner, they're coming.*

There was nothing else, as many times as I typed in his name. I never did get to that pop quiz. I didn't get to anything else, either, not even after-school practice. I guess they got a sub for my last class, or maybe the kids just came in and enjoyed a free period. Whatever, I didn't care. I got in my car and drove to the police station. Their idea didn't help at all. The texts couldn't be traced, and they tried. It turns out the Center runs their own phone service, and all the phone information is proprietary.

Is everybody an idiot in this town?

All of them, too, with no exceptions. The police, the phone companies, the Center, except for Jill, of course. She helped me last night, and she said she was running a trace through her computer systems. I drove out to the Center, certain she would be there. She might have an idea about the phone, how to find out where the texts were from. Find that, I thought, and we find Cam. The receptionist called her to the front, and she looked almost as tired as I felt. She'd been at it all day, and all the leads had been dead ends. I showed her the phone, and she recognized it immediately. It was a standard issue phone for the employees, as well as for the orphans to use when they were off campus. In the press of the moment, she'd forgotten about Cam's, assuming he'd had it with him when he was abducted. When I told her the police had me carry it that day, she was skeptical. The kidnappers wouldn't allow him to text anyone, she said. The abductors would know that the police would be able to trace the text back to its origin, first to the phone number, and then to the phone's location.

"Not with this one," I said. "It's the Center's phone." My tone told what I thought of that. She gave a deep sigh, saying Cam's abductors wouldn't know that, she didn't think. She went to hand it back to me, until I told her about the texts I'd received from Cam.

"He texted you today?" She turned it on to look, only to have it chime before she could open anything up. I knew that chime, and it was for me. My boy knew I was here.

"That's the sound," I said, taking it from her. "He's doing it again." I tapped the icon and got an eyeful. It wasn't the one liner I expected.

I'm sorry, Mr. Turner. I can only do this when they leave me alone. It hurts, and I can't think clearly. I don't know where I am. I think close, because we didn't stop any on the way. I'm hungry, but they've got tubes hooked to me, and they said I don't need to eat. It's my brain that hurts. My head. They want something in my head, and they suck and suck and suck, and I try so hard to remember me and you and school and it's hard. Find me, Mr. Turner. Please. They're coming back. I've gotta go.

Cam, be strong. I sent it fast, hoping he would get it.

I'll try. And that was all, no matter what I did. I handed the phone to Jill.

"I can get our people here to try and trace the texts." Jill looked up after reading the messages, offering me at least something. "It is our system, and we do have access rights."

"Do I have to give them the phone? He might send me another message, and I have to be ready."

"They'll need the phone's ID. That's all. Let's go see what we can find out."

We learned there was no incoming number. Cam had to have a phone to send with, they said, and it would leave identification on the system, but it was as if the texts originated outside the system and were just dropped onto the phone, pretty as you please.

"That would be Cam," I remarked, as Jill and I headed to the cafeteria. We found two seats away from anyone else.

"What would?" She still had the phone, and she was scrolling through the messages. I guessed she hadn't gotten to the first ones he'd sent me.

"Keep scrolling." I reached and moved the list to the top. "See?" I pointed to one phrase. *They don't know I can do this, so I better go. I don't want them to find out.* "Who are *they*, Jill?"

She read the text slowly, and she looked at me. "Us. The Center. This is amazing, Jake."

"That's not the word I would use right now. Disastrous is more like it."

"No, you don't understand. This makes it clear Cam can send a text without access to a phone." Her voice was very excited.

I looked at her with skepticism. "He had a computer, then."

"No, you weren't there. That weekend, Cam was in surgery, and he was in surgery *all* weekend."

"Maybe afterwards. He's fourteen. He probably snuck access to a computer when you people were distracted." I was pretty disgusted by then, tired, too, and I tried to back off, to be nicer. "I'm pretty sure you can text on a computer, as long as you can access the Internet." She seemed very certain, but I knew she had to be wrong. I had the texts to prove it.

"No. Not possible. I'll tell you what. I want to get some people on this. If Cam can do what I think he can do, we might be able to find a way to track him down."

"What do you mean? GPS?" Phones had that, I knew, but this being the Center's equipment, I wasn't betting the bank.

"No, no. This phone, yes, but if Cam's not using a phone, we can't track it with GPS. I'm talking triangulation. If we can get Cam to send a signal, and we can measure its strength, the stronger the signal is, the closer he is to us."

"Or us to him. I don't think he's going to be moving around very much. Tubes, remember. He sounded pretty stationary."

"The picture is bigger. We, and I don't mean just the Center, have cell towers everywhere. Buildings, power poles, the tops of windmills. If we can get something specific from this signal, something we can track, we might narrow our search, even locate him."

I was beginning to follow her. But with no number, I didn't see how. My head wouldn't get around it, and I was so exhausted I couldn't think.

"I'm sorry, Jill. You guys'll have to figure this out. I'm hopeless at high-tech stuff like this." I held the phone in front of me, just hoping for another text.

"Not high tech, Jake." She reached and put her hand on my wrist. "It's a phone."

As tired as I was, that hand made a difference. It shot slivers of fire through my body, almost as if her touch told me that what she offered was possible, when her words had said a bunch of mumbo-jumbo.

"Okay, Jill." I looked at her hand, willing her to leave it there. "I'm game. How do we do this?"

"We don't have a number, but I bet that signal is coming in on a specific frequency. If we can identify that, we might have a chance."

"Okay. Here it is. How do we find the frequency?" I placed the phone on the table.

"It's not going to be that easy." She pushed it back to me. "When we looked up the calls, there was nothing on the phone. We need to get a live feed as the signal is coming in."

"Then you'll be able to track it?" It sounded doable, as long as she had her hand on my wrist. However, I didn't know just when the texts were coming and had no way to predict one in advance. I couldn't exactly text Cam and tell him the day and hour.

"Yes, but if this works, we can only track the signal when he's sending. We may not have long to get a fix on him." She lifted her hand from my wrist.

I felt the life go out of me. I was simply tired once again, and her plan seemed little more than wishful thinking.

"So, this isn't a sure thing." I felt hope fading, also.

"It's a chance, a real chance we might be able to find him, and all because of something special Cam can do. No one else has ever done this, and it might be what saves his life." Her face was intense, and I knew this was important to her.

"So, I need to stay here." Oh, but my eyes hurt. What I needed was sleep.

"I'm sorry, Jake." Her hand found my wrist again.

I wasn't sorry. Not at that moment. I would have done anything

132

she asked me to do, including dancing under the stars to get them to locate Cam for me.

I would have to sleep sometime, though, whether Jill was holding my hand or not. My last thought before my head hit the table was to wonder if it would be okay if I danced under the stars in my sleep.

Then I don't remember anything else.

Chapter 36

Being an Expert Isn't the Same as Being Smart

It was the bright light that woke me. I'd been wandering in a dark place, a labyrinth of interconnected rooms, where banks of blinking machines kept sending wires and hollow tubes my way, chasing me, and my only hope was to speak into the communicator attached to my shirt.

I kept yelling, "Anyone! Beam me up!"

I lay there quite a while, aware of the hubbub of noise around me. It was muted, though, and not unpleasant. I had a pillow under my head, and a warm blanket over me. I pulled it up under my chin, and I turned to my side.

"Pleasant dreams, Jake?"

I opened my eyes. The ceiling overhead, the steel beams, and looking sideways, the vast expanses of glass and lawn beyond. An angular fountain of square tubing sputtered water that ran into a holding pond that was equally angular. I sat up, looking for the voice and pushing the blanket off at the same time. Jill was all business, a tablet in her hand, as she walked up beside me.

"How long have I been asleep?" I didn't feel any better, but maybe I would, that was if I'd slept long enough. The problem was that I never felt better just after I woke. My brain seemed soaked in molasses. Ten minutes or ten hours, both left me groggy and in a fog.

"Let's just say you missed the cock's crow." She smiled and carefully placed her tablet on a small table at the end of the leather sofa I'd been sleeping on. She pulled my blanket to her and began to deftly fold it into repeated squares until it all but disappeared, and she dropped it onto the arm. She sat beside me. "We received another text."

"The phone!" That jarred me awake. I patted my pockets and began to search the sofa, feeling under the cushions.

Jill reached to the table and handed me the phone. It was hooked to a charger that disappeared somewhere under the furniture. I turned it on and scrolled through. There it was. Short, from Cam, and with a reply I hadn't made.

"Who?" She knew what I meant. Who sent the reply?

"We did, or rather, Racine in Logistics. While you were asleep, we had the phone, hoping something would come through. Racine tried to keep the texts going, but Cam never replied to her. I'm sorry, Jake."

"Did it work?" Cam's latest text on the phone ripped at me. *I'm tired, Mr. Turner. I want to go home.*

"We had hoped it would, but no. We're not sure why just yet. Maybe the input from Cam was too brief. All we could pick up was the signal from this phone."

"This phone?" I didn't know enough about how all this worked to do anything except repeat her words. I was scrolling through his old messages, looking for anything that might be a clue, except I knew there wasn't anything. It was only making me more aware of the boy I'd lost, and how determined I was to get him back.

"We can pull signal strength from sources all over the country," Jill reminded me.

I remembered the Secure room.

"Cam's text came through in a fraction of a second, a pulse, if you will. It registered as full strength right at this location. Only your phone would do that."

"The text Racine sent. Does it, or did it register in the same way as Cam's?" Jill looked surprised, and she smiled. I guess she's seen that I'm not very technically savvy.

"Yes, and we tracked that, as well. The signal in and the signal out were almost identical in location. The variances were so small as to be inconsequential."

"Inconsequential?" I was grasping at straws. Here was the person who knew what she was talking about, but straws were all I had. "If it's not the same, it's not inconsequential."

"Within standard parameters, if that's any clearer. And remember, this is something completely new, for one of our children to be able to communicate in this manner. We won't know how it all works until we have a chance to study it."

I caught her words, though. One of our children. They were orphans, not "their children." Just because you're an orphan doesn't mean you belong to someone. Slavery went out with the Civil War. Plus, it made it sound as if they had built them on an assembly line, like saying, it's unusual for one of our cars to get forty miles per gallon. But look, what a pleasant surprise! I didn't badger her, though. I had done that enough the evening before. I intended to be very cooperative. I remembered her hand on my wrist, and I wouldn't mind that again, not at all.

"So, when Cam drops a message on my phone—" I could tell I was taking ownership of both him and his phone, "—the message causes a signal spike on your power gauges—"

"On every power gauge within a reasonable distance." She interrupted, nodding.

"It causes a spike on all the gauges within a reasonable distance." I guess that clarification made a difference to her. One. A hundred. I pictured old-fashioned needles like on a mechanical speedometer jumping to the side and immediately falling back down, and then I pictured every car in Denver doing that all at once. "Then when Racine sent a reply, it did exactly the same thing." All the speedometers jumped, and all the drivers called the Center and reported in.

"Not exactly the same, Jake. This is very technical, and I'm not the expert here, but the incoming signal and the outgoing signal were not exactly the same, just within acceptable parameters."

"Then they weren't the same." I didn't know what that meant, but it didn't mean inconsequential.

"Perhaps not, but both originated at the Center, and look around you. Cam isn't here, and we'd know if he were. Every part of this facility is monitored. No, the most likely scenario is that the phone sent out a companion wave when Cam sent the text. Perhaps that's how he does this. He can trigger the phone's carrier signal, and he can ride the text in on that."

"All that's over my head, but different is different, that's one thing I know. Remember, I teach science. Granted, it's eighth grade, and you people are the experts. But in science, different is different, no matter how slight."

I leaned my head back, studying the ceiling. Every beam up there jutted out at a different angle. How had the architect managed to get every one into place without making a mistake? All that metal, all those angles to catch workers' hands and clothing. It was fortunate no one was killed putting all this up. Or maybe they were. Who could tell?

I knew one thing, though. I needed a shave. And a shower. I wondered if it was safe for me to visit my apartment for a while. Jill answered that question for me. She stood and picked up her tablet and the blanket.

"Jake, there's nothing for you to do right now. Why don't you head home, and we'll let you know when we find out something."

"But the phone. I don't want to miss Cam, and you'll need it." I held it protectively, thinking if he contacted me right then, they'd miss it, because the phone wasn't wherever it needed to be for them to identify the signal, however they did that.

"We can track the signal changes anywhere you are."

"Both of them?" I narrowed my eyes at that, in case she'd forgotten they were different.

"Both of them. In spite of what I said, we have recorded the differences in the signals, and if they diverge, we will be able to tell. In fact, with you at home, if Cam does send, that may tell us something new."

"Like what?" I stood, tired from inadequate sleep, and moody from having slept.

"If we knew, well, that's what will make it new." She held out a second phone. "For us to contact you, or vice versa. Be sure to unplug the charger and take it with you. We want to keep the phones topped off." She smiled, but it was clear I was being dismissed.

I knelt to do so, noticing Jill had very nice legs. I had also noticed the condescending tone. Sometimes I thought she liked me, and other times I was a grain of sand in her shoe, nothing more than an irritation. Jared was probably the cause of that. I could punch *him* in the face.

I carried the charger with me, only remembering I had another at home when I was in the car. I was aware of one thing as I drove away. She didn't even shake hands with me as I left. Was I that repulsive? Maybe after I took a shower and shaved, and then I thought, nah. She has Jared, and I'm just another thing on today's agenda. I'd better let her go.

But I couldn't. I'd noticed those legs, and they kept me preoccupied as I maneuvered into traffic.

Chapter 37

Help Comes in the Unlikeliest of Places

I was almost home when I remembered. Science teacher. I'd reminded Jill I was a science teacher, and it never clicked in for me. I had classes to teach. That was a pain, and I couldn't get to work any later, except not to show up at all. I turned around and headed to the school. I straightened my clothes before I went in, sniffing of my shirt in hopes it didn't smell too rank. Maybe they'd let me run home to change.

"Sharon," I called out to our school secretary, sitting at the front desk. "I am so sorry."

"Oh, no, Jake. We're the ones who are sorry." She looked at me like she couldn't believe I was there.

Then, with no hesitation, she stepped from behind her desk and gave me a quick hug. I didn't envy her. I must have smelled awful. No, I take that back. I knew I smelled awful, and there was no way she couldn't tell. I cringed. She didn't seem to mind, though.

"That missing boy, Cam." She patted the front of my shirt, straightening my pocket. "We know he's only yours until the Center gets him all situated, but still, to have him kidnapped like that. And from right under your nose." She moved back to her desk. "Those of us on staff who believe have been saying prayers for you. Now, did you need anything?" She looked at me and smiled.

"My class?" Why wasn't she asking me about being so late?

"Your class?" She frowned, and then with a quick laugh, she reached to her desk and pulled a half-sheet from inside a manila folder. "I understand. We have someone in your class today. All of your classes, in fact. You are completely covered." Sharon is very perceptive, the best front office secretary in the district. She handed me the paper. The name on it was Miranda Lamb. "The Center contacted Beth Ziegler, and you're all set up for the rest of the week, and next, too, if you need it. Miranda has agreed to stay as long as we need her. You might be aware," and she leaned forward conspiratorially, "the police were in here today, and I did not like that young one. Big, with a bit of an attitude? He suggested that you having Cam living with you, um, that perhaps you were, um, I can't even repeat what he suggested. I put in a good word for you, don't you think I didn't. He was the rudest man, and I did not like him one bit. If you run into him, you be sure to give him a piece of my mind." She nodded at me as if that settled it.

Good old Sharon Lakey. An understanding woman who doesn't mind sharing her faith, even in a public school setting. Sometimes schools get good people, and sometimes they get the best. Lucky Bruce Randolph. Lucky me. I headed out the door, only then remembering the phone was in the car. I rushed to get the door open, but there were no messages. The little icon at the bottom was as empty as empty could be. I tossed it aside and started up the engine. I got a surprise on the way home, Kenny Urbringer, walking down the street. I slowed and rolled my window down.

"Kenny. School's in session. Or did you think it was Saturday?" By then I had stopped, and he had stopped. He had his hands in his pockets, and he was slumped over. When he saw it was me, he backed away. I called to him, "What, Kenny?"

"Um, the police were at school today."

"And they were at my house, too. How much do you know about what's happened?" He spoke as if the police were news to me, and as if it said something that I should have taken into account before stopping to talk to him. His reasoning escaped me, but then most things Kenny did escaped me. Somewhere in there was probably a genius, but it never managed to get out that I could see. If he hung around Cam enough, then maybe, but right now Cam was nowhere to be found.

"They said . . ." He worked his mouth, as if he didn't know what to say. Then he vomited it all out. "They said you like boys, Mr. Turner, and you probably killed Cam so he couldn't tell." His face had gone white, with blotchy patches on his neck, and his eyes were red.

I knew I was going to be angry at someone, but it wasn't Kenny. I turned the key off, opened the door, and got out. I shut the car and leaned against it, making sure not to approach him. If anything, he was hunched even more than before, as fragile as a butterfly in the face of an impending tornado, and about to disintegrate. I couldn't afford to be the cause of that.

"Kenny, how long have you known me?" I waited until he looked at me. "Kenny?"

"A long time, Mr. Turner." He reached his sleeve and wiped his nose.

"Have I ever given you any reason not to trust me?" Work with me, kid.

"No." He was down to a sniffle. That was progress, at least.

"Now, exactly who told you I killed Cam?" I pictured Jerry. He was nothing but a blue-suited bully. I had seen that the first time he opened his mouth. It would be like him, but who knew? Maybe even one of my neighbors had tagged along with stories of Cam and me outside in the rain. But that I killed Cam? It boiled my blood just to say that. I also knew that if this was going around school, I might as well kiss my job good-bye. The liking boys part? If possible, that was even worse, what with Cam staying with me, a single male teacher.

"That policeman. I was late, because my grandmother's sick, and I needed a pass." He was on a roll, but he took time to wipe his nose on his sleeve again. "He was in there, and he told Mrs. Lakey that people like you need to be in jail. He just didn't have any evidence, yet. Mrs. Lakey hadn't seen me, so I ran out the door." He drew in a ragged breath, and he looked like he was going to crumple.

"The policeman, Kenny. He was big? My age?" After a moment, he visibly got himself under control, and he nodded. I sighed and looked up at the sky. I knew who he was talking about. "What did the old man say?"

"The old man?"

"The other policeman. There should have been two." Focus,

Kenny. Focus.

"He was writing stuff down on a little note pad."

Something chimed. I looked around, moving away from the car, forgetting it was Cam's phone. I guess I was expecting it to vibrate. In my pocket.

"Your phone got a text, Mr. Turner."

I glanced at him and yanked the door open, sitting inside and reaching for it. I clicked it on and opened the message.

Mr. Turner?

That's all it was. My palms were sweaty. I started typing, and I kept hitting the wrong letters and having to back up. "Why can't I get this thing to work?" I muttered under my breath, exasperated.

"Mr. Turner, you can talk to it." I looked up to see Kenny at my window. "Here." He touched an icon on the little keyboard, and a pulsing red circle appeared. "Now say what you want to send."

"Cam. Cam, are you there? It's me. We're trying to find you, but we can't locate your signal." I looked at the phone, then to Kenny. "It's not doing anything." It did, though. As I was speaking, the words scrolled across the screen, and I tapped send.

"Where is he?"

I looked at Kenny blankly. He thought I knew? Didn't he listen to anything I said? I turned back to the phone, hoping to see a reply from Cam. Nothing. I glanced at the second phone. Should I call the Center? Or would they call me?

"You didn't really kill Cam, did you, Mr. Turner?"

"Good grief, Kenny, shut up!" I looked at him to see shock in his face. "I'm sorry, Kenny. I shouldn't have said that. Get in the car. I'll take you home."

He did. He got in without a word. He watched me start up the car, and I turned to him.

"You said your grandmother's not feeling well. Do you have somewhere else I can take you?" School was probably not an option, not in his state. He'd shatter at the least provocation.

"I want to help find Cam."

His words were little more than a whisper, and I barely caught them. Still, they told me one thing. He no longer believed I had killed Cam to cover up my unhealthy interest in him. And he no longer believed I liked boys, I hoped. At least not in the way Sharon Lakey had described. Otherwise, he wouldn't have gotten in the car with me.

"Sure, Kenny. Any ideas?" I sat with the car running and not going anywhere.

"Can we get something to eat first? I didn't get breakfast."

"Sure." I smiled at that. Missing friend, warped teacher, and skipping school. And he was hungry. Fourteen, too. Kenny was all very real boy, without any hint of a bionic brain or titanium skull. Not like my Cam. "I have Oreos, eggs, and mustard at my house. How does Oreo cereal sound?"

"Fine, Mr. Turner." He rolled his window down, and he put his face outside as I pulled away. "I like Oreos a lot."

And you get my stamp of approval, Kenny. One hundred percent, very-real-boy Kenny. But he wasn't Cam, and finding Cam was going to make for a very tough climb, all the way to the top of Mount Evans. Still, I had Jill, and now I had Kenny. Between the three of us, we'd find him, or someone would suffer because of it. I'd see to that with my bare hands.

It did surprise me the Center didn't call. However, I guessed they didn't feel the need to let me know the text couldn't be traced.

Again.

Chapter 38

The Morning Show Goes on a Snipe Hunt

"That's right, Brian. Just take two of these a day, and you can be assured of regular bowel movements, no matter how irregular your week has been."

The camera shifted slightly, and a second commentator appeared by the first. The Morning Show was segueing from its health segment to current news.

"Thank you, Stella. I never thought of that as a cure, not one that I'd want to take, in any case. That shows you can never tell about modern medicine." Both commentators laughed. "In local news, there's a report of a Denver school teacher under investigation for possible involvement in the case of a missing student. Do you have more on that, Stella?"

"I do, Brian. It would seem the missing student was in the teacher's class on Tuesday and has not been seen since. Blond hair, five-three, and an eighth grade student at Bruce Randolph School." Cam's current school photo appeared on the screen beside the commentator. "The police are searching for him now. You can call in with any information you have to RESCUE-1733. There's a $1,000 reward for any information that leads to the successful return of this boy."

"Stella, I remember this young man." Now was time for the chatty part of the show. It was a key trademark of the Morning Show for the hosts to chat about each news item, bringing the content down to a human level. "Isn't he one of the Center's orphans? Placed in a home after the Center's dormitory wing was damaged?"

"Yes, Brian. You may remember I was there that night. Camden Archer is his name. If I remember correctly, he's been living with one of his teachers during the interim, and with the school district's approval."

"The same man that's under investigation?"

"Yes, although the teacher's name has been withheld pending further investigation and possible indictment."

"How unfortunate for young Camden to have been tossed from the frying pan into the fire, and at such a young age. In other news, a greyhound near Houston, Texas, is now the oldest living survivor of the racetrack in the world. Can we get a picture of that dog, Randy?"

Chapter 39

All Is Darkness in the Middle of the Day

Camden Archer was not at home, not far from home, and at home, too. It depends on how you define the word home. Is home where the heart is, where the body resides, or where a child is born?

He was in a room, brilliantly lighted, with tightly packed computer equipment lining the walls. It wasn't a large room, but it was spacious enough for a surgical table and all the paraphernalia needed to keep a body alive, even when it wanted to die.

Cam didn't want to die. Of course not. What fourteen-year-old boy, full of enthusiasm, with people around him who care, wants to exit this life without experiencing it first? Yet, in this room, he had no choice. Tubes connected his life processes to machines that kept them pumping along. One fed a proprietary and very unique electrolyte solution into his arm, the minerals balanced to lubricate the electrical responses along his neural pathways. Another removed wastes, meticulously strained from his system. Various wires snaked to his groin, chest, and head, attached by adhesive pads that clung like an octopus' arms. Fat straps held his arms and ankles to the table, and a larger, metal one ran over his forehead. The largest of all kept his chest firmly in place. His eyes were wide open, and from time to time his head jerked. It was clear he wasn't looking at anything above him.

"Queenie!" A burly man in a tailored suit walked in the room, stopping beside the boy. His voice was heavy with latent power, like someone used to authority.

"Yes?" A late-middle-aged woman, a little manic around the eyes and wearing a white lab coat, strode in, a donut in her hand. "Do you need something?"

"This . . . process must be speeded up." The man spoke with a Slavic accent, and he had to pause to choose the correct word. "The boy's disappearance I have seen on the, what do you say, television discussions of the news. If there is discovery of this—" He motioned around the room.

"We are well hidden, right under the Center's nose." The woman snorted in derision.

He spat, "What good is it to spend all my rubles outfitting a, how do you say, remote facility, if you are determined to remain here?" He turned to her, his face hard. His voice had the sound of metal on stone, a scraping, rasping quality that was painful to listen to. He didn't seem to recognize how superbly outfitted the space was, even if the machines were cobbled together from a previous generation of cast-off equipment. Results, screamed the clenching of his jaw. Nothing else could be a higher priority.

"If you'd done a better job with the car, he wouldn't be on the news," Queenie jabbed. "We could have picked him up at the morgue. Cognitive resuscitation would have been simple, and we would be finished already. No, instead, the trauma team got to him first, and you had to terrorize an old woman." She actually smiled at that. "We lost two full days, Arkady. That was not my fault, so don't blame me."

"I offer you . . . simple solution." He walked to the bank of pumps feeding life into Cam's body. "Turn off the machines. I will gladly take care of this detail for you. Why must we keep the child alive? The information is, as you tell me, in the cells, not in the, how do you say it, consciousness. We harvest what we need, and in a more secure location." He looked confident, as if she would change her mind and go along with him in this.

"You are crude, Arkady. You have failed in what you wanted to do. Now you will have to be patient while we do this my way. My process gives me more accurate results, and accurate results equal more money. Remember that, Arkady. I am earning you money."

147

She smiled, but her expression was shot through with daggers.

His hand rested on the switches, although he didn't flip them. After a defiant pause, he dropped his arm and strode to the door, his steps hard. "Faster, or I will do as I say. I do not wish to lose what we already have." His accent had grown thicker, but his words came more easily. He was gone in a cloud of anger.

"Give us what we want, my young friend, and perhaps you can live again, in a thousand different bodies." Queenie walked to stand beside Cam, and she gently stroked his face. "However, I am afraid this will be very painful. Prepare yourself."

She stepped to a computer, and she tapped several commands onto the keyboard. A set of vertical bars appeared on the screen. Each was split into red and green. Where they joined told the current power level for each of the electrodes attached to Cam's body. She reached both hands to the screen and began to raise them. As the green diminished, and the red grew, Cam began to quiver, then the quivering turned to a violent shaking, with one leg vibrating enough to bang against the top of the table.

The computers were reading the electrical pulses Queenie forced along Cam's nerves, picking up minute signals in the surging flood of energy. However, each pass of electricity provided little more than a fragment of the total information needed. The puzzle would be filled in one painful surge at a time, the process repeated over and over, until the picture was complete. It was a crude way to decipher the ground-breaking and quite revolutionary codices etched into each and every one of Cam's cells, but with Queenie's limited resources, it was the only one available.

She walked to stand beside his leg, and she checked the strap, pulling it tighter until it was secure. Then she pressed her hand to his face once more, her arm shaking with the violent movements of his head.

"Give in to it. Let us have what we want. We know it's in there."

Then she turned to sit at a monitor, watching the information, only occasionally glancing up to see that Cam was still tethered, and all her equipment was firmly in place.

She never once bothered to look into his eyes.

Chapter 40

Kenny's Brilliance Peeks Out

My phone rang, and it caught me off guard. It wasn't my real phone. It was my fake one, the one from Jill that really wasn't mine. The ring was unfamiliar, a song I'd never heard.

After begging off and taking a quick shower, I had fixed Kenny my promised Oreo cereal with what little milk I had left, and I was able to scrounge up a couple sandwiches from two old biscuits and a package of week-old pepperonis. It wasn't bad. The phone went off as I was wadding my dirty paper towels to drop in the trash.

"Kenny?" I looked at him. "Is that you?" Boys at fourteen do stranger things than burst into strains of metallic rock and roll.

"Not me, Mr. Turner." He handed me his bowl. "That was good. I think it's your phone."

I looked at my black one. Nothing. No blinking light. Kenny saw my look, I guess, because he leaned over the table and grabbed the Center's phones from the chair. One was flashing, and he handed it to me.

"It plays music, too?"

"Sure, Mr. Turner. All phones do. Answer it before it hangs up."

"How?" I'd never had to answer Cam's. I'd barely learned to

click the text icon, that and connect to the Internet. Those things were easy. Kenny reached up and swiped his fingers sideways on the screen, and a green bar appeared with the word answer on it. I tapped it, and the singing stopped. I put the phone to my ear.

"Jake Turner speaking."

"Jake, send me a text, now, on Cam's phone."

O-*kay*, I thought. I was pretty sure it was Jill on the line, although she hadn't said so. I picked up the phone, turning it on.

"You have to send me one first," I countered. Wasn't that what Cam did? He sent and I replied. I wasn't a rocket scientist.

"Good grief! How can you know so little about simple technology? Where are you?"

"Home. Why?"

"Neighbors. Do you have anyone in the building who might be familiar with using a cell phone?"

"I don't know all my neighbors, so I'm not sure. Why?" Then I caught Kenny holding his hand out. He'd known what to do in the car, and I was pretty sure he'd heard everything Jill said. "Hold on. I think I found someone." I shrugged and handed Jill over to him.

"Hi. This is Kenny." He looked at me for a minute, listening, then he said, "Sure," and took the phone from his ear. He held his hand out for Cam's, taking it and tapping on it a few times. Then he handed them both back to me. "I sent Ms. Compos a text for you."

Masterful Kenny. His genius was peeking out, and I was glad I'd stopped and brought him home. Of course, it could just be the Oreos. If so, I was eating Oreo cereal every day for breakfast from now on.

I held the phones out, staring at the screens, and wondering what to do next. When I heard Jill's voice on one of them, telling me she was still there, I put it to my ear and started to tell her about the text from earlier. She cut me off.

"We know, Jake. About an hour ago. Now, shut up and listen."

That took me by surprise. Jill never barked at me, and she had turned into a Rottweiler. Before I could frame a sharp retort, she tore ahead, and it didn't take me about two seconds to get on the same page. It wasn't pretty, either.

"We caught Cam's text, and we weren't sure our triangulation was working. Your phone showed up halfway between the school and your house. Cam's showed up here, at the Center. A glitch, we thought, until you sent us one back. It's the same. Your phone, the signals are different, just as you said. Cam's originated here at the Center. Dear God—" She became faint for a minute, yelling instructions to someone else with her, something with hall numbers and building names. "Jake, I think he might be here on campus. Dear God, who would do this?" Her voice was shaking. "We've got security combing the complex."

I wasn't much better, standing there, sick to my stomach, and my throat frozen. I had been there all night, and she was telling me he had been within yards of me? My brain was shifting her into idiot category. There were only two smart people left, me and Kenny, and I wasn't too sure about me.

"Jake, are you there?"

Cam's phone chimed, and I looked at it. I opened the message, almost afraid to look.

Mr. Turner, I think they're moving me. Please hurry.

I tapped the screen, and when the keyboard came up, I tapped the microphone. "Keep broadcasting, Cam. We can find you that way." I watched, waiting, the words taking so long to come up. Then I hit send. Cam's reply was immediate.

I can't. They're— and that was all I got.

I put the other phone to my ear. "Did you get any of that?"

"More texts?" She called to someone, her voice distant, "There were more texts. Do we have a location? When? Just now." Her voice grew louder. "Jake, what did he say? Does it give us any clues we can use?"

"Yeah." I was seated by then, with my head bowed, and the fingers of one hand buried in my hair.

"Jake! You've got to talk to me!"

"They're moving him, Jill." They knew they'd been found out, and they were moving him. It was the text that just cut off in the middle that worried me more. Was that the last one I would ever receive from him? Would the next thing be a finger in a box, with a demand for money I didn't have? If they asked the Center for money, would the Center write him off and go looking for new orphans for their little pastime experiments? I was convinced of that, now. They hadn't been only housing the orphans that lived there. They'd been experimenting on them. Using them. Abusing them. Making them into no more than guinea pigs. Cam wasn't a guinea pig. He was a fourteen-year-old boy, a human soul who deserved to be allowed to grow up in a normal family doing normal things, and that didn't mean getting "fixed" every four months. He deserved a chance at life, and at going to heaven when he died, if he chose to believe in God.

Even if I had to give him up for that.

I was well aware I didn't constitute a normal family. Denver's finest had made that very clear. But I was going to give him a chance. By everything I knew to do, Cam was going to have the chance to be a normal boy and live a normal life, because he deserved it, and I loved him too much not to.

I didn't even realize I'd thought it at the time. I was just angry, angry at the man in the red car, angry at Jill, the Center, the policemen, everyone except Kenny. Kenny had done nothing except prove to be the most helpful person around.

He was the only one I trusted at that point.

Chapter 41

The Feathers Come Out of the Nest

The door to Cam's prison burst open, and Arkady flung himself inside. No one would have believed a man of his size and impeccable dress could move with that much nimble speed, but he was at the switches before Queenie could rise from her chair.

"Arkady! Stop that!" Her voice carried a level of authority that had been missing before. His hand hesitated. "What do you think you're doing, and in my domain?"

Clearly, Queenie ruled in this underworld cavern.

"Have you checked the security feeds?" Arkady pointed at her computer. There was a game of solitaire on the screen.

She reached to it and touched two buttons in succession, and the screen separated into sixteen very small images. Each represented a different real-time camera feed. Each one also showed the Center logo in the lower right-hand corner. On a full third of the screens, security guards could be seen unlocking doors, appearing on different cameras, searching. Queenie touched a key, and the image scrolled to sixteen new images. There were fewer security guards, but they were there. She scrolled twice more, then three, until no security were present. Once more, and they could see themselves with Cam's body jerking on the table. That camera was off line in the system. Routine maintenance. Repairs had been scheduled, but of course Arkady and Queenie would be long gone before the maintenance men showed up with their unneeded repair tools. It was the computer geeks that would need to solve this broken camera feed.

"We've got time."

Queenie tapped her keyboard several times, and the bars showing the power feeds to each of Cam's electrodes came up. She reached and slid them all down. Cam's body lay still for the first time in a very long time, his skin pale, his eyes blackened, and his hair limp. He was covered with sweat, and only his quivering fingertips revealed life inside.

"Time for what?" Arkady's voice rasped with irritation.

"To unhook him and prepare him for relocation. You will need to have transport ready."

"It has been in preparation since the first news of his disappearance." He seemed relieved at her newfound willingness to move the boy. "What manner of assistance may I provide?"

However, she was already pulling out IVs and ripping off electrodes, and she ignored his belated request, muttering, "This won't be good for him, but he's a tough one. He'll survive."

She wasn't being gentle. Her willingness to save his life had nothing to do with gentleness, kindness, or mercy. The information she was extracting was in a purer form if he remained alive and conscious. Dead, God forbid, and the finer nuances of his cellular matrices would have to be rebuilt. The boy being unconscious would be almost as disastrous, as the flow of information would be stunted virtually beyond repair. Only perfect information would bring the highest prices when the bidding wars heated up. For that, she intended to ensure her subject lived to see another day and that he remained fully awake throughout the entire extraction process. Then, if the bidding went the way she wanted, many more Cams would one day walk the face of the earth, even if this one was an empty shell when she finished with him.

And she would be richer than God. She would *be* God, purveyor of a new race. Arkady? He might not survive, either. The world didn't need two gods.

Chapter 42

Jake Takes Kenny for a Ride

There were ten thousand reasons for Jake to give up at that point. He was too far from the Center to be of any help. The Denver police force thought he was interested in Cam for only one reason. He didn't have any money. He wasn't Cam's parent. He didn't even have a bedroom to offer Cam. Then, there was each day of the boy's life that he had left to live, ones that would be better spent with a real family, not with a single teacher who was turning out to be a loser.

There was only one reason for Jake not to give up. Cam needed him.

He flew towards the Center, with Kenny white-knuckled at his side. This was do or die. When the need is desperate, the actions must be equally desperate, and unacceptable risks become acceptable.

Everything was acceptable to Jake at that point.

Chapter 43

Two Guns and a Bird Take Flight

Deep in the Center's bowels, far underground where even the backups to the backups dared not go, Queenie released the wheels to Cam's surgical table. He was totally free from the machines and ready to roll.

"Is transport prepared?" Arkady stood to the side, speaking into a walkie talkie. "Did you acquire the Sikorsky, as I instructed?" It was the S-76D, EMS version, one specifically designed to meet the needs of the medical field. And it was fast. He nodded at Queenie in satisfaction. He returned to the walkie, pulling up his coat sleeve and glancing at an elaborate gold watch. "The elevator will arrive, your location, precisely two minutes. I wish to have liftoff thirty seconds from our arrival." He clicked the unit off. "Ready, Queenie?"

"Ready." She folded back the sheet they had draped over Cam to show a Beretta Storm, a handgun noted for its use in law-enforcement as well as personal defense. It would do the trick in any emergency they might encounter.

"It is the same as I carry." Arkady patted a bulky item underneath his jacket. He reached beside the elevator and flashed a very convincing-looking ID card before he hit the button. The doors slid smoothly aside, and once inside, he touched the icon for the rooftop helipad, once again flashing the card. The doors closed, and the floor pressed hard against their feet, the express car moving with blinding speed.

"Will your precious Sikorsky truly make it offshore?" Queenie watched the numbers flash past. She didn't look confident.

When they started slowing, she looked at him to find a preoccupied look on his face, and she shrugged, then began undoing the straps holding Cam down. They would not be able to take the table. It did not matter. She had more equipment waiting. Not as good, but workable. Her laptop carried the information she had already extracted, and more powerful computers would be available when they reached their destination.

"Not without refueling," Arkady belatedly answered her, his preoccupied look still on his face, as he picked up a large bag, hefting the strap onto his shoulder.

"We are taking a chance." Queenie looked truly worried for the first time.

"All we must carry aboard is the head." Arkady placed his big hand on Cam's neck, tightening his massive grip just below his jawline. "Less weight is to mean less fuel consumption. It will be, what do you Americans say, hunky dory that way." He smiled cruelly, his preoccupation now clear.

"Stop that." Queenie slapped his hand away. "We need all of him. We've lost too much time to repair the download before it's sold. You can dispose of the body however you wish when I have my information."

Then the doors flashed open to brilliant sunlight, and two Center employees, or so they appeared, grabbed the surgical table from both sides and began to force it across the landing pad.

"Just the boy, fools." Queenie pulled her gun from under the sheet. "Carry him. We leave the rest."

One of the men hefted Cam over his shoulder, grunting under the unexpected weight, and they began to run towards the sleek Sikorsky. The rotors were already clawing the air as Cam was dumped inside, and as the clock clicked over to thirty seconds, the wheels separated from the blacktop, and they began to fold up into the belly of the craft.

The helicopter surged forward, and it was not long before it was lost to view, with the hopes, dreams, and love that Cam embodied for so many people carried securely inside.

Chapter 44

An Ace up the Sleeve, and It's Still a Draw

I spun my wheels turning off the highway, barely missing the left gatepost leading into the Center. Poor Kenny. I was pretty sure he was wishing he'd stayed at school by then. I actually felt hope that if Cam were here, I'd be the one to find him. Some connection would leap out at me, some thread of recognition. He had contacted me on his cell phone, hadn't he? And no one else. If he could do that, we could find each other. Then I'd smash some kidnapper face, and they'd know just how it felt. Even Jesus had turned over the money changers' tables in the temple. There were times the best of people lost it, and I was about there.

I didn't make it, though. I realized that as soon as I saw the helicopter lift into the sky. The name of the Center was emblazoned like a taunt on the side. It tilted forward, shooting west toward the Pacific Coast. I knew immediately that's where they were headed, somewhere outside of the continental U.S. I figured in my head, by aircraft, nine hundred, plus or minus. It would be farther to drive. I could do it in eighteen hours. That helicopter? Cut that time in half. I had lost him. No matter how determined I was, he was gone and out of my reach. I was out of options and had probably been out of options from the moment he disappeared.

I slowed down the rest of the way. What was the point in hurrying? To continue scaring Kenny? I pulled up and stopped. Still no cars. Did no one drive to work here? Or did they shuttle in from some hidden lot? I realized it didn't matter, so I let it go.

My phone rang. Rather, it sang a rock ballad to me, one with a metallic beat.

"Jake." I held it to my ear, ready for the bad news.

"Liftoff is in three minutes. Follow Mike at the front door. Hurry." The phone went dead.

I turned to Kenny, renewed. "Looks like this is the end of the line for you." I felt sorry for him. His hands still gripped the edge of the seat. He looked at me, and a grin spread ear to ear.

"I never knew a teacher could drive like that. That was fun, Mr. Turner."

I laughed, slapping him in the chest with the back of my hand. "Gotta go. Look for the helicopter in the sky. I'll be waving."

"How will I get home?"

It was a fair question, and I couldn't just walk away, no matter how big a rush Jill was in. I took the two phones, and I pulled out the one she had given me. I handed it to him.

"Call your grandmother. Call anyone. You're the best, Kenny. You've helped me more than anyone else."

He beamed, and I was gone, running towards Mike. When I reached the top of the steps, he was holding the door open.

"Mike," I said.

"Jake. Time is very limited. If you don't mind running." He already was.

"I can do that. What are we going on?" What kind of helicopter, I meant, having seen one just take off, but this was the Center. Who knew? Air Force One, anyone?

"AgustaWestland 139, known as the AW139, but the point is, we're following a Sikorsky 176, D, I think. They max at 155. The 139 can hit 165."

We were coming onto the tarmac, and I was out of breath. Mike was still talking normally. How good a shape was he in? I was no slouch, although I didn't have a cardiac regimen. But this guy was a machine.

As we hit the helicopter, I leaped aboard, and Mike was right after me, closing the door as the big craft surged into the air and threw me to the floor. He helped me up and into a seat. White

159

leather, headrests, and red carpet. I looked around, impressed. Jill was next to me.

"Did you bring the phone, Jake?" She was all business.

"One of them." I pulled it out of my pocket.

"Which one?" She took it from me and looked at it, hitting the power button.

"The right one. Cam's."

"And not the other one. Did you think you wouldn't need it anymore?" She fought a smile, but I could see it on her face.

"Someone else needed it more than me." I looked away, a little perturbed. She hadn't given me a chance to explain.

"Oh?"

I turned to see her grinning.

"Yes, ma'am." That was from Mike. "He put the phone to good use. You don't have to worry about that."

Good. He *had* been paying attention. Then I realized there were cameras all over the complex. She already knew.

Smart aleck.

I didn't mind, though. In my head, she moved from the idiot category to the other one. I wasn't sure just what it was yet. Valued companion. Conspirator in crime. Sidekick. Girlfriend. Whichever, I was glad she was in the seat next to me. I guess I'd read her wrong all this time. She wanted to save Cam as much as I did. This helicopter was proof of that.

She handed me back my phone, telling me there was a charger in the arm of the seat. It wouldn't do not to have it ready when our boy called.

Our boy. Even if I had to give him up when we got him back. It was all about Cam, not about me. He needed a family. That was something I didn't have to offer.

But I could imagine, just for a little while, even if I knew it wouldn't come true.

160

Chapter 45

A Transponder Takes a Flying Leap

"What are our chances here?" I asked the question of Jill, leaning towards her. I could hear the helicopter outside, and I used that for my excuse to lean in. However, the leather-wrapped interior was surprisingly hushed. Just so she didn't see my posture as anything other than upfront and aboveboard, I whispered, "Just between you and me? Mike back there said this baby is ten miles per hour quicker than the one we're chasing. How much difference can that really make?"

"Everything, Jake." She turned to glance behind her, probably at Mike, a smile toying with her lips just for a second, and she looked back to me. "Mike Szczepkowski is our resident transportation expert. This is his baby, as you say. If he has faith in it, I have faith in it."

"Tell me, though. Why are we doing all this?" I pointed to the people with us—there were several I didn't recognize—and at the expensive aircraft. "Don't get me wrong, I'm glad to be here, and I'm especially glad you're here. You know, talking with me."

I wondered if that look back at Mike had meant anything. Perhaps they were an item. How would I know? I was the odd man out, the one who wasn't part of the team, who was here by omission. If anyone didn't fit on this rescue mission, it was me. I was lucky to be driving up at just the right time, and I fell into this. Almost literally.

"Why are *you* doing this, Jake?"

Jill's question surprised me. It was obvious, I thought. When I didn't respond, she went on as if she hadn't expected an answer.

"We've raised him for fourteen years. You've had him a month. Do you think we don't care about him?"

She turned to me, looking directly into my eyes, and I saw Cam looking back at me. Only, I couldn't afford to fall into these eyes, not like I'd done with Cam.

"It's not the same thing." I coughed and cleared my throat, sitting up. Her words were exactly what I'd been thinking, and they left me feeling found out.

"How is it different?" Her question, so civil, and so reasonable, spoken with poise in this very civil and reasonable environment. We all have manners because we all must have manners. Well, Cam's abductors didn't have manners.

But I couldn't bring myself to be rude, not and mess up the good thing I had going for me. These people were spending bookoos doing what I wanted to do and couldn't. That counted for a lot.

Still, I couldn't look at her, and I turned across the aircraft, letting my eyes drift outside. The day was very bright, with a smattering of light clouds, like wisps of cotton candy floating in a blue sea. Cam's eyes blue. Jill's eyes blue. How was it different, me being here, than everyone else in this sumptuous cabin? That was easy. I really did care about the boy.

For these people, what was their motivation? Was it as simple as an experiment gone wrong, or maybe right, disappearing into the western sun? Maybe a government regulation tripped over, one that needed to be neatly lined back up? And the money. They were spending more money flying this luxury yacht than I made in a month of Sundays. They could simply let him go, if money was the issue. Then they wouldn't have to pay me, and their bank accounts would be fatter all around.

"Jake?" Jill. So civil. Still exuding impeccable manners. Not demanding I answer, just knowing I eventually would.

And I felt it working, too. Even that irritated me.

"How is it different? The most important way." I glanced at her

162

and looked away again, wondering if she would get my meaning. I didn't have a choice. It was those eyes. I had fallen into them, and you know the rest of that story. I still hadn't crawled out. Perhaps I could have once, but not after he'd moved in with me. It was that dendrite thing, and that was the Center's fault. I didn't regret it, though, not anymore. How could I? It was Cam we were talking about, not just any kid.

"And that is?"

I looked at Jill, and hard this time. She wouldn't let this go, and I felt I had to make my position clear. She was questioning my involvement, but it was the Center that had tangled me up in Cam's life. I hadn't chased after him.

"You forced him on me. Do you remember that?"

I felt my eyes begin to burn, and I turned back to the cotton candy clouds, refusing to look at Jill, and remembering. Forced? I let the sour taste of the word savor on my tongue. Maybe at first. I hadn't wanted the responsibility of a boy living with me. It was different, now. I wanted him back. However, I hadn't begged for Cam to come live with me. Not once.

"We did?"

"You know perfectly well what I mean. All that paperwork, then, oh, we're not opening up the dorms again. How can you not know what you did?"

I heard the amusement in her voice, like everything they'd done had been what I wanted. Like I hadn't had a life before, and they'd given me one. Gratis. Well, I had had a life, even before Cam, although I was no longer sure how much of a life it really was. I kept that inside, though. Besides, I was getting really irritated about that time. Just when I thought we were coming to an understanding, a meeting of the emotional minds, so to speak, we hit a brick wall. Again. I didn't want to punch Jill, but maybe Mike. And I'd really admired the guy on the way to the helicopter. I felt like he'd betrayed me, letting Jill look at him like that.

"Can a boy fall in love?"

I looked at her, surprised. She'd certainly changed direction with that question, yet there she sat, still so demure, so sensible. I didn't exactly follow her.

"I don't know where you're headed with this, but I'll bite. Yes. Of course. Anyone can." I was a bit testy, but I tried to remain polite. It was hard, though.

"With an adult?"

"Don't make me cringe. I've already got a cop accusing me of moral depravity." I snorted, making my disgust clear. I remembered Sharon Lakey's careful words, and then Kenny hadn't minced his rendition at all. I was angry all over again.

"We heard about that, and we're sorry. We're trying to contain the fallout."

Just what were these people? I felt my chest tighten at her response, so polite and so considerate, filled with concern and a willingness to correct something that wasn't the Center's fault. Her words revealed more than she must have intended. No way were they simply a rich think tank, not with all I'd seen. It was like bamboo. You only see what's above ground, but buried where it's invisible, roots are shooting out everywhere, right under your feet, and you can't tell, not until they burst from the ground, catching you completely off guard. These people had their fingers in everyone's pie.

However, I did notice one thing. Her apology, so completely unexpected, managed to evaporate my anger, just like that. I looked at her and then dropped my eyes, letting them rest on her hands. They were beautiful hands. Very beautiful.

"Jake, can he?"

"You're not going to let me pass on this one, are you?"

"I need you to be on the same page with us. You're chasing after Cam because you think you have his best interests at heart, and you think we have another agenda." She paused, and after a moment she continued. "Maybe we do, but our agendas overlap. I hope they're not so different that we can't work together."

"Trust me," I muttered, a knot growing in my stomach. I wanted to know just where she was going. Agendas. Boys falling in love. They were simply carrots. I knew that, just not where she was leading me. "If you're rescuing Cam with this million-dollar copter, then there's a whole lot of overlap in our agendas." That was one thing I knew for certain.

"Add about ten million to that, but that's beside the point. You've agreed a boy can fall in love. Let's narrow down the choices. With what?"

"No adults?" I suspected we were going back there, but I couldn't figure out why. If these people abducting Cam were involved in the exploitation of young boys, then I wasn't sure I wanted to know. Not yet, when I would only worry. But once I found them, I'd do more than punch their faces. Too bad I forgot my pocket knife. I'd slice some stuff off.

"No people at all. We're keeping it simple. Things only." Jill spoke with a low voice.

It was at that point when I realized everyone else was talking, and I couldn't make out what they were saying. Sound-cancelling technology. Nice. I relaxed a bit, turning to her.

"Video games." I pictured Cam hooting at one especially hard-won digital victory on the screen, having finally beaten me, and thrusting his arm ceilingward in exultation, the game controller still in his fist. He had adored *Warcraft*. I caught myself. I was already thinking of him in the past tense, and I knew that had to be squelched.

"What else?"

"Clothes." For most kids. However, that wasn't Cam. Not clothes. One pair of pants and an enforced trip to the washer once a week, and he was just fine.

"Anything else?"

It was as if she was giving me time to process. I used the same tools in my classroom. This woman should have been an eighth grade teacher, except she would have made less money. Too little to survive on and wear the nice clothes she seemed to change into on a regular basis.

"Animals. Machines. Anything wheeled that goes fast." I stopped and looked at her for a minute, wishing I understood her purpose in all this. "Look, all this isn't really love. It's preoccupation. I know words." Some, at least, although in this situation, I was willing to let her think I was an expert. "Our society uses the word love too liberally. We love our hair for the day, or the chocolate we eat for a snack. It's not love, though. Do you see what I mean?"

"I get it, Jake. It means *like*."

"Yeah. With people it's different. It's like the phone signal. I couldn't get you people to see they weren't the same. We could have found him, if you'd listened." I could tell my eyes were blurring. I tried to laugh and cover it up. "Cam loves mustard, one particular video game that he plays to all hours, and people. Helping people, to be precise." I remembered Mrs. Osgood, and that made me think of Kenny. Kenny was a new man after interacting with

165

Cam. Well, he was a new boy, anyway. Cam loved people.

"You want to talk about Cam, Jake, so let's do that. Cam loves mustard, video games, and people. Does that sum it up?"

"Pretty well." I'd fallen into her hands, and I didn't even know it.

"Does he love those things romantically?"

"He's fourteen. Get a grip, Jill. And I know you're not talking about video games or food. You're making a point about the people he cares about. What is it?" With her question, an image of Cam and me during the storm popped into my head, reminding me once again of Officer Simpson's accusations. The jarring memory made me squirm. She was a rubber band, pulling me one way then another, and I didn't know how to respond. I looked for another seat, but I didn't want to sit next to Mike, not right then.

"You said Cam loves people. Why?"

"I don't know. I can't see in his head. He finds someone, he makes a connection, and bam, he's all over them like white on rice. He brings out their best, too. When Cam chooses someone, they become better than they were before, just because of him. I don't know why he makes the choices he does. He just does." That was all I had. She had pulled up emotions that didn't fit in this white and red bastion of prestige and power. She had managed to get me to vomit up things I knew I'd have trouble swallowing back down.

"How are you better, Jake?"

I looked at her, and long, too, the memory of the rain and Officer Simpson's disparaging accusations melting away with her words. Her question shifted something in my head. Or perhaps it was in my heart. In spite of my reluctance to admit it, I knew what she was saying. However, Cam hadn't chosen me, not like she was suggesting. Fallen in love, even if not romantically? Not Cam, not with me. Kenny, maybe. Look at how he'd improved him. Me? I was still Jake Turner, eighth grade teacher, loser. Well, mostly a loser, a loser at keeping boys in my custody safe from virulent purveyors of unabashed mayhem and violence.

I turned away. My eyes had started to really water, and I wanted to hide it. How was I better? Maybe I cared a little more about other people. Like Mrs. Osgood. I'd lived next door to her for five years, and I'd never once sat down and had dinner with her. Since Cam came, I'd done that twice. And Kenny. I'd never noticed him before, other than to mark him present at after-school practice. Back at the Center, I'd told him he was the best there was, and I meant it, too. Did that make me better?

"Are you seeing it, Jake?"

I felt her hand on my arm, and the same electric fire was there. I froze, not wanting her hand to move. I saw it, but it wasn't true, not for me. A storm had forced Cam to stay the night, the dorms at the Center had been damaged, and I was his only option. Couldn't she see that? He was sleeping on my sofa, for heaven's sake. What boy would choose that for a life?

"Ms. Compos?" It was Mike, and I was irritated. His hand was on her shoulder, and he leaned in close. "We've lost their transponder. We think they ditched it."

I looked at him, and he had his other hand at his ear. I saw the cord running down his neck and disappearing into his collar, and I knew he was wired in, just like on all the movies I'd watched a decade ago when I could afford cable. Transponder? Wasn't that what allowed us to track them, to know that the helicopter we were following was the one that carried Cam?

"GPS, then." A hint of a frown creased Jill's forehead and was gone, even as she looked up. She glanced at me, then to Mike. "We should be able to pinpoint them—"

"Sorry, ma'am. Apparently these people know just what they're doing. The pilot tells me they've simply vanished." The aircraft jerked, and it began to turn.

"And that?" Jill glanced out the window, but there was nothing unusual to be seen.

"Just a moment, ma'am." Mike stepped away and spoke into his collar. After a moment, he turned to Jill. "We're picking up something on the ground. Metallic. There's a chance they may have gone down."

At that, everyone inside the craft went to the windows. I looked for smoke. That's what you always saw in the movies. Follow the column of smoke, and you find the wreckage. Here, we were already deep in the mountains. How else would we find them if they'd gone down?

We discovered one thing. There was nothing wrong with the transponder. It was working fine, or it had been when it left the helicopter. They located it on a ridge, and then lost it almost immediately, the signal dead. That's why we were circling back, to pick it up on radar, visual, or however they found lost transponders.

It seemed to me that transponders were for emergencies. This was an emergency. Why hadn't they planned on batteries?

There was no helicopter wreckage where the transponder was found, either. There was the transponder, but that was all. They had escaped us, free and clear, gone into the wild blue yonder.

And I was just letting myself trust these people. Couldn't they do *anything* right?

Chapter 46

Crow Comes in Multiple Flavors

The two policemen walked in the door of Bruce Randolph to find Sharon Lakey standing beside her desk with her arms crossed. She didn't look especially pleased, either. The building principal, Tim Smith, stood at the door to his office. He didn't look much happier.

"Ma'am." It was the big one, Jerry, baby-faced with all his fat, his hat held respectfully in his hands.

"Mrs. Lakey, thank you for taking time to see Jerry and me." The older officer stepped in front of Jerry. "I apologize we didn't introduce ourselves properly earlier. Officer Prouty, here, and Jerry is Officer Simpson."

"Pleased to meet you, ma'am." Jerry looked past his partner, nodding his head.

"Well, this is certainly a change." Sharon's arms were still crossed.

Jerry just ducked his head. He should. The Center had long arms and very convoluted strings they could pull. Their monetary contributions to Denver's civic functions had eased the city's budget crises several times in the recent past. When Mrs. Linkston saw the broadcast with Stella Whittinger and Brian Darling on the Morning Show, she was furious. She might be just one cog in the elaborate machine that made up the Center for Innovative Software Specialization and Intellectual Enhancement, but she knew Camden Archer, and she knew exactly who had been accused of improper behavior. She wouldn't have it, either, and she had made a few phone calls. City Hall's ears were pinched, and then Jerry Simpson's ears were pinched. He was eating crow for being out of bounds.

"Ma'am, I just plain stepped out of line." It was Jerry's best, aw, shucks, routine, and he meant it, at least as far as he could mean something that would get him out of hot water.

Sharon pointed her finger at him. "I'm planning an assembly, and I expect to see you here to tell our students how to know a child molester when they see one. You can do it with Christian love this time. You, too, Officer Prouty."

"But," Jerry started, glancing at his partner.

"Thank you, Mrs. Lakey. You just let us know when." Officer Prouty pulled on Jerry's arm. Both men nodded respectfully and backed out the door.

On the way to the car, Jerry groused, "You know the department won't give us time to speak in public schools, Rick. There's already a liaison officer for that."

"Then we'll do it on our own time." Rick Prouty slammed his door when he got in the car.

"What? You can't blame me if that broad can't see what's right in front of her eyes." Jerry climbed in and slammed his own door.

"Officer Simpson, the day I got assigned to you was the worst day of my life." Rick twisted the key in the ignition, and the engine roared to life. He pressed his lips together, glaring at his partner.

"What do you want me to do about it?" Jerry glared back.

"Nothing." Rick took a deep breath. "Neither of us makes the duty assignments, and I guess some days you have to take the fertilizer with the sunflowers." He shifted into gear and backed out of the parking space, much more in control.

"What does that mean?" Jerry reached his big hand to the floorboard and pulled a donut out of a sack. "What does all this have to do with sunflowers, anyway?"

"Just shut up, Jerry. Got that?"

"Okay, Rick." He raised his hands in a defensive posture. "I'm shutting up. You drive, I shut up." He put the donut in his mouth, and the car was quiet, at least until he passed gas, but by then, they were well down the road to Channel 7, with more crow to eat.

Chapter 47

Jake Finally Tells the Truth

I sat in the seat and wished I could stretch my legs. At over six feet, small places begin to get claustrophobic after several hours. We had picked up the transponder, contacted every department of everything from here to the coast, and even stopped to refuel. Nothing. Helicopters, I learned, are perfect for flying under the radar. Duck behind a mountain, and nothing in God's arsenal of Seeing Eye dogs can find you. I traced a circle on the leather armrest, hoping to wear a hole through it. When I got out, I wanted someone to know I'd spent hours sitting in this spot.

Jill had been talking with Mike. Sweet-boy Mike. But I didn't care about that anymore. They could have each other. I looked up when she returned to her seat.

"Not giving up, are you, Jake?" She adjusted her legs, then slipped off her shoes. "Oh, for a good pair of flats. What I wouldn't give for a good pair of flats right now."

I kicked one of my shoes off and held it out to her. But I wasn't being funny. Who cared about flats when Cam was out there, God knows where, in the hands of a crazed maniac? At least I hoped God knew where he was. We weren't making much progress.

"Thank you, but no." She laughed softly. "How are you doing?"

"He's going to wind up in a shipping crate in Russia, isn't he?" I felt my eyes welling with tears, and I leaned my head back and squeezed them shut.

"A shipping crate? Why would you say that?"

"I know what happens to kids who disappear. They sedate them and put them in shipping crates so the port authorities can't find them and ship them overseas to sell them to the highest bidder."

"My heavens, Jake. Do you really think that?" She sounded horrified.

I looked at her. It was so clear to me. "Do the math. He's a good-looking kid, blond, and fourteen. Why else would they take him, his prodigy-level space-time-theory equations that will allow us to emigrate to another galaxy in a matter of hours?"

"*You* have been watching too much science fiction." She shook her head.

"Okay, you tell me where I'm wrong." That rubber band was working again. Pulling me toward her. Those eyes. Yeah, I was blaming it on those eyes. And those feet, too, without her shoes. I began to count off on my fingers, "One, ordinary boy. Two, wears torn jeans. Three, eats too much mustard. Four, sings like a frog in the shower. Five, not once has he ever clipped his own toenails since he's been with me. How's that for a model teenager? Nobody would want this kid for anything except exploitation." I fell back in my seat. "And that scares me. He'll be in Croatia or Afghanistan, in some dingy hut, with strangers all over him."

"I think he'd fight back."

"They give them drugs, you know. They can't fight back." Was she making fun of me? For sure, she was irritating me again. Every time I started to like her, she did this.

"I can assure you he's not being stolen for exploitation. Not the sort you're talking about, anyway." She laughed. "You make it sound so funny."

"Well, it's not funny!" I looked away, trying to control my irritation. I needed pretty-boy Mike to come up here and control his woman.

"No, it's not, and you're right. However, the way you describe it. Mustard frog boy with six-inch toenails. Of course no one wants him."

"I didn't say that." She was twisting my words, making me look silly. Worse, making Cam look silly. And, of course, no one wants him? That was the ultimate fighting phrase.

"What's bothering you, now? Frog boy, or that no one wants him?"

"I don't know how to answer you. Everything I say turns out wrong." I worried my fingernails, remembering the one that had been torn. I had pictured Cam as torn and repeatedly having the damage reopened. He needed someone to close the wound and keep it closed until it could completely heal.

"Who wants him, Jake?"

"I do. Is that what you want to hear?" I turned to glare at her, my face hot. She had ripped my heart and soul right out of my chest. Now it was exposed for her to see. I hoped she was happy.

"Took you long enough." Mike's hand was on my shoulder. "We're all rooting for Cam, you know. You stick with us, Jake, and you'll see him again."

I looked at Jill, and she was smiling. Somewhere in that jumble of twisted emotional outburst, they'd found something they seemed to approve of. I'd be a horse's behind if I could figure out what, and I don't care if I'm a teacher. Sometimes to be crude is the only way to express exactly where you stand.

Chapter 48

Cam Is Invited to Supper

Cam's world was a semi-consciousness stupor, filtered through occasional glimpses outside the helicopter. He did feel the change in the throp throp of the engines and pulled himself together enough to peer through drug-glazed eyes through the window at his side.

The ship they approached was quite large. He recognized it as a U.S. Navy Diver-class rescue and salvage vessel from World War II, boasting the remnants of a third-world Coast Guard logo down one side, and a giant, peeling medical ship red cross on the bow. It was a near wreck, now. Even in his medicated haze, Cam could tell that. A weathered communications satellite perched like a forlorn bird on the deckhouse. It had an elevated landing pad for a helicopter, one that barely appeared large enough to land on. Farther away, glints in the fading light could be seen coming off distant fishing and shipping vessels, and far out to sea the sun kissed the horizon.

The inside of the sleek Sikorsky blurred in front of Cam's face, in sharp opposition to the rugged sea-going rescue and salvage ship just outside. Things were not in his favor. To look disreputable, even unseaworthy, would make them harder to find. The old woman and the rough-voiced man had argued continually, his words proud

174

of where they were going, while she had quipped back with barbs in her voice that what counted was the duplicate computer equipment she had installed on the inside. Without her, his foul ship was useless.

Cam sensed they had traveled a long distance, but where, he was too groggy to work out. Drugged was the correct word. He knew drugged. The Center had done that to him enough.

He faded back into the inconsistent awareness of whatever they'd given him, vaguely following but not making sense of what was happening around him, and unable to call out to Jake to come for him.

As the Sikorsky powered down, ship's hands, roughly dressed and rougher in personal care, appeared aboveboard, and in the gathering gloom, Cam was manhandled out and carried by two of the coarsely-shod workers into the ship. Eventually they came to a room with a wall of gleaming computer equipment: massive mainframes that were tied into a series of substantial circuit breakers on the adjoining wall. Nearby was a metal gurney, narrow, with dirty straps in a heap on the floor. The rest of the room was just as filthy.

Cam was more cognizant of the people around him by then. "Let me go," he cried, as he fought to escape. The words hurt his throat, and even yelled, they came out hoarse and barely above a whisper. He hit out with his fists, certain he would never make it out if they tied him down again. He made contact once or twice, aware of the curses that followed.

His handlers were prepared, though. A few rough slaps alongside his head, a bloody nose, and plastic straps around his wrists made it clear who was in control. Besides, he hadn't eaten, and the lack of food over the past day didn't help. His moment of defiance took everything from him. He was forced into a chair, and he sagged against the metal surface, raggedly drawing in the dank air.

A needle was jammed into his arm. He jerked away, but massive hands clamped over his shoulders. He held his balled fists between his legs, breathing raggedly, waiting for whatever they'd injected to take control. Desperation clouded his vision, and bile filled his throat.

As he felt himself coming alert, he sensed the movement of the room, and he remembered landing on a ship. Getting free from this room was not the sort of freedom that would do him any good. Still, if a chance came up, he'd run like his life depended on it, because he was starting to suspect it did.

Queenie came in, and Cam jerked against the hands, the sight of her twisting his gut inside. The first thing she did was put a wicked-looking gun on the gurney, letting it hit roughly and loudly. Her point was made, and he melted in weary resignation, the cold of the chair pressing against his skin. He made one last try to shrug the hands off. They were manacles, holding him until he could be strapped down once more.

The pit in his stomach grew heavier. He couldn't live through the torture again. *Jake, where are you?* He reached out, and with a rising sense of helplessness, he fought against the desperation burning in his eyes.

From inside a bag, Queenie pulled out a commercial container of fruit drink, one noted for its high levels of electrolytes. It was an individual-size serving in a flexible pouch, with a straw attached to the side. She pulled the straw loose and stabbed it into the pouch, holding it out to Cam.

"Drink this. We can't have you dehydrate, not yet. We still have a job for you."

His eyes tracked it. Clearly, she knew just how thirsty he was.

"Go on, boy. It's not drugged."

He took it in both hands and began to slurp the juice as quickly as he could get it through the straw. Within moments, he sucked at empty air, devastated to find it all gone.

"Well, Queenie. You have missed a grand occasion, no, as you would say, a perfect party." Arkady sauntered in with a large sausage wrapped in greasy paper. His English was awkward, but his meaning was perfectly clear. He was mocking her. In his free hand, he had a white towel. He took a bite and wiped his chin with the towel.

"For sausage? You don't know me, Arkady. Go back to your galley and let me get to work."

"No, you did. It is true." He walked to Cam and waved the sausage under his nose.

Cam watched it hungrily. His eyes blurred with the need. The smell . . . his stomach churned with sour dread, even as he wanted to reach for it.

"You should have slipped some calming medicinals in your

176

little packet of juice. Did you see how he sucked it down? Like a baby bird eating a worm." He turned and waggled the sausage at her. "Use your opportunities wisely, my love. Then we do not need these zip ties. Nasty things." He reached and pulled at Cam's arms, then dropped them back into the boy's lap.

"And if he is knocked out, then what good is our information? I have China, North Korea, and Russia still in the game. My contacts now tell me the minimum bid is rising and should be at $100 million soon. We must have the best results possible when we make our delivery. That is only achieved when he is awake and fully conscious."

Cam heard that, the awake and conscious part. Then, the number hit him. $100 million. They wanted what he was, and he was unimportant to them, alive at least. He fought against the despair that threatened to consume him. He tried once more. *Jake!* It was as if they had isolated him from the rest of creation.

The big man let out a sigh and closed his eyes. "Ah, Mother Russia." He smiled, visibly awed by the new numbers. "Citizen soldiers, all alike, and all programed from one template. As many as the Motherland wants to build. Unstoppable."

"Breed, build. It is all the same." Queenie had her laptop out, and she opened the bag Cam vaguely remembered the man loading onto the Sikorsky. She began pulling out the equipment to hook Cam to the computers.

"What about the big recirculating machines, the ones with the IVs? I do not see them." Arkady took a substantial bite of his sausage, chewing it hard. "You stated we have to keep the boy alive. That has changed, now?"

"The medical equipment aboard this vessel is rubbish. Even if that were not so, our power generating capacity is insufficient to run both the extraction computers and the life-sustaining equipment. Your generous funds provided my computers, but not sufficient generators to run them at speed."

By the tone of her voice, that goaded her. Even Cam could see the truth in her words. By the condition of their surroundings, the ship's mechanical systems were probably outdated and barely functional, which, by her tone, she had most likely not discovered until the mainframes were already installed.

Before Cam could take any satisfaction in his observations, she went on, her strident words now infused with mocking laughter. "In any case, once I am finished, I will no longer need the boy. If you care so much, give him the sausage. You will smell better if you do."

"Do you want it, boy?" Arkady held it out.

Cam would have taken it. In fact, he made to reach for it, but the hands on his shoulders held him firmly. He nearly cried when he saw the big man pull it away.

"See, Queenie? He will not share my gift. I try to make my generosity his, and what do I get in return? So American, this ungrateful little piece of garbage that does nothing but sit in his underwear and take up the air I need to breathe. Are there not clothes you can provide him?" It was a long discourse in English for Arkady, one filled with disdain. He paused to take a bite from the sausage, chewing it hard and swallowing.

"They are in the way, Arkady. I have to monitor the sensors, not worry about dressing and undressing a child. If you don't like the way he's dressed, we're on a big ship. Go elsewhere." She was turned away, already tuning him out.

"Ahh, yes, even in the old country, we must remove the clothes to reside in the hospital. You are right in this, my love." Arkady smiled ingratiatingly, turning back to Cam. "Since he will not share my food, perhaps he can provide for us some entertainment? In my homeland, I had, do you say, a reputation with the fists. The boy should be given the opportunity for practice. I think about here." He pointed with the sausage to Cam's midsection.

Each of the men holding him leaned around and punched Cam hard in the stomach, one at a time. The first time he doubled over, coughing, with the suddenness of the unexpected hit blanking every thought from his mind. For a moment, his world was a white ball of searing pain. Then his head was pulled up, and he was hit again. Red juice splattered all over the floor. It was bitter as it came back up, and he began to cough violently.

Jake, Cam jerked out in a sharp rush of barely coherent pleading. *Now is a good time,* and he shivered, well aware nothing was getting through. He searched for a connection, but the machines around him were not powered up. Anything else was still too far away. He could hope, though. He had to hope and keep trying.

"Arkady, you fool," Queenie called after the big man, as he exited the room laughing. "I have no more juice. Now I may have to hook up the IV after all." She didn't sound much like she intended to follow through, however.

She motioned, the movement abrupt, and the two men standing over Cam yanked him up and wrestled him to the gurney. This time he had no energy to resist. One moved the gun to a nearby shelf, and together, they picked him up and held him to the table. In a final burst of defiance, Cam kicked for all he was worth as they began to strap him down. The straps were ratcheting straps, though, and as the men worked them down, the harder Cam struggled, the tighter they forced them.

Finally, Queenie stopped them.

"He has to be able to breathe. Can you see that? Look there, his hand is already blue. Loosen that one. And that one." She pointed, waiting until the plastic ties were cut and the straps were adjusted. Then she dismissed the men to leave her alone.

"So, my little friend." Queenie had her white lab coat back on, oddly angelic in the filth of the old ship. She reached and patted his face, taking time to wipe some of the fruit drink from his chin. "Now you get to give me the rest of what you know."

"Please," Cam whispered, his voice cracked and dry. "You don't want to do this."

"Oh, so you *can* talk." She looked at him in surprise. "I wondered if you had become mute. Burned out conductive tissue can do that." She ran her fingers down his chest and past the straps that held him immobile. "Too bad you didn't keep that juice down. You'll truly need the additional electrolytes. It helps with the transfer of information. It lessens the discomfort, as well. Even so, your body will give me what I need, either way." She shook her head, almost as if in regret, and she began adjusting her equipment. "Our power levels are limited here, no matter what that fool Arkady says. I shall be forced to do this at a reduced pace. Perhaps you may even retain the use of your voice when I'm finished, although with Arkady present, that may not benefit you for long. He thinks if you are dead, this will be easier. He's a fool, anyway. I'm the one who knows you inside and out."

"You don't know me." Cam licked his lips, the skin painful and tasting of blood. "You don't know me at all."

"Oh, but I do. You may not know me, but I'm your mother, you see." At his horrified look, she laughed. "Oh, not in that way, but I made you just as surely as any natural mother could. A DNA snip here and DNA snip there. Add someone else's DNA in just the right spot, and voila! I have a little boy. Of course, Pinocchio's not a real boy, but he's as close as I could get. Now we have to make sure someone besides my employers gets access to this technology. We can't have the Center keeping it all to themselves. For making me laugh, perhaps I can share one small bag of lubricant with you."

With that, she held up a bag of fluid clearly stamped Concentrated Electrolyte Solution, and below, in smaller letters, it listed the ingredients potassium chloride, potassium phosphate, sodium chloride, and magnesium sulfate. It was a standard issue bag, although the printing was coarse, and from its appearance, it was unclear just how trustworthy its origins were.

"This is not the proprietary mixture I used at the Center, but it will suffice. When resources are limited, then we must all make do, mustn't we, my boy?" She clipped it to the wall with a magnetic hook. Feeding a line over to Cam, she grabbed the back of his arm. He struggled against her hands, but without success. On the front side, she worked the needle in, continuing to talk the entire time.

"Others achieved partial success, but they were all failures, short-lived failures. Oh, they thought they had success for a time, but they lost them in the end. You? Organic self-replication. And I developed the process. It's mine. They tried to steal it from me. I kept a secret record, however, fooling everyone. I did it right in front of their eyes. The coding is written in your body's cells, mostly here." She tapped his forehead with her fingertips. "The only way for me to get my rightful property back is to take it, pulling the patterns from the electrical signals transmitted by your nervous system. The stronger the signals, the better the information. So, we must force the signals to be strong."

She paused for a moment, her expression clouding, even as she continued to work. Her next words were softer, muttered even, as if not intended for Cam, and as if they expressed a level of frustration she had kept inside for some time.

"Better equipment could read the DNA patterns in fewer passes, and this would be completed by now." She glanced around the room, clearly disgusted by the filth of her surroundings. "It is all Arkady's fault for bungling the crash and forcing me to do this in secret. It is the Center's main servers that I need, not that hole I was forced into with all its mismatched equipment, and certainly not this floating cesspool.

"However, you, my dear boy, are the only functioning copy left.

The only one, and you are mine, my chance to change the human race forever."

Her words had brightened, as if she once more spoke to Cam. By that time she had the IV on a steady drip into his arm and was untangling the electrodes. As she attached the first one to his groin, and began moving up his body, the maniacal look around her eyes began to take over her face.

"Did I say you will change the human race? I don't think so. You are the first of a brand new race, and you are my invention. You are the start of homo supremus, the finest humans who will ever live, and I am the mother of you all."

Cam gagged at her words, tasting the final remains of the red juice, before he got the spasms under control. If Jake didn't get here soon, there wouldn't be anyone to rescue, not anyone by the name of Cam, anyway.

"That fool, Arkady. What is he up to now?" Queenie fumbled with a panel on the wall. Punching a series of buttons, she found one that brought up Arkady over a speaker, the clink of an iced drink in his hand identifying him, with the sounds of winches and hydraulic jacks in the background. Queenie muttered, "Ah, they are removing the evidence."

Arkady's voice agreed with her, as he called instructions to his men, unaware he had an audience. "The Sikorsky, she is moved towards the back of the ship. No, there! Winch the front side first. I brought you American jacks. They will not break as those from Russia might. Now, tip it with much care. If you damage my ship, it is very far from land to swim." He laughed roughly.

Queenie cackled. "Fools. They will take the ship down, also, and Arkady does not care."

Yet, over the speaker, the successful sounds of the sleek machine going overboard came through quite clearly, metal upon metal groaning, until it became overbalanced and toppled into the water. Going over, it barely made a sound, hardly louder than the noise coming off the ship's engines, as it melted into the depths. The men cheered loudly, most in strange and chaotic languages.

Arkady's ice clinked in his glass as he called roughly, "Cheers, Mother Russia. Or Albania, maybe. Who should know? It is all the same to me. But, what a pity! Such a beautiful aircraft to go overboard. I would have enjoyed the rubles I could have gotten from her."

As the sounds of a closing door came over the speaker, Arkady's voice growled, "It is of no consequence, in any case. She was out of fuel and could fly no longer."

Cam faded in and out with alternating waves of hunger and nausea, but he caught the sound of Queenie's strident laughter as she punched the speaker off. She stepped to her computer, tapping the keys, while vilifying Arkady as the biggest fool she'd ever known. Cam didn't hear that. As soon as she began tapping her keys, all he could hear was the electricity screaming along his nerves, one raw electrical surge at a time.

Or was it his voice? Within his nightmare, even Cam couldn't tell.

Chapter 49

It's All About the Mustard

Mike stepped away from me. Somehow he didn't seem such a pretty boy anymore. Tough Mike was back, the one I wanted at my side. The one who was a machine, who could run forever and not get winded. It seemed no one in this story stayed who they were supposed to be. Jill was Cam's supporter and my confidant, then she tried to undermine everything I was trying to do. As soon as I began to hate her, she turned, again becoming Cam's champion. And look at Pretty Boy Mike, able to leap tall buildings in a single bound. I bet he did a lot more than transportation for the almighty and powerful Center.

Even little Kenny had turned from sports catastrophe to knowledgeable electronics expert, my number one help in my darkest time of need.

What would I find out about Cam? Was he really Wonder Boy with aerated titanium bones and woven glass tissues, or was he the real boy I had come to believe in, the one who cried when he hurt and who needed his toenails clipped because he was too lazy to do it on his own? Nothing about the people I had come to know was what I expected it to be, or maybe I was just seeing them differently. I admitted to that. It was entirely possible that the real difference was me. All of these people had been all of these things all along, and I had been too blind to see it. Too blinded to see it.

That got me thinking. Blinded by what? Youth? I didn't have much of that anymore. My job? What could teaching blind a person to, except the realities of having real money? Love? I liked Jill, but I wasn't in love with her. I hardly knew her. Adventure? Maybe that. I had been given more adventure in the past thirty hours than I had seen in all my thirty years.

I noticed Jill quietly tapping a pencil on the arm of her seat. I realized she wanted my attention, and I looked her direction.

"Yes? That is for me, I assume."

"You assume correctly."

Jill actually smiled, and it looked very pretty. Not condescending. Not mocking. Not so much, *you finally get it,* but friendly, nice, a genuine smile.

"You deserve some answers from me, and I apologize."

"Answers?" For which question, I thought. Questions was more like it. She'd answered hardly any of them, from the very beginning.

"Cam is not what you think, Jake."

She paused, and I sat for a moment. How did she know what I thought? Even so, in a moment of clarity that seemed to flood over me, I knew what she was going to say. He was genetically flawed, and he needed regular treatments, hormones for growth, or perhaps he had growth plate deficiencies. Both would explain his visits every four months, as well as his spurts of sudden growth. It would also explain the Center's desperation to retrieve him. He might die without treatment. Maybe it would never stop, and he would be the tallest basketball player in the world for two years, then keep on growing until he could no longer stand upright, collapsing in on himself. There were stories of real people who had done that. Instead, I wanted her to say *Spideyman* or something similar, or use the word *piston*, or *titanium*. Something, please, Jill, just not real boy, because that's exactly what I think. And no real boy should have to deal with those issues.

"Understand," she began, hesitating from the start, "that there are certain legal lines I cannot cross, even in this dire situation, but I can tell you this. The people who have taken Cam are former employees of the Center." She had her face hard, as if it pained her to say that.

"Former? I saw the copter take off. The logo on the side was the Center's." I wasn't angry. I just wanted her aware of how much I knew.

"Not former then. Former now. A very important former employee."

"How important?" I took a risk. "He has your eyes, you know. And your laugh."

She put her hand to her face, and when she took it down, her eyes were red. It was the first time I'd seen her break her professionalism. I had hit close to home.

"That's important, huh? You don't have to answer this, if you don't want. Is he yours?"

That got a laugh out of her, and she reached with one hand to wipe under her eyes.

"No, Jake, Cam is not mine, not in the way you suggest. But his eyes, I'm willing to claim those."

"You told me you'd answer my questions, and all you're doing is giving me more. When does the answering part begin? Like, who has him right now?"

"We've nicknamed her Mother, but," and she held up her hand for me to be patient, "she's no more his mother than I am. She's a geneticist, Dr. Marie St. Laurent-Deville, called Queenie by those in her inner circle. For a very long time, I worshipped her. We now suspect delusions of grandeur."

"I understand the delusion part—" Why else would she kidnap a boy and whisk him away in a helicopter? Love? "—but not how it fits. Connect the dots for me. I'm not a geneticist. Just eighth grade science." I hoped I was being funny, but I was no longer sure.

"When Cam was with you during the storm, the devastation on the Center's campus was total."

"From that lightning strike in the news reports? What damage?" Now I was really mystified. I was there the next day. The place seemed in perfect order to me. Oh, the news reports, sure, and the comedians, but total devastation?

"We were working on a product line. Decades of research, with over twenty years of actual product in hand. Do you know what that means to a research facility? Field trials were under way, and we were ready to present to the entire world." She turned her head, her mouth tight, and her eyes pressed shut. She looked like she was attempting to maintain control. Then she relaxed and opened her

185

eyes, giving a little laugh, like she was embarrassed at her gaffe.

I shivered. Her intensity had been almost scary for a moment. Pictures flashed in my mind of Cam's wrists, his sudden growth over one weekend, and his undamaged legs after the accident. Then, the texting with no phone. The Frankenstein jokes didn't seem so far-fetched all of a sudden.

"Jill, I don't want to think what I suspect you're trying to tell me. So don't." Real boy. Real boy. Just say real boy, Jill, because I've changed my mind.

I realized my hands had gripped the armrests, and my knuckles were white. I made an effort to relax them. I'm stupid, I thought. Product. Field trials. What was I thinking? It was medicine or miracle soap or a new fuel to power the world's cars. Wasn't that what research centers invented? Maybe Cam was the guinea pig for new medical procedures like I'd thought, and if he survived, all the cancer centers in the world would shut down. A lot of people would lose a lot of money. Enough to kill for? Probably.

"Cam was all that was left, and we entrusted him to you."

Crikey, how could she say that? And I lost him. It was time for me to be irritated, but I couldn't be. She looked like this hurt her as much as it hurt me.

"Are you following me, Jake?" Her hand appeared on my wrist again, and all I could do was nod. "That's why we can't lose him. All the things you like about him," and she squeezed my arm, "the mustard, the awful singing, and the laziness, well, that's just who he is. We got lucky there."

I glanced at her, and she was smiling. I guess she loved him, too. Too? Let me retract that. I was hardly ready to admit to loving him. He was just a kid who had come to live with me, and now I was used to him in my life. Clearly, though, Jill cared about him very strongly, in spite of her position at the Center. Somehow, I felt grateful for that, like it was important, and like it made a real difference.

In the silence, I ventured, "I agree with you. He's not going to be in Croatia, drugged, and sold to strangers, and thank you. I'm very relieved." She squeezed my arm. "Any more answers?" She was offering, and I'd better take while the taking was good.

"You asked if that was what I wanted to hear." No expression. No clue as to what she meant.

"What did I say? I was busy, and I can't recall it."

"You said," and this time she was smiling as she looked at the ceiling, like she was remembering, and it was a good memory, "that you wanted him."

"I did say that, didn't I?" I remembered the intensity of my response, too. I didn't regret a word of it. However, there was a broader question, and the only one who could answer that one wasn't conveniently handy. I whispered, "The real question is, does Cam want to be with me? All I have to offer him is a dumpster sofa."

"And mustard."

"And mustard." I smiled. She'd been listening. I was thinking she just might be okay, especially if she found Cam as loveable . . . then I caught myself. What I meant was, as *likable* as I did.

For a time, it was pleasant sitting there, the camaraderie flowing between us. It reminded me of that last night with Cam, there on the sofa, as if all was right with the world, the emotions flowing between us as if we were connected inside. It was that way with Jill right then, as if we understood one another, and we were in complete agreement on something very important, even if it was just mustard.

Then the sound of the engines began to change, and I could feel the wheels lowering. I wondered if my car would still be out front, and if Kenny had remembered to shut the door. If the battery was dead, would Jill ask the pilot to land out front and give me a jumpstart?

She promised to keep me updated, getting me another phone from a cabinet inside the facility. Keep Cam's phone on and charged, she reminded me, and by all means, get some sleep tonight. The search was on for Cam, and there was a whole team of experts looking all over the world. Mike even came by and shook my hand as I exited the copter, assuring me he already had leads he intended to follow up on during the night.

See? I said he was more than just top dude over transportation.

It was in the car, heading home, that I hit myself in the head. Jill never did tell me why Cam would want to live with me. He can get mustard anywhere. And part of mine is just left over from Mrs. Osgood's. I don't see how it even tastes good anymore.

And she never told me why she was willing to claim Cam's eyes. Then there was where Cam had been held overnight in the Center. How had I not thought of that? Surely it would give us some clues.

Dang. I wish I could think of everything when it was important.

Chapter 50

The Rusty Nickel Late Night Chat Line

"Welcome, Michelle from Mississippi. You are live on the Rusty Nickel Late Night Chat Line. This is Rusty. What do you want to talk about tonight?"

"Do you remember me, Rusty? I was on before, and I asked about Frankenstein."

"Hello again, Michelle. I do remember you, and if you'll turn your radio down, I'll be able to hear you much better."

"Oh, I'm sorry, Rusty. I had to do that last time, too."

"Ah, much better, Michelle. Now, what's your question tonight? The floor is yours."

"So, I can ask about Frankenstein again?"

"Certainly, Michelle. What do you want to know about Frankenstein?"

"Could Frankenstein see through walls?"

"I don't think so, Michelle. Why?" Over the line Rusty could be heard chuckling, something he rarely did.

"My dad has an old comic collection, and in one back from 1992, Superman died. What if Frankenstein got Superman's eyes? Then he could see through walls."

"That's interesting, Michelle. What else do you think Frankenstein would be able to do?"

"I think he would be able to send telepathic messages."

"Who would have to die for Frankenstein to send telepathic messages?"

"Maybe no one. Maybe he's in so much pain he just does it."

"Thank you, Michelle. If that were so, then I think a lot of people would be able to send telepathic messages. Welcome, Claire from California. You are live on the Rusty Nickel Late Night Chat Line. This is Rusty. What do you want to talk about tonight?"

"My brother works on a deep-sea fishing boat just off the coast. Do you know anything about fishing boats?"

"I'm certain I do. What do you wish to know, Claire?"

"Do helicopters float?"

"I thought this was about boats, Claire." Rusty chuckled again.

"It is, Rusty. My brother, the one on the fishing boat, says a helicopter landed on a big ship not too far from his boat, then he saw people pushing it overboard. I told him it might be a submarine. You know, like in *Titanic*."

"Is it possible the helicopter was only delivering a submarine to the ship, Claire?"

"Rusty! He watched it land, and they pushed it right over-board."

"I see, Claire. Did your brother notice anything special about the helicopter, except that it was also a submarine?"

"That's why he called me. He thought it was funny. He had his binoculars out, and on the side he thought he could read the word *sissy*. I don't like to make fun of people, Rusty, but who would write that on the side of a helicopter everyone sees? I'd die if I had to ride in it."

"Thank you, Claire. I'm sure there are people out there who would be glad to ride in a helicopter slash submarine, no matter what word is on the side. Welcome, Frank from Utah. You are live on the Rusty Nickel Late Night Chat Line. This is Rusty. What do you want to talk about tonight?"

"You been hearing about these UFOs outside Provo? One just buzzed my house a bit ago."

"Did you get a picture, Frank?"

"Jeepers, Rusty! I ain't running out there to be zapped by lasers. Besides, I couldn't find my shoes quick enough, and Marti, that's my girlfriend, couldn't get the camera to work. Too dark once she got outside, she said."

"Maybe if you can get a picture next time, Frank . . ."

Chapter 51

The Game Goes Into an Extra Inning

My phone was blinking when I got home. It wasn't my usual light, either. It also wasn't ringing, and that confused me for a minute. I was getting used to the cell phones, and I had begun to wonder why people kept regular phones tethered to their walls anymore. It sure was convenient to carry them with you.

I picked up the receiver and got a dial tone. I pushed the button, and a voice purred at me, "You have one new voicemail message, and thirteen old messages. Press one to listen to your new messages now, or two to erase your old messages."

I had voicemail? It'd been so long I'd forgotten it did that. I pressed one. It was my mother, asking if I knew anything about that boy who had been kidnapped from my school. She'd heard from my Aunt June that he'd been taken from the school parking lot, kicking and screaming, right in front of the police. I'd know about that, wouldn't I? Since I taught there? If I didn't, Aunt June said I could look it up on the Channel 7 website, because that's where she saw it. And she wanted to know if I'd found a girl yet, and when was I going to come visit?

Thanks for calling, Mom, I thought, pressing the two. The phone just beeped, unwilling to accept my input, and I hung up.

Tossing my keys on the table, I pulled out a glass and put it under the tap, saving the water bottles for Cam's return. That made me feel like I was offering him hope. Kenny's bowl was still in the sink, and I set it on the counter. The package of Oreos was out and opened, with two cookies left, and I rolled the end and clipped it shut with a plastic clothes pin. I was hungry. Very hungry. Digging in the fridge only reminded me how long it'd been since I'd gone shopping. I knew Mrs. Osgood kept stuff for stew, so I went to her bathroom door, forgetting it was locked now, and banged my head. I had no choice. Store or starve. Besides, ten minutes, sandwich stuff, and I was good for another three days. It wasn't rocket science. Grabbing my keys and wallet, I pulled the door to after me, using my house key to lock the deadbolt. I hadn't forgotten the breaking-in thing at Mrs. Osgood's. I wasn't headed anywhere without locking up. It had started to sprinkle, and I didn't have an umbrella, so I ran to the car, starting it up and heading in the rain to the local mart.

I was gone less than ten minutes. Maybe nine, and in that length of time, everything changed. I got home, and my phone was blinking again. My first thought was, aw, Mom! Then I saw the cell phone blinking. Mom didn't have the cell phone number. I grabbed it and turned it on. A new icon had a number above it. I tapped it and got a play button. I touched that, and Jill's voice started up.

"Where are you, Jake? We've got a lead. If you want to join us, you have to get here now. Call me at this number." Then she was gone. There were all sorts of activity going on in the background. I wondered just how good this lead was. The last one had been a bust.

I located her number on the screen and tapped it. It answered immediately.

"I told you to keep this phone with you. Where have you been?" Then, to someone else, "Do we have anyone north of McKinleyville? Yes? Get them out there, and Mike? Pull whatever strings you have to in order to get us on a military vessel, one with real armament, if possible. I'm told Arkady Vodovos might be aboard, and we don't dare take chances with Arkady." Her voice returned to me. "Now, Jake. We're in the air already. Do you want to go?"

"Where?" Duh. To find Cam. I felt really stupid for asking that. But then, maybe it was the hunger. My stomach was empty. "Of course. How do I meet you?"

"We're coming to you. We can put down at the park, but we

need you there when we arrive. Bring a coat, if you have one. You'll want it." She was gone.

I grabbed my keys and dropped them in my pocket, and then I looked around the apartment. My coat. It was on the back of my bedroom door. I flung the door clear, pulled the coat off the hook, and held it in one hand. I paused for a moment, considering if I had time for fresh clothes. I decided I didn't, and I ran back to the kitchen. What else, I wondered? I threw my phones in the bag from the mart, and with my coat in the other hand, I headed out the door, pulling out my key and locking it before I darted out of the building and down the walk. I could already hear the copter and see the lights in the distance. I tore towards the park, hoping they didn't beat me.

Thank you, God, I thought. Thank you for pointing these people the correct direction. Now, help me find Cam and bring him home again.

I didn't know where we were going—McKinleyville? Never heard of it—but I wanted to be there when we arrived, maybe give some ex-employee a black eye.

That'd feel good for a change.

Chapter 52

Jake Gets a Gift

"You people don't have an off switch."

I fell back into my seat, a different one than before, but it was the same white leather and red carpet, so I felt at home. I dropped my sack and coat into the seat beside me. Unlike earlier, only three of us were present this time. Jill was off to the side speaking into her phone, and she lifted a hand to acknowledge my presence.

As the craft surged up and forward, Mike smiled and pointed, "Shopping expedition?"

"Supper. I haven't eaten." I clipped my seat belt in place with a loud snap. "Where are we headed?"

"You remember I said I had some leads?" He tapped the wire still in his ear. "While we were off on our goose chase, security was scouring the part of the Center where our boy was held, and it was very revealing. But one thing was especially helpful." He leaned forward with a very pleased and expectant look on his face.

"And it was?" I leaned forward, also.

He reached into his pocket and pulled out Cam's stainless steel wallet. Then he opened it to extract a business card. It was stained, and I could just see something written on the back. He held it out to me.

"The Rusty Nickel Late Night Chat Line? What's this?" The letters were bold, and at the bottom it gave a nightly schedule and a phone number.

"More importantly, read the back."

I flipped it over to see a hand-written comment. *Really good stuff.* It was in Cam's cramped script, but that was all. I turned it over again, perplexed, and I looked at Mike. "So?"

"The *so* is that any lead can be a good lead." He reached into a briefcase at his side, and he pulled out a stapled sheaf of papers. He handed them to me. "This is a transcript of tonight's broadcast."

A number of the lines were highlighted in yellow, and Mike pointed to them. I scanned my eyes over the words, finally understanding.

Caller: My brother works on a deep-sea fishing boat just off the coast. Do you know anything about fishing boats?

Rusty: I'm certain I do. What do you wish to know, Claire?

Caller: Do helicopters float?

Rusty: I thought this was about boats, Claire.

Caller: It is, Rusty. My brother, the one on the fishing boat, says a helicopter landed on a big ship not too far from his boat, then he saw people pushing it overboard. I told him it might be a submarine. You know, like in *Titanic.*

Rusty: Is it possible the helicopter was only delivering a submarine to the ship, Claire?

Caller: Rusty! He watched it land, and they pushed it right overboard.

Rusty: I see, Claire. Did your brother notice anything special about the helicopter, except that it was also a submarine?

Caller: That's why he called me. He thought it was funny. He had his binoculars out, and on the side he thought he could read the word *sissy.* I don't like to make fun of people, Rusty, but who would write that on the side of a helicopter everyone sees? I'd die if I had to ride in it.

"What do you think *sissy* really means, Jake?"

"I take it I only get one guess." CISSIE. The Center. "You're not just the resident transportation expert, are you, Mike?" I looked up, and he had an amused twinkle in his eye.

"Nominally." He reached for the sheaf of papers, and he slipped them back into the briefcase. He held the wallet to me, nodding to me to take it. I did, slipping it in with my things.

"A lot must come under that heading." I looked at his arms. Solid muscle. His neck? Even thicker. I was really warming up to Mike. I decided if we got in a firefight, I wanted to be in the seat next to him. "So, I gather this new information can help us find Cam."

"We've located Claire. She lives in Crescent City, California, just south of the Oregon state line. She hooked us up with her brother's ship, and we know exactly where they were when the sighting was made."

"We can find them, then. Right?" He was like an eighth grader, answering questions with a rambling discourse on everything but the answer.

"We can get closer."

"Why only closer? What about their transponder, or whatever ships carry?" I glanced at my food. I'd feel better if I ate. Then I wouldn't be so short-tempered. However, I wouldn't have to be short-tempered if Mike would just tell me what I wanted to know, that we could find Cam, and he would be whole and in one piece, and this nightmare would be over.

Jill relocated to my side as I asked my question, her phone put away. She moved my sack and coat into the next seat before sitting next to me, and I watched my supper warily. I didn't want it to get too far away. It might save these people from a bear mauling in about five minutes.

"Jake, when people want to hide very badly, and they are as smart as the people we're chasing, they can be very difficult to find."

"But, you can find a ship, right?" I mean, it was a *ship.* One ship out on the water. How could we miss it?

"It's night." She motioned to the windows, as if I couldn't tell that for myself.

"But they have to have headlights on . . . to see where . . ." Mike and Jill were smiling. "No headlights?"

"No headlights, not in the ocean."

"Duh," and I hit myself on the forehead. "Radar. They drive

195

with radar. Pilot with radar, right?" I was a science teacher, after all. I should know these things.

"Among other things." Jill held out a plastic case to me. "Can you use one of these?"

I took it and opened it. Inside was a black gun. I looked at her in dismay. "Me?"

"It's a simple gun to use." Mike leaned in, lifting it from the case. "SIG Sauer P225. Here's the laser. It turns on here. Point. Pull the trigger. It won't miss. 15 shots."

"Safety?" It would miss if I didn't have it set to fire. I reached for the gun. It was heavier than I expected.

"Automatic release. Point and shoot."

Point and shoot. I pictured a hole in my foot, and immediately I imagined trying to get it out of my holster, and I accidentally shoot myself closer to home. If that happens, they'd better give Cam to me, because he's the only kid I'll ever have.

"And if I have to use it?" I slowly put it back in the case. "What then? Like, if they die. I like my life, and I don't think I'm suited to prison."

Jill looked at Mike, and she pressed her lips together. Something went between them, but I had no idea what. Perhaps they didn't want to die, and they realized that if they gave me a gun, the odds increased tenfold. Anyway, I expected Jill to take it away.

"If we locate them, and that is an if, then we have to be prepared. Do you want to do this, Jake?"

"Do I have a choice?" I meant to find Cam or not to find Cam.

"You can stay on the plane. Mike and I will handle this, and you'll be safe and sound."

I was irritated that she thought I might not be willing to help rescue Cam. Then I caught her obvious mistake.

"Copter, you mean."

"Listen, Jake. We're landing." She was right. The engines had changed. "We're at the airport now, and we'll be transferring within five minutes. We need to get all the way to the coast, and we're not getting there in this. Not in time."

When the door opened, I expected a Boeing 747, or maybe a 787. What I saw was the sleekest thing I'd ever laid eyes on.

"What is it?"

"Gulfstream G150. It'll do 500 knots and take us across the continent without refueling."

196

I could hear the pride in Mike's voice.

"His baby. He handpicked it." Jill pointed. "Now, Jake. All aboard."

I thought the helicopter was luxurious. When I stepped aboard the Gulfstream, we were wrapped in leather. Polished wood tables. There were even laptops out, ready for us to use. My grocery bag and coat seemed very out of place in the extra seat. Then my eyes landed on the parachutes.

"We're not doing that, are we?" I knelt and lifted the smaller of the two off the floor. It was lighter than I would have thought.

"We hope not." Jill was in her seat and snapping her seat belt.

"So, those are just for emergencies." I took a deep breath. "Mike?" He was already buckled in, and he had his eyes closed.

"Define emergency."

"Now you're turning into Jill. Don't do this, Mike."

Jill laughed.

"No, really. I want to know."

"Settle in." Jill patted the seat across the aisle from her. "You can trust Mike, and we have two hours for him to explain it all to you."

I wasn't especially reassured by her explanation. However, the seats were very comfortable, and once we were in the air, I had plenty of time to eat my supper. It wasn't like I didn't want to share, but Mike got up and brought some food items back from the galley for him and Jill. After I finished, I asked if there was a refrigerator. I wanted to take my extras home. They were all I had for the next few days. Sure, Mike said, and he put it all away. When he returned was when I began to wish I hadn't eaten anything at all.

"Now, Jake," Mike started, reaching for the bigger of the two parachutes, "have you ever done this?" He held the 'chute up.

I shook my head.

"Don't worry about it. If we have to jump, you and I will be together on this one." He seemed so calm and collected, like he did this every day.

Me? All I could see was a greasy spot on the deck of a ship, ready to be washed off by the next big wave. I didn't want to be a greasy spot. Besides, what about when I landed? I was certain the shock of the landing would set off my new P225, the ship would be compromised, and we'd all sink to the bottom.

If the bullet didn't take out something more personal, first.

I wondered if I should have visited the confessional on the way home from the Center. This might be my last day to live. I didn't want to die with any sins on my record.

Then I pictured Cam and reminded myself I was doing this for him. Still, I couldn't stop the thoughts that flashed through my head. You'd better be grateful, Cam. I'm doing this for you, but I'm only doing it once. The second time, I'll already be dead.

Chapter 53

Sweet Dreams Are for Children

About forty-five minutes in I noticed Jill was asleep. Mike had been great, treating me as if I could actually do what he was telling me, rather than assuming I was an idiot who would automatically fail. He would have been smarter to assume failure, but this felt better, like I was now a little bit of a machine, one that could run a little farther, shoot a little straighter, and survive in a firefight just a little longer than a normal human. Of course, he made it clear I'd be standing behind him all the time, but I had no problem with that. That was when he tapped his chest and showed me his armor-plated vest. Now he was loading ammunition into magazine clips for the guns.

"What's Jill's job here?" I nodded at her, her head on her arm, her seat reclined. She was beautiful, even asleep. I admired that. I've never seen myself asleep, but I've seen myself just after climbing out of bed. It isn't pretty, either.

"You've been watching her do it all along."

That was another thing about Mike. Sometimes I didn't under-stand his answers. Not about Jill, anyway. He'd been great when explaining weapons and survival gear. Now if he could just merge his techniques, he'd make a great eighth grade teacher, able to keep the kids intrigued and maybe teach them a thing or two at the same time.

"So, she'll stay behind if we have to parachute?" I assumed the small parachute was intended for me, if I'd known how to use it.

"Jill." He lifted the second parachute.

"She can do this?" I looked at her in amazement. "In a business suit?" I understood, though. If I wasn't willing to jump with Mike, it would be me staying on the airplane. Alone. That's what Jill had meant when she said she and Mike would handle it.

"You don't get the full picture. No one at the Center is just the Center. We've all come from somewhere. Jill's ex-FBI."

"Jump out of planes, catch the drug dealers, ex-FBI?" That was a jaw dropper. It would explain her on-going and very efficient professionalism. I'd only managed to break it once, and then she'd recovered almost immediately.

"Any text messages on that phone of yours?"

"No." It was on the table, but it was blank, and I understood what he'd done. He'd shifted the conversation away from Jill. I'd barely scratched the surface, but I was on his playing field, and I knew that. No sense in antagonizing the man who would be standing in as my shield when the bullets started flying. Still, whether he intended it or not, the reminder cut. Here I was all jazzed about paratrooping out of a luxury corporate jet, gun in hand, saddles blazing, and Mike had stuck a needle in my balloon.

I picked up the phone, and I turned it on. "Just all the old ones," I muttered. I scrolled through them, and they reminded me just what was at stake here, as if I needed reminding.

"I don't expect anyone will get much sleep once we get there, so now's our time. You leave that phone out and see if you can get some rest. It may just be an hour, but you'll be grateful for that hour if we have to bail out of here and head down there." He held his hand to the window and pointed down.

"And you?" I laid the phone out in plain sight. "You planning on sleeping?"

"I'm ex-Special Services. I don't sleep." He grinned when he said that, and I laughed. I think he was serious, though.

I tried to sleep, even closing my eyes for a while. It was easier with them open. I didn't see the texts that way, Cam's words, how much he was hurting, and him begging me to come rescue him. It was easier to watch Mike. He was on and off his microphone repeatedly, working on one of the computers, once stepping to speak to the pilot, at which point I felt the plane make a course correction. A couple of times I felt his eyes on me. The last time he said, "We'll bring him home, Jake. We never leave our men in the lurch. Our motto? To free the oppressed. We do whatever it takes."

I appreciated that. I didn't remember anything else until Mike was shaking my shoulder to wake me up. Mike's pretty good. His bedtime story had put me to sleep. Or maybe it was really a prayer. If I start to believe in angels, I tell you what, Mike's going right to the top of my list. Well, maybe right under Jill, but right at the top, nonetheless.

Chapter 54

Jake Learns to Fly

Cam's next text caught us all by surprise. To tell the truth, we'd gotten so used to the screen staying blank that none of us were paying any attention. We were over the ocean, hoping beyond hope, in the general area where Claire's brother had seen the Sikorsky go overboard. There was nothing. It was dark outside, and the seas had grown rough. The radar images coming in could be anything. We crossed some off because of their transponders, filtering their signals through our database, and marking them with a firm identity. Others? Less helpful. We knew they were there, but who or what, we couldn't tell. Even the air support we had combing the area had come up with nothing. We? I have to retract that. I couldn't claim any credit. I was sitting and taking it all in. Mike and Jill, they were the heroes here.

The phone shattered everyone's concentration. It vibrated on the polished wood, jumping noisily. Then it was still. We all froze, everything else gone from our minds, and we stared at it. Me, too, like it was a foreign object, electrified, and if I touched it, I would find out some truth I didn't want to know. For a moment I thought, not now, Cam. We're busy saving you. I was pumped, imagining jumping using a parachute, and Cam seeing me be all hero and stuff, and of course, that'd make him love me, and so on. Then the phone happened, and I knew what I'd pictured wasn't real. He was dying down there. People were ripping his life from him, and he would hate me for taking so long. He would feel abandoned. I knew abandoned kids. They tested the adults responsible for them. First they loved them, then they tested them, then when the adults failed to live up to the kids' expectations, they ran from them. Abandoned kids were too badly damaged to know that families aren't perfect on the inside, not the way you see them from the outside. Sometimes people let us down, and we have to understand and love them anyway. Damaged people can't see that, and Cam was an orphan. Orphans are damaged, even if other people can't tell. It's that fingernail thing. They all have one that's never healed.

That phone said all that to me, and I was frozen. At a time when I should have grabbed it in ecstasy, I didn't want to turn loose of rescuing hero. If I did, I'd become no more than a man who hadn't been able to rescue Cam from his tormenters, even when he'd pleaded for help.

"Jake? That's for you." Jill pushed the phone my direction.

"It's Cam." I still didn't take it.

"Get a grip, man. The boy needs you." Mike shoved the phone into my hand.

I touched the power button and clicked on the text icon. Then I looked at the two people watching me. "It's nothing."

Mike grabbed the phone and turned it his direction. "Jill, look at this. Interference?" He handed it to her.

"Code, perhaps." She began scrolling through the previous ones. "There may be similarities in an earlier text. Acronyms, perhaps. Or it may be nothing."

I understood their confusion. There was a text there, except it was unintelligible. *Oe horst so myod!* Random letters.

"Jake, try a reply." She held it out.

I typed, *Cam, it's Mr. Turner. Is that you?*

It spit back, *Hurts! Plas dpfj asd,* and it ended.

Cam, I typed frantically. *We're here. We've come for you. Tell us where you are.* I shook the phone when it didn't answer, and I began pounding on it with the side of my fist. "Say something, you piece of junk!" I no longer cared if I was an avenging angel, or simply the man who was too late to save Cam from all that he'd endured. I just wanted him safe, even if he never wanted to see me again.

"Jake, he's gone for now." Mike took the phone from me. "Look at my computer. We have triangulation capabilities here, too. His signal is gone."

"But there's more." Jill looked up with a smile on her face. "We don't need to triangulate his signal. We know exactly where it originated." She turned her laptop around, and there, centered inside a blinking red circle, was one particular blip that said, Here I am, Mr. Turner. Come get me. That's all I want, just for you to come get me. I've shown you the way. Now all you have to do is show up.

"We know that's him?" My words were rough, and they were angry. I wanted them rough and angry. I was ready to burst with rough and angry.

"That's where his signal originated." She turned her computer back and typed into it. "Moving northwest at nine knots. We can catch her, fifteen minutes, tops."

"Are we jumping?" I wasn't afraid, anymore. In desperate circumstances, any risk is acceptable, and this was a desperate circumstance, if I'd ever seen one.

"I'm checking, Jake. We have support in the air and on the sea, both military and private. We'd hoped to transfer to an armed vessel, Navy preferably, but I can't see that now. In our favor, we trump everyone else in speed, even if jumping is dangerous, both from this plane and in the dark. Let me see where our support teams are."

Not close enough for me. Cam was right there on the screen, and I couldn't get to him. Two feet away, and it might as well be a hundred miles. *Do* something, woman! I was going to burst.

"The closest with the ability to board and assume control is forty-five minutes away. Coast Guard, a medium endurance cutter." She looked at me, then at Mike. "Your call, Mike."

I spit out, "He could be dead in forty-five minutes. He could still be alive in fifteen." I looked at Mike. I got it. Jill had said dangerous, and she trusted him to make the best call. Jump, Mike. Jump.

Mike nodded.

Jill smiled. "I'll be suited up in ten. I hope you chose a capable pilot. He's got some fancy maneuvers to keep us off the wing."

Mike just grinned at her, and I could see something going on between them that I couldn't read. I'd wanted him to make this call.

Now I wasn't so sure. Keep us off the wing? Just what did she mean by that? Wouldn't we simply fall toward the ocean and open our parachutes? Then my eighth grade science kicked in. Velocity. Motion. Momentum. We would jump and immediately start to slow down. However, the plane would keep on moving, as in the wing would come at us at hundreds of miles an hour. We had to be out of the way before it got there.

Oh, crikey! Cam, I may not be able to rescue you after all. I may be dead before I get there.

But by then Mike was suited up. He held out a separate harness to me, one with no parachute attached, and he showed me how to put it on over my coat. My stomach churned. We were really doing this.

The copilot joined us as Mike secured our guns on our bodies. I could see Jill with hers at her side.

"So, we can do this?" I asked the copilot. Maybe he would talk to me, tell me the real deal, even try to talk me out of it. Heck, he might even be successful. At least I would know when I was going to die, whether it would be when I jumped from the plane or when I hit the ship.

"Yes, sir. We'll slow to just over a hundred knots before opening the door, then drop a flare to give you visual on the ship. Then we'll stall just as you jump."

"Has anyone ever done this before?" I felt like I had run-on mouth, the kind that asks more questions than is good for it. It was nerves, I knew, but I had no way to shut it up. The more he told me, the more I wished I didn't know.

"Off a 150? No sir, not successfully."

"Is he serious?" I looked at Mike, then I turned to Jill. I didn't know if my eyes were burning from sleep deprivation or desperation.

"You did ask, Jake." Jill shook her head. "Sorry."

I felt the plane shudder.

"Door open," called the copilot. He wrestled with it, forcing it outward.

It vibrated in the onslaught, but I was reminded that on the ground it should withstand a hundred-mile-an-hour wind. They were no faster here. He held on tightly, looking out over the water. Then, with a level of judgment I never could have duplicated, he dropped a flare overboard, and as it fell, the ship far below became a dark object against a darker sea. It was no bigger than a postage stamp. We weren't over it, but we were close. The sea blew sideways as the wind whistled past.

The noise was deafening.

"Jake." It was Mike, and he was loud and right in my ear. His hand was on my shoulder. He held up Cam's phone, and then he slipped it in my coat pocket and buttoned the flap. "You might need this, just in case. Now it's time to buckle together. Remember this: I know what I'm doing, and the pilot knows what he's doing. That storm out there? That's what makes this possible. We'll go off the end of the ladder, and the wind will carry us directly to the ship."

"And if we miss?" I suspected he wasn't sharing everything with me, and I pictured my regular confessional back in Casper. It was looking pretty good to me at that point.

"We swim." I looked back, and he was grinning. "But we won't. Trust me. I can control this parachute like you ride a bike."

"I never ride bikes!"

However, he had us hooked up by then, and we were moving to the door. I saw my life flash before my eyes, and it was all in black, the black of the night just outside the plane. The plane shuddered again, differently this time, and a warning buzzer sounded. Then the nose jumped up.

"That's stall. Now, Jake." Mike leaped forward, and we were aloft.

I couldn't see Jill, and I hoped she made it off successfully. I had my eyes closed, so I had no idea how close the wing came. After what seemed like a hundred years, I heard the jet engines kick in with a whine, and I knew we were on our own. When I opened my eyes, the wind buffeted my face, but I could see the flare and the ship floating in the distance. I tried to console myself that Cam was down there. I was finally going to kick some abductor backside. But it wasn't doing much good. It was all I could do to keep my underwear clean.

"Get ready," Mike yelled.

Then I was jerked in two pieces, and all my air was gone. I coughed, and hard, before I finally managed to breathe again.

"Where's Jill?" I yelled it into the wind, not sure if Mike would hear me.

"Behind us. We're heavier. We'll get there first."

"Oh, great! They can shoot at us first." I didn't know I was also the point man. I thought Mike was going to be my shield. Now Cam wouldn't know how hard I'd tried to find him, because I'd be dead when I did.

"They won't even know we're there. In this weather, we'll land like a butterfly, and sting like a bee."

Tears filled my eyes. I was glad Mike was at my back, because I didn't want him to see. That was exactly what Cam had said to me.

Mike threw an arm around my chest, and he yelled in my ear, "You're a brave man, Jake. My father left my family when I was eight, and he never came back. You're going after this kid, and he's not even yours. He's lucky to have you watching out for him. Hang on, now. It's going to get rough."

Going to get rough? And it hadn't been rough so far? I looked for the pearly gates, certain they must be at hand. Death by ship impact. There it was, floating in the ocean, and it was going to be the last thing I ever saw before shaking hands with St. Peter. I screamed, and then we hit, rolling across the deck of the ship. When we came to a stop, Mike immediately began working out of the parachute and getting me free. Faster than I thought possible, the chute was gone over the side of the ship. Then Jill came in, and I watched her land on her feet, Mike jumping forward to give her a hand. With both of them together, her chute was off. It caught on an elevated helipad for a moment, then it, too, disappeared into the blowing wind. Mike pulled us together into a huddle.

"This is it, Jake. We're going down there to rescue your boy."

Oh, but my heart felt big at those words, even as my legs shook in absolute terror. I could feel the jelly in my knees, and my response choked in my throat. Mike looked at me, and I guess he saw the fear in my eyes.

"Remember, you stay behind me at all times. Do you recall how to turn your laser on?"

I nodded.

"If you need to fire, hold the gun up until the laser is in the middle of the chest, then fire. Don't bother watching them. They'll already be dead. Jill, you find the boy. Make sure he's okay. We'll have company in," he spoke into his collar and checked his watch, "twenty-six minutes. I want us here and on this deck, package in hand, in twenty-five. Got it?"

Golly, but Mike was good. Mike was really good. Still, I wished I'd brought that extra underwear, because I was sure I was going to need it.

Chapter 55

The Rusty Nickel Late Night Chat Line

"Welcome, Justin from Oregon. You are live on the Rusty Nickel Late Night Chat Line. This is Rusty. What do you want to talk about tonight?"

"You listening to this, Rusty?" In the background a shortwave radio crackled, and garbled words punctuated Justin's question.

"It seems I have no choice, Justin. You might need to turn that down."

"Don't get smart with me, Rusty. We're getting attacked by the Japs here in Astoria. There's activity all out there."

"There is, Justin? And just what activity is out there?"

"Freakin' listen to it, man! I'm picking up all sorts of radio traffic. I was in the Gulf War. I know how these things go down. We've got bogies swarming the ocean out there."

"How can you tell, Justin? Any explosions, yet?" There was just a hint of amusement in the words.

"Nah, Rusty. Got my telescope out, though. My father-in-law's condo sits on the Columbia River, you see, and I have a direct sight right out to sea. They come my direction, and I'll know."

"Then we're safe for now?"

"Not sure, Rusty. Weather's rough tonight. I'm keeping a

lookout."

"Well, Justin, call me back if you sight anything ominous. Welcome, Delilah from Nevada. You are live on the Rusty Nickel Late Night Chat Line. This is Rusty. What do you want to talk about tonight?"

"Have you ever done a Vegas show, Rusty?" The words purred over the line, sultry and low.

"Is that an invitation, Delilah?"

"What do you think, Rusty?" If anything, the voice had grown even throatier. It oozed with appeal.

"I think I don't live anywhere near Las Vegas, so I'll have to pass this time. Thank you for calling, Delilah. Welcome, Debbie from Dallas. You are live on the Rusty Nickel Late Night Chat Line. This is Rusty. What do you want to talk about tonight?"

Chapter 56

Sibling Rivalry Threatens to Boil Over

Arkady was holed up in the ship's galley. He'd pulled up a metal stool and sat hunched over a stainless island, a tumbler of American Jack Daniels and his Beretta in front of him. Just above his head pots hung from a rack, also stainless. In a previous life, the ship had catered to numerous crew and passengers, and the galley was set up for the myriad dietary needs of the ill and infirm. However, now a coating of greasy dust covered the cookware, and a filthy fry vat off on one wall was all that really got any use.

The pots over Arkady's head shifted position and clanged as the ship rolled.

"Mother of Lenin, can you not just *shut up*?" He yelled the American phrase, one he had learned and especially enjoyed using, while hitting at a particularly low-hanging pot within easy reach.

The clattering only got worse, and the one he hit worked loose, falling to the metal island before skipping to the floor. He jerked out of the way, knocking his stool over, and making the noise even worse. His drink survived the calamity completely unscathed, sitting right where he'd left it next to his gun, calling him seductively.

"Mr. Vodovos. Is everything okay?" A wire-thin man in grimy, baggy clothes leaned into the room. The face was dark, although not African. His voice was terse and curt. It was also heavily accented.

"This weather. All this noise. I can no longer stand this floating, how do you say, tin can." He picked up his stool and set it upright, reaching for his drink. "Everything is okay. I thank you."

The face disappeared, but Arkady was correct. It was noisy. The ship was old, its last retrofit had been before he was born, and the wind came in everywhere. And everything was broken. Even the toilets. The storm had garbled all the communications, and he hadn't been able to pull up his email or the ship's satellite phone service.

He straightened his coat and felt at his collar. His tie was loose, and he wrapped his fingers around it to tighten it, but his drink was in his other hand by then. The amber fluid caught his attention, and he let go of the tie, heading into the corridor and grabbing the doorframe as the ship rolled, then waiting for the floor to level again before stepping through. One hand felt beneath his coat for his gun, only to see it still on the counter.

"We are at sea. Who is there to shoot?" he muttered.

He walked away, pausing as the floor once again shifted. His hand against the wall stabilized his massive bulk. At the old operating theater, Queenie's download room, he paused at the door, simply looking in. The boy lay on the narrow metal gurney, the straps tight around his lower legs and his chest, his head and arms immobilized with yet more of the same. He was tethered to Queenie's bank of computers by the intricate maze of wiring from back in Denver. His skin was bruising, both from the rough treatment he'd received, as well as the lack of fluids.

"Shark meat." Arkady sauntered into the room, stopping to put his hand against the wall as the ship shifted position.

Queenie stepped from behind a cabinet, glanced at Arkady, and dismissed him with a shake of her head. She looked down at her monitor and tapped a key, smiling in satisfaction.

"Shark meat, I tell you."

"I heard you." She didn't look up.

Arkady walked to the boy, and he placed a hand on one of his shins, wrapping his fat fingers underneath the bone, and squeezing the muscle before letting it go. "Not much left. Is perhaps still usable for scrap."

"Scrap?" There was no other indication Queenie recognized

Arkady's remark, other than that one word.

"High-grade metals, polymers yet unavailable to Mother Russia. Might get many rubles for this boy, even when you are finished."

Queenie laughed. "You have no sense of what I've accomplished, have you, you fool? That's small change next to the programming, the ability to take scraps of DNA, infuse it into self-replicating cellular tissue, and create a real body, one that functions like a live person, and even thinks for itself. The possibilities are limitless."

"It does feel quite real. In that, you speak the truth." Arkady's hand was back on the leg, and he was up to the thigh. "Can it reproduce?"

"Unimportant. Don't you get it yet, Arkady, or is your head thicker than this boy's? We build them from scratch into just what we want them to be."

"But I feel, how shall I say it, interested now, Queenie." His tone had changed. He could charm, if needed. "You always want me to share your enthusiasm, and now you do not want me to ask questions. Which it is, my love?"

She sighed heavily and checked several things on her computer. Cam was stiller than not on the gurney, his eyes open, the pain coming through as quivering muscles, especially in his fingertips. They hadn't strapped those down.

"What do you want to know?" She moved to the gurney.

"This is no *mal-chik*, or as you would say, little boy. Can your . . . walking dolls truly create more of their own kind?" He grinned, shaking Cam's leg hard, forcing the muscle to jerk under his hand.

"He is alive, Arkady. No matter what part I have had in it, he is alive—"

"Except every four months," he sneered. "Then he is—" and Arkady paused as he searched for the correct phrase, his hand held in the air like a traffic officer, "—*dismembered* to make him grow. Over two hundred bones, and you must extend every one. On Lenin's grave, that is a machine, not a person." He gave Cam's leg a rough slap to illustrate his point, laughing when the boy's body jerked hard against the restraining straps. The gurney slid sideways for a bit before coming to a stop.

"Hardly dismembered, Arkady. True, I haven't mastered normal

bone production at the growth plate, but he remains in one piece."
Her face looked pained, as if his reminder slandered her abilities,
and she was cut to the quick. "Give me enough time, though, and
even that will be resolved."

"Just not for this one." Arkady grabbed Cam's thigh and
squeezed hard, his meaty fist biting into the flesh. When he
removed his hand, he left red marks where his fingers had been. "I
want to cut him and see whether he bleeds blood or the fluid for
lubrication."

"He is not a machine." Queenie was back at her computer.
"Now be quiet, Arkady. I am in the final stages. This is important,
and I have to monitor carefully. Without this, independent cell
replication in the new hosts will fail, and all we've done will be
useless."

"We will have our money, though." He was at Cam's face, and
he grabbed his jaw in his hand. "You, boy, will make me very
wealthy. I will live like a Tsar." He squeezed the jaw, forcing his
grip tighter under Cam's chin, until the boy began to choke. Arkady
froze, looking down to see a gun pressed into his side.

"You kill him, and I'll see that you don't get off this ship alive."
Queenie's voice was hard. "Let him go. I need to be at my
computer, and I can't spend my time babysitting you. Now,
Arkady."

That was when gunfire elsewhere in the ship got their attention.

Chapter 57

Gun Up, Jake

I was grateful for the laser. It gave me something to focus on besides the possibility that I might die. In the dimly lighted corridors, with only part of the old and filthy lights burning, it danced like a brightly-burning fire. I did learn what Mike's shirt smelled like. His hair, too. To me, any man standing in front of me to catch incoming bullets smells pretty good. Mike was my new best friend, and he could come over and play at my house any day.

Jill was off searching for Cam, so it was just Mike and me. I didn't know who was in the better situation, because we caught someone's attention almost immediately. My gun was pointing at the floor, and I was watching the laser dance around, when Mike grabbed my hand, pulling the gun up to where the laser hit an empty doorway.

"Always assume someone's coming out."

Just then someone did, right out of that doorway, someone big, in dirty clothes, with a massive gun in his hand. It was, like, a rocket launcher. In retrospect, I knew it wasn't a rocket launcher. Maybe an AK-47, but it was bigger than mine. What do they say? My daddy is bigger than your daddy? Well, his daddy was bigger than my daddy. He didn't live to brag about it, though. Mike had my gun in his hand, and I had my finger on the trigger. The laser zeroed in on the man's chest, and Mike hit my finger. The gun exploded, and so did the man's chest. He slammed into the doorway like a rag doll, his arms flailing, and his gun went down with him. I watched as we walked on past, and I could see it was strapped around his body.

"Jake, what did I say about looking?"

"Fire and look away."

"Are you looking away?"

"It's my first time to kill someone." I felt my stomach coming up, and I wished I hadn't eaten back on the plane. I also wondered if St. Peter would count this as murder. Could I still make it in if I claimed self-defense? My stomach roiled again. "Can I throw up, Mike?"

"Not on me. Now, let me see that laser. Every door, Jake. Every door."

That gave me focus. I tell you, Mike's good. He should take a position at Bruce. He'd probably get teacher of the year. Maybe even at state level. He wouldn't get paid enough, though. The things you give up just to get a pat on the back.

"Mike, what time is it?" I whispered the words in his ear.

We were coming up to a bend in the corridor, and he placed his gun at the corner, then whipped around, his laser hitting each doorway, open or not. I leaped after him, unwilling to be left all on my own. Mike was my only shield, and I wanted a shield. Desperately.

As we moved forward, I repeated my question, "Do you have the time, Mike?"

"Why?" Very tight, very terse.

"You said twenty-five minutes." It seemed like it had been forever. Forever and one dead man.

"We're okay. Gun up, Jake. Doorways."

"Gun up. Doorways. Right, Mike." I hoped I hadn't just dirtied my underwear. I didn't want Mike to think I was a sissy.

I let the little laser bounce from doorway to doorway. Mike's laser was like a machine, jumping from opening to opening. Mine played Red Rover. But it got there. We heard some voices and clanking metal sounds, and moving up to an open door, we realized it was the galley. Two men were inside talking in a foreign language, and they were banging things around. It was probably why they hadn't heard us. Poor dead guy, I thought. His friends don't even know. It never occurred to me that they were most likely not friends and they wouldn't care one way or the other if he was alive or dead. I just don't think that way. I hadn't known Mike but a day, and if he got shot, I'd care very much. And probably run away screaming like a girl.

I squeezed my buttocks together. No leaks, please. I hoped God was up there listening to me. Let me get shot, God, but no leaks, not here in front of Mike. But, just in case you take that literally, God, I don't want to get shot, either.

Mike had his finger to his lips, and he looked at me, making sure I understood. He motioned with his hand for me to follow, and he began moving past the door. Heck, did he think I was staying behind without him? He was my lifeline to a continued existence. He could climb into a shark's belly, and I'd just yank out the shark's teeth and clamber in on his heels.

Our worst problem was the pitching of the ship. Every time we took a step, we had to adjust for the tilt of the floor. Once or twice I bumped an open door, only to have Mike freeze, then move on when there was no one chasing us. Each time I did, I thought, gun up, doorways, right, Mike, like that made up for my idiocy.

As we successfully made it past the galley, the ship must have hit an awful wave, because the floor dropped out from under us. Mike took it in stride, his knees bent already, and he started to step forward again. I wasn't so smooth. I stumbled, and in recovering, fired my gun at nothing. I had no idea where the bullet went, but there was no way those guys in the galley missed it. Mike whipped around, slamming into me, his arm outstretched. The two men from the galley leaped into the corridor. Only one had a weapon, but Mike's gun went off twice, and both men dropped to the floor. I was in a total sweat by then, and too late, I raised my gun, the laser jumping all over the corridor.

"Look away, Jake."

I couldn't.

Then another man leaped out of the bend we had just passed, and he had his AK-47 up and ready to fire. I closed my eyes and squeezed the trigger. I jumped when the gun fired, and that caused me to squeeze the trigger again. Mike pulled my arm down.

"Just one bullet, Jake. When a man goes down, you don't fire a second time."

That time I didn't look. I'd killed him all on my own, and I didn't want to see. I didn't want to go back to my science lab, and see my eighth graders come in, and try to teach my classes, all the while picturing a man I'd killed, just because he'd been there in front of me. And this one I'd done on my own. I sensed heaven growing dimmer by the dead man. Kill another one, and I was pretty sure they'd lock all the confessionals and throw away the keys.

I was shaking, and I couldn't move.

"You did the right thing, Jake. You acted before I could, and you did exactly what I would have done. You saved us both."

"I'm sorry." I sniffled. "I can't believe I did that."

"If you enjoyed it, I'd worry about you." Mike smiled. "Now, we've got Jill in here somewhere, and she needs us for backup. Are you still with me? We've got a boy to rescue."

I wiped my nose with my sleeve, and I nodded. I guess I'm not so grown up after all. My eighth graders wipe their noses on their sleeves, and they're just kids. I'm not so different from them. I appreciated Mike not calling me a baby. He's really good. When I go back to school, I want him for my teacher. I think he's the best there is.

Somewhere a gun went off deeper within the ship. Then there was an explosion that rocked the floor, and the lights went out. We stood in darkness for a moment before emergency lighting flickered on.

I forgot about being a baby. I looked at Mike, and he was looking at his watch. He slapped me in the chest with the back of his hand, motioning for me to follow him, and he took off at a run. I didn't know how he knew where he was going, but I was trying to memorize the way we'd come. If this ship went down, I didn't want to be caught in the belly. I wanted up top. I remembered *Titanic*. All those poor kids drowned because the gates were locked. They didn't know any other way to get to the lifeboats. Lifeboats? Lifeboats? We were in the middle of the ocean. I wanted to ask Mike about lifeboats, but we were running so hard I could barely breathe by then.

And that's when we caught the distant sound of water rushing into the ship.

Chapter 58

White Lightning Doesn't Go Down Well

"Move that, woman, if you entertain the desire to keep your hand attached to your arm. You will not hold a gun against Arkady's side." He grabbed it, his accent heavier than usual, even as he continued to crush Cam's throat with his massive paw. He pulled the gun up until it pointed at the boy.

Queenie tugged at the weapon, but she was powerless against the bigger man's muscle.

"You wish to squeeze your trigger? I give my permission. It will resolve one of my difficulties. Then the boy's body can, what do you Americans say, sleep overboard with the sharks." Arkady laughed harshly. "I have radioed for transport. It will arrive in one hour. If you do not wish to accompany me, I only ask for this small thing. Allow me the head, and the rest of the boy is yours to do with as you please."

"He must not die. Not before I have all I need from him." Queenie's hand on the gun was white with tension.

"You surely understand the situation. If we remain aboard this ship, I do not think we get our hundred million. Circumstances are now changed, and we must go. With haste."

Two more shots went off somewhere. Then, within moments,

two more. Queenie relaxed, and Arkady let go of both the gun and the boy's neck. She laid the gun on the gurney beside Cam's head.

"I am so close." Her face was very intense, but it no longer carried the fire it had shown minutes before. "An hour, or two."

"It is enough."

"Enough?" Her words were bitter. "It doesn't have to be enough. It is all here, inside the boy. We have it all."

"Then we shall move him again, yes?"

"Move him? Of course. Let's do that, Arkady. Where? And how?" She didn't look at him. Her face was filled with defeat.

"You have stated you can withdraw the information faster—" He motioned to her computer encouragingly.

"And kill him." She laughed bitterly. "Likely before the information is complete."

"Then kill him. It is of no concern. Burn his nerves until he dies, and we are that much closer to our goal. You will rebuild the final parts of the process."

"With a decade and a fully staffed research center, yes, I can rebuild the process. However, I am no longer young. I do not have the time."

"I do, woman. I have the time, and I want to be a Tsar." Arkady strode with hard steps to her computer, and he tapped her keys, bringing up the sliders. He put his fingers on them and pushed them up as far as they would go. "There. Now I will get what I want."

"Not wise, Arkady." Queenie stood back nervously. "We have limited power resources." She looked at Cam, his body contorted on the table, and then to the bank of very specialized and power-hungry computers. The machines in the room began to react, readouts changing, and cooling fans increasing in speed. Cam began to react, too, his tortured body flailing against his restraining straps.

"Not wise? It is working. Our *mal-chik* is still very much alive, and the computer is, shall we say, filling up with rubles. The boy shall be emptied before my transport pulls alongside. I will not need the head after all, I do not think." He sneered his last comment. "I should have done this back in Denver. I should have done you back in Denver."

He reached into his coat, only to find it empty. Then his eyes recognized Queenie's weapon. He leaned forward heavily, grabbed the gun, and he turned it on her.

"I will enjoy the rubles, Queenie. Thank you for your generous contributions." With that, he flipped the safety with his thumb and fired.

He looked surprised when one of the breakers across the room tripped, and the nearest of the energy-starved mainframes went down. The smell of fried insulation scorched the air in the room. Tossing the gun on the gurney where he'd found it, he marched over and forced the massive breaker back into place. It didn't want to catch, but then it stayed, and the computer began to blink, quickly rebooting and coming to speed. Within seconds, another breaker tripped, and he repeated the process, only to have it happen yet in another place.

He looked at Cam, to see him lying still. Each time a breaker tripped, the boy relaxed. Arkady muttered, "You ignorant *mal-chik*, give me what is in your head," as he reached to reseat yet another breaker.

The final one he pushed into position didn't want to remain in place. He forced it in, holding it while it crackled and spit white sparks. Then, with a surge of white light, it slammed him to the floor, and somewhere deep in the ship, something shook violently.

The lights went out.

When the emergency lighting came on in the corridors, the room remained dark. Arkady didn't know. He was out stone cold. Queenie was unaware, too. She was breathing, but the hole in her stomach said not for much longer.

Cam was the only one still conscious, although barely, at that. His eyes were open, staring into the darkness. His body was abused, his nerves stripped raw, and he was desperately dehydrated. The saline with its electrolytes had been depleted long ago, and Queenie hadn't bothered to replace it. He had been left horrifically alone, even by those who had abducted him.

Somehow he found the strength to send one more text.

Chapter 59

Cam Wants to Go Home

I felt the phone vibrate. I remembered it later. However, at the moment, we were running so hard that I couldn't think of anything except catching my next breath. That and lifeboats. I knew we must be in the heart of the ship, and what worried me was the emergency lighting. It was flickering. I'm a pretty smart man, what with a college degree and all, and if you remember, I'd had an epiphany earlier. Well, I just had another one. One big boom. The sound of water. Flickering lights. Remember *Titanic*? That was the point at which everyone died.

Then we heard three shots, one, then two in quick succession. That led us to Jill. She was on her knees in the corridor, and there were two men beside her. Jill was alive. The men weren't, not as far as I could tell. However, I didn't look, leaving them to their own fates, however awful that might be.

Mike fell by Jill's side.

"I should have given you my body armor." He put his arm around her and helped her sit up. "How bad is it?"

"I'm alive." She coughed, and then she looked at me and laughed, before coughing again. "I see Jake's still with you."

"And he took out a few baddies." Mike grinned at her. "You,

though, need treatment."

"And we have a boy that I think is somewhere in here." She pointed to where the corridor split just ahead of us. "These goons were determined I wasn't getting past this point, and I showed them otherwise. I've gone as far as I can, though, and I suspect this ship has suffered irreparable damage."

"The explosion a few minutes ago?" Mike watched her face.

"Just as the lights went out? Most likely. I'm not sure what it was, but the whole place rocked. These two," and she nodded at the dead men, "seemed to think it was something big."

"Engine room, I expect. We heard water earlier."

"We can still do this." Jill coughed again. "Have we heard from Cam?"

That was when I remembered the text, and I muttered to myself, "Dang it, Jake. You're an idiot." I'm getting good at that lately. Not the remembering part, the being too free with the careless language in front of others part. Still, I thought God would understand this once. I grabbed at my pocket, and when I couldn't get it loose, I tore at it until the button flew off.

"Does that mean yes?" That was Mike, with a look at Jill.

"Yes," I said. "It vibrated while on the way here." I got the phone out, and I tried to turn it on, but my hands were sweaty, and it slipped from my grasp, clattering to the floor.

Mike swept it up in his hand, holding it out to me.

"You do it." I wiped my hands on my pants, shaking my head. I couldn't. I was about to come apart.

He flipped it on, tapping it to bring up the message. He smiled, and he showed it to Jill. Then he held it up to me.

Mr. Turner, are you here, yet?

I could no longer see the corridor with its dying lights or the rust stains eating into the walls. Almost, Cam, I wanted to scream. I'm just around the corner, and I've come for you.

"What do you want me to say?" Mike prodded me, gently, too, like he understood. I loved Mike at that point.

"Tell him yes." I could hear my voice shake. It was all I could do to focus on standing still. I looked at Mike typing, and I took in Jill watching him. The two of them together jumped out at me. Maybe there was something between them, after all. I didn't know. I didn't care. They'd risked their lives for something important to me. I loved them both, and I intended to tell them, just as soon as we were out of here.

"Do you want to see his reply?" Jill, really pale, I noticed for the first time, smiled at me. She took the phone from Mike and gave it to me.

Good. I'm tired. I want to go home.

"Mike," I said. "How do we find him?" I kissed the phone, and I didn't know what to do with it. I started to put it back in my pocket, but I was afraid Cam would send me another message, and I'd miss it. I know adrenalin must have flooded my system, because I was all over the place.

"Jake, let me help you." Mike took the phone and put it in my jacket pocket. He turned to Jill. "Are you okay alone for a few minutes?"

"For six and a half. That's when we have to be topside."

"We'll be there, and with our boy, too. You have ammo?" When she nodded, he turned to me. "Jake, come along. We're not going home without everyone."

"Foaming mothballs, we're not." I grinned. I'd done it again, but I was proud of that one. I remembered that experiment from my bathtub. Sometimes it's the words that tell your true feelings, and that time, it said exactly how I felt.

Jill shook her head, but that was okay. I knew what I meant. After that, I was better with my gun, more focused, perhaps. The smile had faded, but the adrenalin was still pumping. The laser seemed brighter in the gloom. Together, Mike and I circled the corridors. Most of the rooms had dim lighting inside; some didn't. That was why we almost missed him.

I had stopped Mike, asking him if the ship felt funny. Sluggish. Heavy. He scared me. It does that, he said, when it's about to sink. He should have said, Oh, don't worry about it, Jake. All ships do that in a storm. Still, I'm glad he was honest, because that was why I went in a pitch black room. I was determined to search everywhere, as quickly as I could, because I wasn't climbing off this ship without Cam, and I didn't want to go down with it.

At first my laser caught a man on the floor. Mike stepped up behind me and said, "Arkady Vodovos." He spat the words at the inert form.

"Cam?" I called out, which I hadn't done before. I wasn't afraid any longer, not of making noise or being shot. He had to be somewhere. In this dying ship he could be anywhere, and I had to find him.

"Mr. Turner?"

I barely heard the reply, but I knew that voice, even cracked and broken.

"Cam?"

I danced my light across the room, seeing an older woman in a white coat crumpled on the floor. Red colored her dead, or so it appeared. The mutilated body I saw on the gurney, well, I didn't think it was Cam, at first. A corpse, I thought, strapped down and almost naked. Then I saw the electrodes, and I ran to him, pointing with my gun, the laser illuminating each bruise and hand print, telling me more than I wanted to know.

"Don't shoot me, Mr. Turner."

"Cam! How can you think that?" I had tears in my eyes as I began loosening the straps. I glanced up to see Mike at my side removing an IV from Cam's arm.

"Look at his face, Jake." Mike chuckled. He tossed the IV aside, reaching to release one of the straps.

Mike was right. Dang it, if the kid wasn't smiling. It wasn't much, but it was a smile. He was teasing me.

"When we get out of here, Cam, I'm going to hold you upside down under a downspout until you scream for me to let you go."

"I won't," he whispered. "I won't ever scream for you to let me go."

"C'mon, Mike, can't we do this any faster?" Cam was working me, just like he always did, getting me to do just what he wanted. And just like every time, I fell right into it, and I couldn't climb out.

Well, this time I didn't want to climb out. He wanted me to get him out of here, and he wanted to spend time with me, and, well, that's exactly what I wanted, too.

"Downspout?" Mike whispered.

"You had to have been there," I whispered back.

Chapter 60

Four Makes a Package

Getting Cam off the gurney only made things harder for us. He couldn't stand, not without help. I didn't know what those people had done to him, but I was furious they were already dead. I wanted to give them a little bit of my mind, and I wanted to do it with my fist. Who in their right mind would do such a thing?

It was only later that I understood my question had also given me my answer. Who in their right mind would do such a thing? No one.

I had Cam's arm around my shoulders and my arm across his back. Being tall, I have long arms, and they fit around him very easily. What got me was that every time I touched him, he cringed or whimpered.

"Cam, how can I make this easier?" I asked, when I realized tears were running down his cheeks.

"You can't, Jake." Mike had pushed the gurney aside. "Let me help." He leaned to put Cam's other arm over his shoulders when the gurney moved on its own.

"No!" The word was as much a gasp of pain as anything. We turned. The woman in the lab coat was holding to the gurney and trying to stand. "He's mine. You cannot take him." She had a gun in her hand, but she could barely hold it.

I felt Cam's arm tighten on my shoulder. "Please, Mr. Turner," was all he said to me. It was real fear I heard in his voice.

"Go, Jake," Mike called, moving between the woman and us.

However, in that moment, hearing her voice, my feet had become frozen, and I couldn't move. Conflicting emotions flooded me. This was the chance I'd waited for. I wanted at her, and it was almost uncontrollable.

"She doesn't matter." It was Mike again.

"No!" Her voice grew stronger. "He is the beginning of everything. You must not take him." The gurney skidded away from her, and she fell to the floor.

I didn't know what she meant, but I held tight to Cam. I wanted to run, for Cam's sake, but my pent-up anger was about to boil over. I was shaking with the adrenalin flooding my system, and I could barely suck in air. I knew if I let go of him, my hands would be around her neck.

"I know what you're thinking. She's not worth it." Mike stepped up to me, placing his hand on my shoulder. He looked right in my face, blocking my view of her. "Your boy is more important."

I swear it was almost dark in that room. How Mike could have seen the hate on my face, I don't know. He read me like a book, though. Cover to cover, that's all I could feel, what I wanted to do to her. Then Cam did what he does best.

"Let's go home, Mr. Turner."

"You've got a smart boy there, Jake. Let's go home."

I swept him up in my arms, calling to Mike, "We're moving out." I turned, and I felt Mike's hand on my back just for a moment as we moved into the corridor.

We were jarred by the sound of a gunshot behind us, but I didn't stop to see. I could hear the woman's voice, but I kept moving, and Mike was right with me the whole time.

It was only later that I realized exactly what Cam had done for me with those five words. In that moment, my focus shifted, and I was able to dismiss that woman from my life, because I was taking my boy home.

"How long, Mike?" I was walking sideways, watching for Cam's legs, enjoying the feel of his arms around my neck. They were real-boy arms with real-boy warmth, and they were holding tight to me.

"Four minutes till rendezvous."

"Can we make it?" I had memorized every crook and turn, and I was going to be there, even if I had to run the entire way.

"We can make it. Jill's just ahead." He called, "Jill?"

That was when our feet hit water. In the next corridor, Jill sat in a foot of cold, swirling sludge, and dark stains circled her like sharks of death. I pulled Cam's head to me. He knew Jill. I didn't want him to see her dead.

"Jill?" Mike knelt, picking up her hand and patting her face. "Jill, are you with us?" She didn't respond for half a minute, then her head jerked.

"Mike? Did we get the boy? Is he safe?"

"Let's go, Jill. Our ride's waiting."

"No, Mike. I don't think so. Not this time." Her eyes caught me standing to the side. They looked glazed. "Jake, you've got him. Good. Is he okay?"

I started to say, he's not okay. He's been tortured and abused, and it looks like he's been beaten. No, he's not okay at all. But, as unending waves of emotion boiled up in me, my words caught in my throat, and all I could do was pull Cam closer.

Cam answered for me. "I'm okay, Ms. Compos." His arms tightened around my neck.

He was alive. That's what she'd really asked, and Cam's answer told her what she needed to hear. I'm glad he answered for me. I couldn't have said it so well.

"Come on, Jill. We'll get you fixed up." Mike lifted one of her arms and put it over his shoulder. "Just outside a boat is waiting."

The water had risen another six inches in the time we stood there.

"I'm bleeding out, Mike. You've got to let me go this time. It was a good ride, though."

If I hadn't had Cam in my arms already, I would have picked her up and carried her out. But, I guess my prayers to God worked. Mike stepped up to the plate, doing his Mike thing, and I didn't have to.

"I'm not listening, Jill, not this time. I'll let you bleed out, but I won't let you drown. You're going up top with us, and if you want me to leave you there, I will, and you can bleed out all you want. But it's not happening here." He swept his arms under her, and with water everywhere, he began to slog his way back to the deck. I

227

discovered I hadn't needed to memorize the way to the top. Mike didn't make even one wrong turn.

His timing was impeccable, too. At each set of steps, we thought we would find our way out of the encroaching water. However, it was rising faster than we could fight through it. I was waist deep as I started climbing the final set of stairs, and as you know, I'm pretty tall.

As Mike broached the deck, he spoke into his collar, "Package ready for pickup."

I was at his back, and I could see his earpiece hanging down over his shoulder. That was when I felt like we were there. He didn't need it any more. I was grateful to see three inflatable skiffs circling the sinking boat. Each had brilliant lamps aimed our direction.

A bullhorn started up, "Is anyone injured?"

Duh, I said to myself. I thought they were stupid back at the Center. These bozos could see us carrying one bleeding woman and a boy who couldn't even stand. They had come to get us, though, so I'd cut them some slack. However, they'd better get over here before this boat went down. I didn't mind carrying Cam, because he was the best thing that had ever happened to me, but dang it, how heavy can a fourteen-year-old be? He felt like he was made of steel.

Chapter 61

Forever Adds Up to About Four Years

Somehow I'd imagined that was all there would be to it. I'd sweep in and rescue Cam, and the next day we'd be back at school, everything the same as before.

Not exactly.

We almost lost Jill. Sitting in that water did about as much damage as the bullet. Maybe more. You can't imagine what diesel fuel and human waste can do when it gets into the human body. She sat in that long enough that it filled her up with poison.

And Cam. Even with all the texts he'd sent, I had no idea. The black eyes, the bruising. The needle marks. And the hand print on his thigh, like someone had grabbed him and squeezed him just to make him hurt. It was like that around his neck, too. He says he can't recall how those got there, but I remember what he once told me. People say babies can't remember, but he remembers every time he was worked on as a kid. I bet he remembers what happened back there on that table, too. Him not telling me? That's Cam, for you. He doesn't want me to know. He's watching out for me.

We kept Cam out of school until his bruises faded. We also avoided Sacred Heart for the same reason. No sense in getting any child abuse rumors in the pipeline. I say we. The Center helped, and primarily by making sure I was off with him. You know, those convoluted strings they were able to pull that first time. I think they pulled some more. I had his books, and I was supposed to tutor him the whole time. Mostly we played *Gods of War* and ordered in pizza. Once a week we sat on the sofa together, and I pulled his legs up into my lap. I took my clippers, and I trimmed his toenails. That's become a thing we do, like some people fix pancakes on Sunday mornings. Well, Cam and I, we trim toenails on Friday nights. It reminds me of what it really means to be a parent. It's not the big things, the summer days spent at the water park. Anyone can do that, even a teacher. A parent trims toenails, just because it needs done.

When we learned that Jill was out of the critical care unit, Cam and I went down to see her. Surprise, surprise to find Mike there. Back when I first met her, I thought there might be something between us some day. I thought I had competition in Jared, but when I brought it up, Jill just laughed at the very idea. Jared is her brother. They'd been trying to get together to organize an estate sale. Their mother had moved to an elderly care center, and her house and furnishings needed to be sold. They'd tried several times to meet over dinner, only to have Center business get in the way time after time.

Mike? That was a different story. They had been shadow boxing for years, and it took Jill nearly dying before Mike was willing to declare his devotion to the woman of his dreams—and Jill to the man of hers. They told me that when you come from a background where emotional attachments are a hindrance, you learn not to let people close. Well, almost losing someone changes that view really fast.

Will I have Cam with me forever? Here's how I look at it. Kids grow up. That's what they do. So, for me, forever is about four more years. I'll only be thirty-four. I'll still have my whole life before me. And if Cam wants to hang around a little longer, well, there's a really great college here in Denver, and Mrs. Osgood's still at her brother's. Maybe by then, her apartment will be available. Who knows?

I'll tell you one thing. I hug my boy now. He's had two more "visits" to the Center since coming to live with me for real. Now he's five-five, and he's really beginning to fill out. When he turns fifteen next month, he's going to be a lady-killer. I've already told him, when he gets as tall as me, I'm not taking him back. The Center will have to do without him after that. Six-two is all he gets.

There is something that puzzled me for a long time. Cam was never able to explain how he sent those texts. He said he just thought them. When they left him alone, he could feel the machines, and he thought them. That doesn't make any sense to me. But then, a lot about fourteen-year-olds doesn't make any sense to me, so what's one more thing?

Chapter 62

A New Pair of Big Boy Pants

"Sir, these pants are simply too large. Let me show you a pair that will fit your son a little better."

I winked at Cam in the mirror. He held his shirt pulled up around his chest as the sales clerk tugged at the waist of his new jeans. They were about an inch too loose.

"And here." She knelt, showing me how the hem was bunched under his heel. "If you buy them this long, the back edge will wear out before he can grow into them. You are better off buying for his height and weight now, and purchasing a larger size when he grows more."

"Oh," I said, "I think these will be just what we need—"

"—next week."

Cam has been doing that, finishing my sentences for me. Sometimes I finish his for him. We like to say that great minds think alike.

You know, I no longer think Cam has titanium bones and piston legs. I don't worry about his soul, whether he has one or he doesn't. All that was just me being stupid. He's not a robot boy or anything like that. He's just a kid that's had his fingernail torn loose too many times, and he's needed a safe place to let it heal. I've tried to give him that. His trips to the Center? We've come to terms with them. I've never asked what Cam's real medical problems are, and he's not offered to share them. I just take a Monday off every four months, and we hang out for the day. Even if Cam sleeps the whole time, he knows I'm there, and I think it makes him feel better. He attends Mass with me when he's home, and he's got me driving up to see my mother on the weekends he's gone. He calls her Grammy now, and she phones once a week just to talk to him. Cam does that, brings out the best in people.

"No, ma'am, we'll take this pair. They'll fit perfectly on Monday."

"Sir, I know boys, and real boys don't grow an inch over the weekend."

Cam and I laughed. This one does. He's mine, and he's as real as they come. I'll bet my life on it. In fact, I already have, and I haven't regretted it for one minute. Cam tells me he hasn't either. Is that how two real men say they love each other?

In our house it is.

www.ingramcontent.com/pod-product-compliance
Lightning Source LLC
Chambersburg PA
CBHW071324250626
47159CB00004B/1458